THE ARDEN SHAKESPEARE

GENERAL EDITORS: HAROLD F. BROOKS
AND HAROLD JENKINS

TITUS ANDRONICUS

THE ARDEN EDITION OF THE
WORKS OF WILLIAM SHAKESPEARE

TITUS ANDRONICUS

Edited by
J. C. MAXWELL

LONDON
METHUEN & CO LTD
HARVARD UNIVERSITY PRESS
CAMBRIDGE MASSACHUSETTS

The editors of the Arden Shakespeare have been W. J. Craig (1899-1906), R. H. Case (1909-44), Una Ellis-Fermor (1946-58). Present editors, Harold F. Brooks and Harold Jenkins

H. Bellyse Baildon's edition of Titus Andronicus was first published in 1904

This edition first published, 1953

Third edition, 1961
Reprinted 1963

3.2

CATALOGUE NO. (METHUEN) 2/4728/10

PRINTED IN GREAT BRITAIN AT
THE ABERDEEN UNIVERSITY PRESS

CONTENTS

PREFACE

DETAILS of editorial method are discussed below in the Introduction. Here I have only to make some general remarks and acknowledge obligations.

This edition is not based on the earlier *Arden* edition, though of course it is among those which I have consulted. The commentary is designed to meet the requirements of relatively elementary as well as of more advanced students. Hence there are glosses on classical allusions and common Elizabethan usages which the latter will not need, while some of the more elaborate notes may presuppose more knowledge than the former possess. But I hope that each note will be intelligible and helpful to those readers to whom it is primarily directed.

Where possible I have acknowledged specific debts in the notes. In addition, I have to thank the General Editor for giving generously of her time and thought, and also the following scholars who have helped me in various ways: Mr. J. M. Nosworthy, Mr. K. D. Paxton, Professor H. T. Price and Dr. Alice Walker. My debt to Professor Dover Wilson calls for special mention. His name probably occurs in the Introduction and commentary more often than that of any other scholar, and a good many times I quote his views in order to question them. But that is principally because his edition of the play is the only really substantial one that there is. I have taken advantage of its existence to cut down the number of parallel passages cited : in this direction I have seldom struck on anything significant that has escaped his notice. He has also helped me by answering privately a number of questions. Among the earlier editors, those from whom I have most often learnt what I should probably not have discovered without their aid are, I think, Capell, Dyce and Delius.

J. C. MAXWELL

KING'S COLLEGE, NEWCASTLE UPON TYNE
UNIVERSITY OF DURHAM

PREFACE TO 1961 EDITION

THIS reprint has given me the opportunity of correcting many errors and of indulging in second thoughts on many passages. I am indebted to reviewers of the earlier edition, especially the late Sir Walter Greg, *M.L.R.* 49 (1954), 360-4; Dr. Alice Walker, *R.E.S.* n.s. 6 (1955), 80-2; and Professor Clifford Leech, *Durham University Journal*, n.s. 15 (1953-4), 77-8. Professor Leech has also given me privately further corrections and suggestions, as have Mr. N. S. Brooke, Mr. John Crow, Dr. G. K. Hunter, Dr. J. H. P. Pafford and Professor F. P. Wilson. But my greatest debt is to Dr. H. F. Brooks, who has not only provided a valuable Appendix for this edition, but has also gone through the original edition, and the draft of my new material, with the greatest care. The closeness of his scrutiny gives me some hope that little that is wholly indefensible has got through into the present edition.

Apart from the correction of positive errors, I have been able to correct and supplement acknowledgements to earlier editors, but, in the light of past experience, I am sure that I have not traced all explanations, and citations of parallels, to the scholars originally responsible for them. I have remedied a deficiency which my critical apparatus shared with those in all other editions by recording in brackets the places where Edward Ravenscroft's adaptation anticipated emendations by later editors.

I have unfortunately been able to make only a very few references to the monograph by Horst Oppel, *Titus Andronicus: Studien zur dramengeschichtlichen Stellung von Shakespeares früher Tragödie* (1961), which has just come into my hands, and which I shall be reviewing in a forthcoming number of *Modern Langauge Review*. [56(1961), 6 29-30]

The three new additional notes on p. 138 are based on the findings of Charlton Hinman, *The Printing and Proof-Reading of the First Folio of Shakespeare* (1963). [1963]

ABBREVIATIONS

The abbreviated titles of Shakespeare's works are those of Onions, *Shakespeare Glossary.* Line numbers as in W. J. Craig's Oxford Shakespeare.

Editions of *Titus* :

Baildon	H. B. Baildon, Arden Shakespeare, London, 1904.
Camb.	W. A. Wright, Cambridge Shakespeare (2nd ed.), London, 1892.
Chambers (1907)	E. K. Chambers, Red Letter Edition, London, 1907.
Delius	N. Delius, Shakespere's Werke (3rd ed.), Elberfeld, 1872.
Herford	C. H. Herford, Eversley Edition, London, 1899.
Hudson	H. N. Hudson, Era Shakespeare, London, n.d.
Lee	S. Lee, University Press Shakespeare, New York, 1908.
Ridley	M. R. Ridley, New Temple Shakespeare, London, 1936.
Rolfe	W. J. Rolfe, Friendly Edition, New York, 1890.
Stoll	E. E. Stoll, Tudor Shakespeare, New York, 1913.
Verity	A. W. Verity, Henry Irving Shakespeare, London, 1890.
Wilson	J. D. Wilson, New Shakespeare, Cambridge, 1948.
Witherspoon	A. M. Witherspoon, Yale Shakespeare, New Haven, 1926.

Other references:

Abbott	E. Abbott, *A Shakespearian Grammar* (3rd ed.), London, 1870.
Adams	J. Q. Adams (ed.), *Titus Andronicus, 1594,* New York, 1936.
Baldwin	T. W. Baldwin, *William Shakspere's Small Latine and Lesse Greeke,* Urbana, 1944.
Baldwin (1959)	T. W. Baldwin, *On the Literary Genetics of Shakespeare's Plays, 1592-4,* Urbana, 1959.
Chambers	E. K. Chambers, *William Shakespeare,* Oxford, 1930.
Franz	W. Franz, *Die Sprache Shakespeares,* Halle, 1939.
J.E.G.P.	*Journal of English and Germanic Philology.*
M.L.R.	*Modern Language Review.*
N.E.D.	*New English Dictionary,* Oxford, 1884-1928.
Noble	R. Noble, *Shakespeare's Biblical Knowledge,* London, 1935.
O.D.E.P.	*Oxford Dictionary of English Proverbs* (2nd ed.), Oxford, 1948.
On.	C. T. Onions, *A Shakespeare Glossary* (2nd ed.), Oxford, 1919 (last corrected impression, 1946).
Parrott	T. M. Parrott, " Shakespeare's Revision of ' T.A.' ", *Modern Language Review,* 14 (1919), 16 ff.
P.M.L.A.	*Publications of the Modern Language Association of America.*
Ravenscroft	E. Ravenscroft, *Titus Andronicus, or the Rape of Lavinia,* London, 1687.
R.E.S.	*Review of English Studies.*
Schmidt	A. Schmidt, *Shakespeare-Lexicon* (3rd ed.), ed. G. Sarrazin, Berlin, 1902.
Sh.Jb.	*Shakespeare-Jahrbuch* (formerly *Jahrbuch der Deutschen Shakespeare-Gesellschaft*).
Simpson	P. Simpson, *Shakespearian Punctuation,* Oxford, 1911.
S.P.	*Studies in Philology.*

Tilley   M. P. Tilley, *A Dictionary of the Proverbs in England in the Sixteenth and Seventeenth Centuries*, Ann Arbor, 1950.

T.L.S.   *Times Literary Supplement.*

W. S. Walker W. S. Walker, *A Critical Examination of the Text of Shakespeare*, London, 1860.

Wyld   H. C. Wyld, *A History of Modern Colloquial English* (3rd ed.), Oxford, 1936.

INTRODUCTION

I. Text

THERE are three Quarto editions of the play before the First Folio.[1]

First Quarto (Q 1). Title-page: THE / MOST LA- / mentable Romaine / Tragedie of Titus Andronicus: / As it was Plaide by the Right Ho- / nourable the Earle of *Darbie*, Earle of *Pembrooke*, / and Earle of *Sussex* their Seruants. / [Device] / LONDON, / Printed by Iohn Danter, and are / to be sold by *Edward White* & *Thomas Millington*, / at the little North doore of Paules at the / signe of the Gunne. / 1594.

Head-title: [Device with initials I. D.] / The most Lamen- / table Romaine Tragedie of / *Titus Andronicus:* As it was Plaide by / the Right Honourable the Earle / of *Darbie*, Earle of *Pembrooke*, / and Earle of *Sussex* their / Seruants.

Running-title: The most Lamentable [2] Tragedie [3] / of Titus [4] Andronicus.

Collation: A-K⁴.

Only one copy is known. It was discovered in Sweden in December 1904, and collated in *Sh. Jb.* 41 (1905), 211 ff. It is now in the Folger Shakespeare Library. Sporadic use of its readings was made by editors in the next thirty years, but it was not until after a facsimile had appeared, edited by J. Q. Adams (Folger Shakespeare Library Publications, 1936), that editions based on it throughout were published: those of G. L. Kittredge (1936), Neilson and Hill (1942), etc. Adams's edition gives full details of this Quarto. It is a poor piece of book-production, and very deficient in punctuation (the rule seems to have been:

---

[1] A full bibliographical description of all the early editions is to be found in W. W. Greg, *A Bibliography of the English Printed Drama to the Restoration*, Vol. I (1939), No. 117.

[2] Sometimes : lamentable   [3] Sometimes : *T*ragedie   [4] Once: *T*itus

" when in doubt, put a comma at the end of the line "),
but it provides what is to all appearance a very accurate
text, and is the only source for a number of lines which
appear in quite a different form in all later editions (see
below on Q2). A number of features of the Q1 text,
such as the wording of the stage-directions (see on I. i. 69)
and the irregularity of the speech-prefixes (see on I. i. 299),
make it fairly certain that the printer's copy consisted of the
author's manuscript (" foul papers "), not always finally
tidied up for the stage (see on I. i. 35a, III. i. 36, 281, IV. iii.
97-8, V. iii. 171, Additional Note on II. iii. 294).[1]

Second Quarto (Q2). Title-page: The most lamenta- /
ble Romaine Tragedie of *Titus | Andronicus*. / As it hath
sundry times beene playde by the / Right Honourable the
Earle of Pembrooke, the / Earl of Darbie, the Earle of Sussex,
and the / Lorde Chamberlaine theyr / Seruants. / [Ornament] /
AT LONDON, / Printed by I. R. for Edward White / and
are to bee solde at his shoppe, at the little / North doore of
Paules, at the signe of / the Gun. 1600.

Head-title: [Ornament] / [leaf-sign] The most lamentable Romaine / Tragedie of *Titus Andronicus*: As it was plaid /
by the Right Honorable the Earle of Darbie, Earle / of
Pembrooke, and Earle of Sussex / theyr Seruants.

Running-title: *The most lamentable Tragedie | of Titus
Andronicus*.

Collation : A-K[4].

" I. R." is James Roberts. Two copies of this edition are
known. One is in the Edinburgh University Library, and
the other, at one time in Bridgewater House, is now in the
Huntington Library, California. The latter copy has the
outer forme of sheet D and the outer forme of sheet I in
a corrected state, thus differing from the Edinburgh copy
in eight readings (Adams, p. 19). The Edinburgh copy
has been unsatisfactorily reproduced in facsimile by Ashbee
(1866) and Praetorius (1886). The Huntington copy was
discovered in 1800, and readings from it transcribed (not
very accurately, and by no means fully) by H. J. Todd are
recorded in the 1803 Variorum. Malone's copy of Q3,
collated by him with Q2, is in the Bodleian (Malone 37).

---

[1] Cf. Greg, *Editorial Problem in Shakespeare*, pp. 117-20; Wilson, pp. 91-4.

Apart from corruptions and minor corrections, Q 2 differs from Q 1 at a number of points. It omits the obscure and contradictory passage I. i. 35 (from *and*) to 35*c*, and it diverges from Q 1 at the following places near the end of the play, evidently because the copy of Q 1 from which it was set up was damaged; v. ii. 71, 106 (line 1 of sig. I4 in Q 1); v. iii. 25 S.D., 60 (third last and second last lines of sig. K2); v. iii. 93-7, 129-33 (last five lines of sig. K3); v. iii. 164-9, 200 (last six lines of sig. K4. Here the last five lines had completely perished, with the result that at the place corresponding to the end of the verso in Q 1, which in Q 1 was blank except for "*Exeunt*" and "*Finis the Tragedie of Titus Andronicus*," Q 2 added four new lines). A single injury to the foot of the page would account for all but the first of these losses. The divergence at the top of sig. I4 involves only one word in each of the two lines concerned, but since the two words are in precisely the same position on recto and verso, there must have been an injury here too.

This edition tidies up the text (and especially the punctuation) here and there, but (with the possible exception of II. iii. 231, *Piramus* for *Priamus*) contains nothing "beyond the powers of an intelligent and ingenious compositor" (Adams, p. 20). The Cambridge editors in 1865 referred to Q 2 as "printed with remarkable accuracy"; most of the credit is due, already, to Q 1.

Third Quarto (Q 3). Title-page: [Ornament] / THE / MOST LAMEN- / TABLE TRAGEDIE / *of Titus Andronicus.* / *AS IT HATH SVNDRY* / times *been plaide by the Kings* / Maiesties Seruants. / [Device] / LONDON, / Printed for Eedward White, and are to be solde / at his shoppe, nere the little North dore of / Pauls, at the signe of the / Gun. 1611.

Head-title: [Ornament] / [paragraph sign] The most lamentable Romaine / Tragedie of *Titus Andronicus*: As it was plaid / by the right honorable the Earle of Darbie, Earle / of Pembrooke, and Earle of Sussex / their Seruants.

Running-title: *The most lamentable Tragedie / of Titus Andronicus.*

Collation: A-K⁴.

Fourteen copies of this edition are recorded. There is a facsimile by Ashbee (1867). Pope was the first editor to make use of Q 3. When Steevens in 1766 brought out his very accurate reprint, he knew of no other copy than the one he used. Q 3 supplies a handful of corrections and a great many more corruptions.[1] The chief interest of Q 3 is that the First Folio text (except for III. ii.) was set up from a copy of it to which some stage directions had been added.

First Folio (F). The text of *Titus* in this was set up from a copy of Q 3 to which a number of stage-directions, especially flourishes, a couple of lines (I. i. 398, and " what booke? " after IV. i. 36), and a whole scene, III. ii (from manuscript) were added. The folio introduces even more errors, and even fewer corrections, than its immediate predecessor. The new stage-directions, as Greg (see p. viii) pointed out in correction of a remark in my 1953 edition, presumably go back to the original production.

The presence of one entirely new scene, evidently from manuscript, raises the question why no further use was, apparently, made of that manuscript. Wilson (p. 97) rightly holds that a scribe preparing copy for the Folio by adding III. ii, and stage-directions, from the prompt-book would not necessarily have bothered to read through the whole play. It must, after all, have been well known that, apart from the missing scene, the Quartos offered a good text. Wilson also points out shrewdly that I. i. 398 is at a point where " stage-directions are thick on the page," so that an omission in the printed text would catch the scribe's eye. There is one folio reading which looks too good for conjecture (though it could easily have given rise to the Quarto reading) and which I believe to be correct: v. ii. 18 (see note). The halting metre, as well as the uncertain meaning, might well lead the scribe to consult the prompt-book there. It remains odd that he did so nowhere else (except perhaps at III. i. 36: see note): but

_____

[1] Bolton (*P.M.L.A.* 44 (1929), 769) notes " 19 errors corrected, 16 new errors made, 56 minor variations introduced." Not all the corrected " errors " are real ones: apart from the most elementary misprints of Q 2, I reckon only 5 genuine corrections in Q 3. Moreover, the distinction between new " errors " and " variations " is arbitrary: they are all errors, even though the 56, as opposed to the 16, may not be *manifestly* false.

this is merely an extreme case of what we find in *Richard II*, *Much Ado about Nothing*, and *The Merchant of Venice*, where, according to Greg, the collation of Quarto used as copy with manuscript was (respectively) " rather perfunctory," " rather casual " and " not systematic." [1]

The Longleat Manuscript. This consists of a drawing representing Tamora and her two sons on their knees pleading to Titus. Aaron stands over the sons with a drawn sword. Beneath the drawing are the words " Enter Tamora pleadinge for her sonnes going to execution," followed by a transcript of I. i. 104-20 and v. i. 125-44, the two extracts being linked " by three lines partly derived from I. i. 121 and I. i. 126 and partly concocted by the scribe " (Wilson, p. 98). The last line is followed by " & *cetera*," and then the name " Alarbus " is written in the margin (where speech-prefixes occur in the rest of the transcript), followed by lines across the page. The source seems to have been the First Folio rather than any Quarto, although the margin contains, in the same hand as the text, the words " Henricus Peacham Anno m° q° g q^to " which a later hand has interpreted as " 1595." [2] Who this Peacham was, and whether the date has any authority, we do not know. The main discussions of the MS. are as follows: E. K. Chambers, *The Library*, 4 Ser. 5 (1925), 326-30 (reprinted in *Shakespearean Gleanings* (1944)); Adams, pp. 31-40; Wilson, pp. 98-9 (and more fully in *Shakespeare Survey* 1 (1948), 17-22); J. Munro, *T.L.S.*, 10 June 1949, p. 385 (reply by Wilson, 24 June, p. 413). Wilson holds that the lines were added to the drawing " by someone knowing very little about the play and at a loss to discover the dramatic moment depicted." I find this rather difficult to follow. The transcription is made with fair accuracy from a good text, and the pains taken to join together the two passages of which it consists point to someone who had a purpose, however obscure to us. I do not see how a scribe at a loss to interpret the drawing would have been made any happier by constructing this cento, which he himself must have realized did not represent any single situation in the play. I

---

[1] *Editorial Problem in Shakespeare*, pp. 121, 123, 124.
[2] This involves taking the "g" as a " 9 "; see Adams, p. 33, for the difficulties.

cannot help thinking that drawing and text belong together. Perhaps the compiler's purpose was to string together (for private theatricals?) two striking and popular speeches from the play, and perhaps it is a private performance that the drawing represents, rather than, as Wilson suggests, " the actual action and grouping of Shakespeare's fellows in Shakespeare's theatre at a particular moment of a play in which he had a hand." But problems still remain: the name of Peacham and the date, and the incongruity between the representation of Aaron and his situation in either Act I or Act v. Our one comfort is that the MS. is of no textual importance.

There are two entries in the Stationers' Register that may refer to the play. On 6 February 1594, Danter, the printer of Q 1, registered " a booke intituled a Noble Roman Historye of Tytus Andronicus " together with " the ballad thereof." It has been suggested (Adams, p. 9) that this may refer to the Prose History preserved along with the ballad in the eighteenth-century chap-book discussed below under " Sources." The same may apply to " a booke called Titus and Andronicus " transferred by Thomas Millington to Thomas Pavier on 19 April 1602. (For later transfers of ballad and, possibly, prose history, see Adams, p. 9.) The subject is obscure, but we may readily agree with Greg (Bibliography, p. xxv) that " it would be quite in keeping with Danter's character to make one entrance serve for two separate publications."

The present edition is based on Q 1. Though not in principle " conservative "—I have no initial prejudice against emendation—it departs less often from Q 1 than Professor Dover Wilson's, the only other edition that follows Q 1 closely.[1] Spelling and punctuation are modernized, but certain features of the text will be novel to anyone accustomed to the usual modernized texts of Shakespeare. In accordance with the principles of this series, I have retained all older forms that are more than variant spellings: hence the reader will find " murther," " banket " and

---

[1] This was written before the publication of Professor Alexander's one-volume Shakespeare (1951). I think Professor Alexander and I are about equally conservative in essentials, but I have retained more archaic forms.

" cur'sy." Absolute consistency is not attainable: I have, for instance, printed " mart'red " at III. i. 81, while stopping short of " tortering " at II. iii. 285. I have also rejected what may be called pseudo-modernizations: forms that were modernizations when they became part of the accepted text but that have lingered on although they are now just as obsolete as the forms they supplanted: a good example is " swounded " (v. i. 119). The most important word in this class is " and." In Elizabethan English " and " and " and if " were both used as equivalents of " if." In the course of the seventeenth-century it became customary to write " an " instead of " and " in this sense, and " an " became universal in the eighteenth-century editions. But now that the usage is completely obsolete, it seems to me high time to return to the original spelling, and I have done so throughout. Where there is some doubt whether " and if " means " and + if " or simply " if," I have left it to the reader to decide if I have no strong views myself. On another point of spelling I have adhered religiously to Q 1. The past tense of a verb such as " scatter " appears in three different spellings (I ignore the presence or absence of apostrophe), " scattered," " scattred," and " scatterd." Whether the difference between the first and the second reflects a real difference of pronunciation I do not know; but I have retained the first form where it occurs in Q 1, even where the metrical norm would be one syllable rather than two, in case the intention should be to slur and not to elide the penultimate syllable. The editorial tendency has been to introduce the third form, which is far the rarest in Shakespeare and in many of his contemporaries.[1] Examples are I. i. 425, 427 and 432, where I have restored " (dis)honoured " for the " (dis)honour'd " of (respectively) F 4, F 1 and Pope. This subject is fully discussed in *English Institute Essays: 1947* (1948), pp. 147-51, by Professor H. T. Price, but for whom I should probably not have been sufficiently alive to this problem.

On lineation I have followed the current practice, for convenience of reference. In the early editions, when a

---

[1] H. T. Price, *op. cit.* in text, p. 151, notes that Jonson and Massinger, however, prefer this form.

speech begins in the middle of a line of verse, there is no typographical indication of the fact. Thus II. i. 45, which is printed here, as in other modern editions,

> *Dem.* Ay, boy, grow ye so brave?
> *Aar.*   Why, how now, lords!

appears in the early editions (ignoring minor variations)

> *Demetrius.* I boy, grow yee so braue?
> *Moore.*   Why how now Lords?

This is purely a change of convention, and it would have been pointless to record it in the critical apparatus. The same applies to the practice, particularly common in F 1, of dividing the opening line of a speech. At I. i. 56, for instance, where Q 1 has as in a modern edition (except that the speech-prefix *Saturninus* is centred in a line by itself)

> Friends that haue beene thus forward in my right.

F 1 has

> *Saturnine.* Friends, that haue beene
> Thus forward in my Right,

I have ignored all such variations, except where there is doubt as to the metrical arrangement intended. The whole subject of lineation, with special reference to the peculiarities just discussed, is dealt with by R. B. McKerrow, *Prolegomena for the Oxford Shakespeare*, pp. 44-9.

One other detail may be mentioned here. Editors have in general been too timid about introducing hyphenated compounds. Writers and printers of Shakespeare's time were not in the least systematic in distinguishing between two adjectives, both qualifying the same noun, and two words, both adjectival in form, of which the first is in meaning an adverb modifying the second. Modern practice in the second case hyphenates the two words. W. S. Walker was particularly fond of introducing the hyphenated forms into the text of Shakespeare. He may have overdone it, but most of his proposals deserve serious consideration. This is not a question of emendation, it is a question of interpretation, and every case must be decided on its merits, with no presumption in favour of retaining the unhyphenated form.

As *Titus* is neither a play with a complicated staging nor one which will ever be widely read, I have thought it worth while, at the cost of a few oddities, to sweep away almost the whole paraphernalia of later editorial stage-directions and return to Q 1, with only occasional supplements. I have, of course, retained the traditional Act and Scene divisions, and have normalized the speech-prefixes, which in Q 1 show the variations characteristic of author's manuscript (see on I. i. 299).

In the critical apparatus I have tried to record, besides all textual variants,[1] any interesting spellings, especially of Q 1. When not all the four early editions are mentioned, it is to be assumed that those omitted have the reading printed in the text. Thus " *morn*] *Moone* Q 1-2 " means that the reading " morn " (in whatever spelling or spellings) is that of Q 3 and F. Where a later editor has conjecturally restored the substantive text, I have sometimes added his name in brackets (e.g. v. iii. 146). When several of the early editions are cited as agreeing in a reading different from that in the text, I give the spelling of the earliest edition concerned. I have sometimes, in the lemma of a collation, given the modernized spelling or punctuation of my text without indicating when it first made its appearance, but only, I hope, when it is the obvious (or at least *an* obvious) representation in a modern text of the original reading.

The subject of punctuation presents peculiar difficulties in a modern-spelling text of an Elizabethan play. I have made no special attempt to represent unusual punctuations by a modern equivalent, and in any case this play presents (in Q 1) few interesting oddities. In the apparatus I have recorded the original punctuation only where it would, according to modern conventions, be definitely misleading. I have ignored minor vagaries of the later Quartos and of the Folio where Q 1 is either correct or at least not misleading. I cannot leave this subject without expressing my indebtedness to the Cambridge edition (2nd ed. 1892). Its critical apparatus is wonderfully complete and accurate (though

---

[1] I omit obvious misprints found in only one edition, where the correction is too evident to be classed as an emendation.

it contains too much that is of no intrinsic interest), and I have relied on it without verification for many minor points,[1] though not, I hope, for any on which the true reading in the text may depend. I have often omitted the word " conj." when I have seen no reason to doubt that the author of a proposal who is not himself an editor would have been prepared to print it in the text. This may be questionable procedure, but it seems preferable to citing without " conj." only editors who have actually printed the reading in question.

2. DATE AND AUTHORSHIP

The date and authorship of *Titus Andronicus* seem at first sight to offer no problems at all. Shakespeare's authorship is vouched for, not only by the inclusion of the play in the First Folio, but also by the mention of it as his by Francis Meres in *Palladis Tamia* (1598).[2] As to date: Henslowe in his diary [3] notes a production as " ne " of " Titus & Ondronicous "[4] by Sussex's men on 24 January 1594. Shortly afterwards, on 6 February 1594, as noted above, " a booke intituled a Noble Roman History of Tytus Andronicus " was entered to John Danter in the Stationers'

---

[1] One detail had better be mentioned here: in my apparatus, " Rowe, 2nd ed." refers to the second edition, dated 1709 but probably published 1710, which McKerrow distinguished from the first edition in *T.L.S.*, 8 March 1934, p. 168; " Rowe, 3rd ed. " refers to the 1714 edition, the Cambridge edition's " Rowe, 2nd ed."

[2] Chambers, II. 194.   [3] Ed. W. W. Greg, I. 16.

[4] The form " Titus and Andronicus " persists in a very odd fashion. It is found in the Stationers' Register for 1602, 1624, 1626 and 1630 (Chambers, I. 313-4; Adams, p. 9), where the reference is to the prose history and/or the ballad. It also occurs in several seventeenth-century references to the play, where it is hard to imagine a direct connection either with Henslowe's diary or with the Stationers' Register: the catalogue attached to T. Goff's *Careless Shepherdess* (1656), in which the play is not attributed to Shakespeare (*Shakspere Allusion Book*, ed. J. Munro, II. 58); and the list in Henry Oxinden's commonplace book (started in 1647) of plays in his possession (*Library*, 4 Ser. 15 (1934-5), 448). J. M. Robertson, *Introduction to the Study of the Shakespeare Canon*, p. 69, pointed out that Titus and Andronicus figure as separate characters in the same story in E. Hellowes's translation of *The Familiar Epistles of Antonie Guevara* (1584). The story is the one more familiar as that of *Androcles* and the lion. Robertson tentatively suggested that this might have been made into a play, and its title might have lingered in people's memories.

Register, and an edition printed by Danter appeared in the same year.

Yet few have been convinced by the whole of this simple and consistent story. The first recorded denial of Shakespeare's authorship comes from Edward Ravenscroft in 1687, in the *Address* to his adaptation of the play. He claims to " have been told by some anciently conversant with the Stage, that it was not Originally his, but brought by a private Author to be Acted, and he only gave some Mastertouches to one or two of the Principal Parts or Characters; this I am apt to believe, because 'tis the most incorrect and indigested piece in all his Works; It seems rather a heap of Rubbish then a Structure." [1] There is no evidence that Ravenscroft had any good authority, and (though it seems unlikely that he simply invented the whole story) his chief motive may well have been to justify his own rewriting of the play. Langbaine was not slow to point out that Ravenscroft had accepted Shakespeare's authorship in the prologue to his adaptation when it was produced.[2] All that the story shows is that the inferiority of *Titus* to Shakespeare's other tragedies made such a story plausible long before wholesale disintegration of the Shakespeare canon became popular. Thus Theobald, in rejecting Shakespeare's authorship, claims to be in the company of " the better judges," [3] and the main eighteenth-century scholars, Johnson, Farmer, Steevens and Malone took the same view, though Malone thought the play was probably included in the Folio because Shakespeare " wrote a few lines in it, or gave some assistance to the author, in revising it, or in some other way aided him in bringing it forward on the stage." [4] Capell, Tyrwhitt (who first called attention in print to Meres's reference [5]) and Ritson [6] favoured the attribution to Shakespeare. There is no need to trace the later history of the play in scholarly opinion—though the spirited defence of Shakespeare's authorship by Charles Knight (*Studies of Shakspere*, 1849) is still worth reading—but the early establishment of

---

[1] Chambers, II. 255.   [2] *Ibid.*
[3] Quoted in 1821 Variorum, XXI. 379.   [4] *Ibid.*, p. 258.
[5] *Observations and Conjectures upon some Passages of Shakespeare*, Oxford, 1766.
[6] *Remarks on the Last Edition of Shakespeare*, London, 1783, p. 158.

an orthodox opinion hostile to the Folio attribution is notable.[1]

Apart from a natural reluctance on artistic grounds to attribute the play to Shakespeare, what are the difficulties about the 1594 date? The first is an allusion in the anonymous play, *A Knack to Know a Knave*, to an incident not known to occur anywhere but in *Titus*: Osric greets King Oswald as being as welcome

> As Titus was unto the Roman Senators
> When he had made a conquest on the Goths.
>
> (Sig. F 2v; Hazlitt's *Dodsley*, VI. 572.)

A Knack is recorded by Henslowe as " ne " when performed on 10 June 1592 by Strange's men at the Rose, and it was registered on 7 January 1594. This is not conclusive—it might be an allusion to Shakespeare's source, not as yet identified with certainty[2]—and I discuss in Additional Notes an attempt to undermine it. Verbal echoes of *Titus* in writings earlier than 1594 are more elusive,[3] but I believe there is one in *The Troublesome Reign of King John*, published in 1591. At the end of that play, John is melodramatically repenting of his crimes, and says:

> How, what, when, and where, have I bestow'd a day
> That tended not to some notorious ill?
>
> (Pt. II. viii. 85-6 in the text ed. by
> F. J. Furnivall and J. Munro, *The
> Shakespeare Classics*, 1913.)

This can hardly be independent of Aaron's speech, v. i.125-7:

> Even now I curse the day, and yet, I think,
> Few come within the compass of my curse,
> Wherein I did not some notorious ill.

Which passage is the debtor? I do not think a confident answer can be given, but the author of *The Troublesome Reign* is a shameless borrower,[4] and these lines seem to me much more at home in Aaron's speech than in John's: " some notorious ill " is happier as a boast than in a penitential

---

[1] Chambers, I. 316, understates the position when he says that " Shakespeare's original authorship has been very generally doubted from the days of Malone onwards."

[2] See below, p. xxx. The prose story contains no ceremonial reception of Titus by the senators.   [3] See also note on II. iii. 39.

[4] See P. Alexander, *Shakespeare's Life and Art*, p. 85.

context. I think there is also a connection between the following passages, though there is nothing that strongly suggests the priority of one rather than the other:

> No funeral rite, nor man in mourning weed,
> No mournful bell shall ring her burial;
> But throw her forth to beasts and birds to prey.
>
> (v. iii. 196-8).
>
> Lo, lords, the wither'd flower,
> Who, in his life, shin'd like the morning's blush,
> Cast out o' door, denied his burial rite,
> A prey for birds and beasts to gorge upon.
>
> (*Troublesome Reign*, Pt. II. i. 33-6.)

A date about 1590 or a little earlier would be consistent with the immaturity of the play as a specimen of Shakespeare's art, and would also be easier to reconcile with the famous allusion by Ben Jonson which must now be quoted. In the *Induction* to *Bartholomew Fair* (1614) he writes: " Hee that will sweare, *Ieronimo*,[1] or *Andronicus* are the best playes, yet, shall passe vnexcepted at, heere, as a man whose Iudgement shews it is constant, and hath stood still, these fiue and twentie, or thirtie yeeres." No doubt Jonson need not have meant his arithmetic to be taken too literally, and he was certainly likely, if anything, to exaggerate the antiquatedness of the plays mentioned, but as far as it goes his remark favours an early date: it would not be so easy if *Titus* had been a bare twenty years old in 1614. Jonson may, indeed, not have known its date with any accuracy, but there is no need to multiply hypotheses of this kind.

One of the other arguments for a date earlier than 1594 is, I believe, a mare's nest. It is the suggestion that Henslowe's " Tittus and Vespacia," produced as " ne " by Strange's men on 11 April 1592, is either identical with *Titus* or an earlier form of it. In spite of all the ink that has been spilt on the subject, I can see no reason to reject the obvious explanation that *Titus and Vespasian* (which is presumably what Henslowe meant) was a play about the two Flavian emperors, probably dealing with the destruction of Jerusalem (so Adams, p. 10; a possible objection (Chambers, 1. 319) is that Strange's men had another play called " Jerusalem " running concurrently with " Titus &

---

[1] I.e., Kyd's *Spanish Tragedy*.

Vespacia " in 1592, but this, as Chambers himself allows
(*Elizabethan Stage*, III. 341), is very likely about the First
Crusade, not about Titus's destruction of Jerusalem). It is
true that the German *Tragœdia von Tito Andronico*, indirectly
derived from *Titus*, substitutes the name " Vespasian " for
" Lucius," but as Chambers (I. 319) says, a natural process
of association would readily suggest that name in a play
whose hero was called Titus.

These considerations, none of them conclusive, raise the
question: how much weight, and what exact meaning, is to
be attached to Henslowe's " ne." Chambers (I. 320)
writes: " Henslowe's ' ne,' whatever its precise significance,
is certainly a mark attached to a play ' the first tyme yt
wasse playde.' Generally it seems to have been a new play
in the full sense. It is probable that it was sometimes a
revised play, and possible that it was sometimes an old play,
given by a particular company for the first time. But there
is no clear case of this last type, and there are several
clear cases in which such a performance was not marked
' ne '." His more detailed account in *The Elizabethan
Stage*, II. 144-6, does not entirely bear this out. For
" Jeronimo," which is universally agreed to be identical
with Kyd's *Spanish Tragedy*, is given as " ne " when produced
by the Admiral's men on 7 January 1597. It is possible that
the play had been revised since its original appearance in
the 1580's, but this is not certain, and the most natural
interpretation is that the play had not previously been
produced by this particular company. Since the title-page
of *Titus*, Q 1, mentions the " servants " of the Earls of Derby
and Pembroke before those of the Earl of Sussex, it seems
reasonable to suppose that it was only to the last-named
company that *Titus* was new in 1594. When and where the
other two companies played it,[1] we must be content not to
know. The Earl of Derby, who succeeded to the title on 25

[1] I know of no evidence in support of the following statement by Hardin
Craig, *An Interpretation of Shakespeare* (New York, 1948), p. 38: " This [the
title-page of Q 1] has caused more confusion than it warrants. It does not
necessarily mean that all these companies had acted this particular play, but
only that they had all acted a play on the same subject. The Elizabethans
did not discriminate among versions, but among subjects." He compares the
non-entry of Shakespeare's *King John* for the Folio, and Danter's prose history

September 1593, had previously been Lord Strange, and performances of *Titus* in which the Chamberlain's company, including many of Strange's men, was associated with the Admiral's men are recorded by Henslowe on 5 and 12 June 1594.[1] Strange's men may easily have produced the play earlier, though not (assuming that " Titus and Vespacia " is irrelevant) in the London season of 1592 which Henslowe records in full. Those who believe in a late date for *Titus* may be conceded the point that it is odd that such a popular play should not have been put on in 1592, if it were already in existence and in the company's repertoire. The career of Pembroke's men is a more obscure one, but they seem to have come to grief in the latter part of 1593, and do not emerge again as an important Company. On the title-page of Q 2, the name of Pembroke precedes that of Derby. If the transposition has any authority, a difficulty arises for an early dating of *Titus*, since Pembroke's men are not recorded as active before 1592.[2] (In my 1953 edition, I suggested that 1594 might be the date of the first London production of the play, Strange's and Pembroke's men having played it on tour. I agree with Greg (see p. viii) that this is unlikely.)

The evidence, it can be seen, forms a tangled web, and I have not tried to conceal what is fragmentary and conflicting about the external evidence for the date and early stage-history of the play. But there does not seem to be anything that flatly contradicts a date of about 1589-90. The internal evidence that has been adduced for a later date is more formidable, and carries us back to the question of authorship, which I have left aside for some time.

of *Titus*. On the latter, see Greg's remark, quoted above, p. xvi. As for the former, I believe that *The Troublesome Reign of King John*, though not strictly a " bad Quarto," is a rehash of Shakespeare's play, so that its publication would make it unnecessary to register the latter for the Folio.   [1] Chambers, II. 319.

[2] A plausible theory according to which Pembroke's Men came into existence in May 1591 has been put forward by J. Dover Wilson, *New Shakespeare* edition of *2H6* (1952), p. xii. Mr. A. S. Cairncross has kindly shown me a number of echoes of *Titus* in the Bad Quarto of *2H6* (see Arden, 1957, pp. 183-4) and the Bad Octavo of *3H6*. These were Pembroke plays, as we learn from the title-page of the latter (*The True Tragedy*). The former (*First Part of the Contention*) was entered in the Stationers' Register on 12 March 1594. Their contamination by *Titus* may have taken place during provincial performances.

A larger number of significant parallels with *Titus* have been found in *Venus and Adonis* and *The Rape of Lucrece*, especially the latter, than in any other works of Shakespeare. It has been argued that this is evidence in favour of a date for *Titus* fairly close to that of the poems, and this (on the assumption that the latter were published soon after they were written) would be 1593-4. I do not see that this carries much weight. *Titus* is, apart from the poems, the work of Shakespeare in which the Ovidian mode is most clearly discernible. Moreover, it is linked in subject with *Lucrece*, so that Shakespeare's mind might easily revert to the play when he was writing the poem. Still, it must be allowed to the late-daters that it is an odd coincidence that the parallels with *Lucrece* are consistent with the obvious interpretation of Henslowe's " ne."

The other items of internal evidence which are adduced in support of a late date for *Titus* are bound up with the contention that Shakespeare is not entirely responsible for the play and must now be dealt with in relation to that contention. In the palmy days of disintegration of the Shakespeare canon, almost all practising dramatists of 1585-95 were called in to take a hand in *Titus*, but at present the only serious candidate for a share in the play is George Peele. There is general agreement, too, that there is much better evidence of his presence in Act I than in the rest of the play. A number of scholars, most recently Dover Wilson, have pointed to striking resemblances between Act I and the plays and poems of Peele, and probably more suggestive than any individual verbal parallels is the tendency to mechanical repetition of words and phrases (Wilson, pp. xxviii-ix; cf. my note on I. i. 294). To this may be added an argument from syntax. At I. i. 5-6 we have:

> I am his first-born son that was the last
> That ware the imperial diadem of Rome.

The construction " his . . . that " is not uncommon in sixteenth- and seventeenth-century English, but it is unusually frequent in this Act, occurring six or seven times in 500 lines, i.e. six or seven times as often as in the rest of the play (four times in 2000 lines). In Peele's non-dramatic poetry the construction is also about six times as common as in *Venus and Adonis* and *The Rape of Lucrece*, and the absolute frequency is not very different. This is not conclusive, but it is at any rate quite independent of the other arguments that have been brought forward for Peele's hand in Act I of *Titus*.[1]

So much for the outline of the case for Peele's hand in Act I of *Titus*. It has been further claimed that the parallels favour a particular date, 1593. There are specially close resemblances between *Titus* and Peele's poem, *The Honour of the Garter*, which must belong to May and June 1593, and Wilson (p. xlv) argues that "despite Peele's habit of repeating his clichés year after year, the parallels with *Titus Andronicus* make it tolerably certain that play and poem were being written at the same time." It seems to me more reasonable to say that in view of Peele's habit it is far from certain. There is one parallel that calls for special attention, since it involves a word found only in *Titus* and in *The Honour of the Garter*. *Titus* I. i. 182 runs:

> This palliament of white and spotless hue,

the "palliament" being thought of as the white robe of the candidate for office. In *The Honour of the Garter* (lines 91-2), Edward III is

> A goodly king in robes most richly dight,
> The upper like a Roman palliament.

Later in the poem come the lines (313-6):

> O sacred loyalty! in purest hearts
> Thou build'st thy bower! thy weeds of spotless white,
> Like those that stood for Rome's great offices
> Make thee renown'd, glorious in innocency.

Opposite conclusions have been drawn from the comparison of these passages. Wilson (who believes that Peele wrote both) argues that the *Titus* passage is the earliest, since the reference to a "palliament" (apparently a quasi-classical

---

[1] For a detailed account, with statistics for some other dramatists, see my paper in *J.E.G.P.* 49 (1950), 557-61.

coinage based on one or both of the words " pallium " and
" paludamentum ") is out of place in the poem, as indeed
Peele himself admits, for he goes on:

Indeed a chaperon, for such it was—

" that is to say," Wilson writes, " it was not a ' pallium ' or
cloak at all but a hood! " This seems a good argument for
the priority of the play, though telling, if anything, against
common authorship. Wilson does not make it clear what he
takes to be the connection between the *Titus* line and lines
313-6 of the poem: the implication seems to be that here
again Peele recalled his own *Titus* line. The same three
passages have been used by H. T. Price [1] to prove that the
Titus line is (a) posterior to the poem, (b) not by Peele.
Pointing out justly that Peele does not identify his " pal'lia-
ment " with the candidate's white robe as earlier scholars
(joined, since Price wrote, by Wilson, p. xlvi) had asserted,
he claims that Shakespeare confused the two Peele passages
so as to produce his white palliament. This ignores the
greater appropriateness of the reference in *Titus*, and proves
nothing. There is no means of telling in advance whether
the original coiner of the word " palliament " referred it to
a white garment or a coloured one such as the Garter robes,
and neither application of the word need be a confused
version of the other. The comparison of these passages,
then, neither proves nor disproves common authorship,
but I think (with Wilson against Price) that the *Titus*
passage is probably the earlier.

The case for Peele's hand in *Titus* is primarily a stylistic
one. The case (from internal evidence) against it rests on
considerations of structure. That the structure of the play
is like Shakespeare and unlike Peele is not a conclusive
argument against all theories which attribute some share
in the play to Peele, but it is an argument against the most
popular type of theory, according to which Peele is the
original author of the play, and Shakespeare a reviser and
adapter. The most recent, and most elaborate, version
of this theory is that of Wilson, who postulates (a) a short play

[1] *Papers of the Michigan Academy of Science, Arts, and Letters* 21 (1935), 506-7;
J.E.G.P. 42 (1943), 61.

by Peele written for a travelling company in 1593; (*b*) an expansion of (*a*) for London production, carried out towards the end of 1593, in which Peele was assisted by Shakespeare, " partly [because] Shakespeare was known to be working just then upon the kindred theme of Lucrece, but mainly [because] the Earl of Sussex's men were in a hurry " (p. xxxvii). Any such theory comes up against the objection that the firmness of construction evident in *Titus* is quite unlike anything in any of Peele's plays. It is true that most of these are preserved in bad texts, but it is impossible to believe that they were ever well-constructed. In an important article, " Plot Structure in Peele's Plays as a Test of Authorship " (*P.M.L.A.* 51 (1936), 689-701), A. M. Sampley has, on these grounds, argued strongly against Peele's responsibility for a number of plays with which he has been associated, including *Titus*. There is only one other dramatist besides Shakespeare writing at the time who might conceivably have plotted *Titus*, and that is Kyd; J. M. Robertson showed a sounder instinct Wilson in invoking him as the original plotter of the play, though in fact there is nothing in the writing to suggest that he had any hand in it. The detailed consideration of the structure of the play (which I rate more highly than Wilson does) must be left to the final section of this Introduction. Meanwhile it is enough to point out that the apparent discontinuity in style between Act I and the rest of the play is not paralleled by any discontinuity in construction, and that the structure of the whole play suggests Shakespeare rather than Peele.

It may seem tempting to assert roundly that the whole play is by Shakespeare and no one else. This has been ably argued by H. T. Price,[1] and may be the right solution after all. My only defence is that I can never quite believe it *while* reading Act I.[2] At the same time the alternative to which I find myself driven is not a very plausible one, since it involves holding that as early as 1589-90 Peele, already a well-established dramatist, acted as a very

---

[1] *J.E.G.P.* 42 (1943), 55-81.

[2] Actually if there is a clean break between the two authors, I should be inclined to put it after II. i. 25.

subordinate collaborator with a writer a number of years
his junior in both age and experience.[1]

3. SOURCE

No source for *Titus* survives in a form which we know to
have been available to Shakespeare. But a single copy (in
the Folger Library) of a mid-eighteenth-century chapbook
giving a version not based on Shakespeare may be in
essentials pre-Shakespearian.[2] It has not been reprinted,
but there is a full analysis of it, with many quotations, by
R. M. Sargent.[3] Its title-page claims that it is " Newly
Translated from the Italian Copy printed at Rome," and it
may indeed be of Italian origin. The ballad, " The
Lamentable and Tragicall History of Titus Andronicus,"
which is printed with the prose story, and is also included
in Percy's *Reliques* as " Titus Andronicus's Complaint," is
entirely dependent on the prose story, though some of the
stanzas have been rearranged to bring the order of events
into closer conformity with the play.[4] All the differences
between the prose story and the play are compatible with
the hypothesis that the former is substantially identical with
the source of the latter.

The vague late-Roman setting of the play is localized " in
the Time of Theodosius " (late fourth century A.D.) in the
story. Italy has been plundered by the Goths. Titus
Andronicus, a Roman senator, raises the siege of Rome, and
becomes engaged in a ten-year struggle with the Goths, at
the end of which he kills the Gothic king in a battle, and
captures the queen Attava. The dead king's two sons

[1] An elaborate attempt at dating the play has recently been made by
T. W. Baldwin, *The Literary Genetics of Shakspere's Poems & Sonnets* (Urbana,
1950), pp. 4-9. (Baldwin had earlier argued that the play was later than
Venus and Adonis: see note on II. iv. 36-7.) He compares the handling of the
image of the sun taking leave of the morning in the following passages: *3 H 6*
II. i. 21-2, *Titus* II. i. 5-9, Spenser, *Faerie Queene* I. v. 2, Peele, *Descensus Astraeae*,
4, and concludes that the order of the first three is Spenser (1590), *3 H 6*,
Titus, and also that Peele (1591) precedes *Titus*. I ought to add that the
passage in *Titus* (cf. the previous note) is one which I incline to attribute to
Peele. (See now Baldwin (1959), ch. 22-26.)

[2] This chap-book was known to Farmer and to Halliwell-Phillipps
(Chambers, I. 321).

[3] *S.P.* 46 (1949), 167-83; see also Baldwin (1959), pp. 427-30.

[4] *Ibid.*, p. 171.

Alaricus and Abonus continue the struggle, and eventually
the Roman emperor decides on a political marriage with
Attava and enters into it against the advice of Titus. After
becoming empress, Attava secures the key-positions for
Goths and vows revenge on Titus, whose banishment she
procures, but at this the people rise in revolt and the
decision has to be reversed. Attava hates Titus all the more
for this. At this point in the story comes the account
of the empress's intrigue with a (nameless) Moor. She
does not succeed in concealing her blackamoor child, but
persuades the emperor that it was " conceived by the Force
of Imagination," [1] whereupon the Moor is exiled, but the
empress later secures his return. It is only now that Lavinia
comes on the scene. She becomes betrothed to the emperor's
only son by a former wife. As the marriage would frustrate
Attava's plans to secure the empire for her own sons, she
decides to make away with the prince. She, the Moor, and
her two sons murder him, and throw him into a pit. Lavinia
persuades her brothers to go in search of him. They fall
into the pit, are discovered and accused of murder, and are
condemned, partly because of the false witness of the Moor.
As in the play, the Moor (but at the instigation of the
empress, not on his own initiative) persuades Titus to
let him cut off his hand by a false offer of clemency to his sons
if he does so, but they are executed notwithstanding and
their headless bodies sent to Titus. The next disaster is
the rape and mutilation of Lavinia by Attava's sons.
She eventually discloses her story as in the play, and
Titus vows revenge. He feigns madness, and shoots arrows
to heaven. The citizens become alarmed at the arbitrary
behaviour of the empress. Titus and some friends ambush
and kill the empress's sons, and the grim banquet takes place.
Titus orders his friends to kill the emperor and empress.
At this stage the Moor discloses his share in the wicked deeds
and is tortured to death. Titus finally, " to prevent the
Torments he expected, when these things came to be known,
at his Daughter's Request, . . . killed her; and so,
rejoicing he had revenged himself on his enemies to the full,

---

[1] This motif occurs in R. Head and F. Kirkman, *The English Rogue*, Part III,
ch. 2.

fell on his sword and died." There is nothing about what happens in Rome after his death.

One part of the political background is clearer in the story than in the play—the purpose of the marriage of the emperor with the Gothic queen. It may be conjectured that Shakespeare, having decided to send Titus's son Lucius (a character not in the prose story) to join the Goths, had to represent Tamora as having cut herself off from her compatriots. That being so, there could be no political end to be secured by the emperor's marriage with her.

The main differences may be summed up as follows:

(1) There is no problem of succession in the prose story. Titus is never a candidate for the throne, and he has no occasion to make the fatal decision he makes in the play.

(2) The sacrifice of Alarbus is an addition.[1]

(3) Lavinia is betrothed to the emperor's son, not his brother, and the murder of her betrothed is not part of the same plot as her rape: nor is either brought into close connection with the intrigue between the empress and the Moor. Here the play shows effective concentration.

(4) The Moor " never emerges as an independent character; he remains, until his concluding confession, the instrument of the Queen." [2] His attitude towards his son, and his defiance at the end, are also peculiar to the play.

(5) The survival of one of Titus's sons, and his flight to the Goths, are absent: " the triumph of civic justice through the instrumentality of Lucius is wholly the creation of Shakespeare." [3] Shakespeare himself (iv. iv. 67-8) makes the comparison with the story of Coriolanus.

(6) The emperor is a weakling rather than the villain he is in the play.

(7) " The play deliberately obscures the clear-cut nature of the foreign-native conflict for power . . . the vendetta between the Queen and Andronicus assumes more nearly the status of an interfamily feud." [4]

---

[1] This has been thought to be indebted to Seneca's *Troades* (Kittredge, cited by R. A. Law, *S.P.* 40 (1943), 145). In *Titus* itself Alarbus has been thought to be an addition to the original version, but see note on i. i. 69. Alarbus and Mutius are both absent from the seventeenth-century Dutch and German versions which are in some way derived from *Titus*.

[2] Sargent, p. 176.   [3] *Ibid.*, p. 178.   [4] *Ibid.*, p. 182-3.

(8) " The play concludes (as the story does not) with the authority of the Roman state once more centred in a strong, just emperor." [1]

Perhaps the most interesting consequences of the assumption that we have in the chap-book what is substantially Shakespeare's source, are that it confirms the impression that Aaron is peculiarly Shakespearian, that it gives to Shakespeare the typical concern both in the first and in the fifth act with civil order and the forces which threaten to overthrow it, and that it makes the notion that Titus's misfortunes follow in large part from a misguided decision of his own, a Shakespearian innovation.

In view of the discovery of what may be, in essentials, Shakespeare's immediate source, speculation on more remote origins becomes of doubtful value. Of the names which are new in the play,[2] Bassianus may have been suggested by the emperor Antoninus Bassianus Caracalla (d. A.D. 217), whose character, however, is more reminiscent of Saturninus's. A Latin university play about him survives.[3] Saturninus is the name of a legate in Germany who raised a revolt in A.D. 88, and also of a third-century emperor.[4] Tamora may recall Tomyris, queen of the Massagetae, mentioned in 1*H*6 II. iii. 6, who revenged her son's death on the Persian king Cyrus. The name of Mutius may be connected with Mutius Scaevola, who burned off his right hand as a proof of fortitude. He belongs to the time of Tarquin, and the name might have been suggested by the story of Lucrece, which Shakespeare clearly had in mind while writing the play. No parallels have been suggested for the name Alarbus, though it is not far from the Alaricus of the prose story.

Of the names that appear also in the prose story, only that of Andronicus calls for comment. It has been thought to point to a Byzantine origin for the whole story. The emperor Andronicus Comnenus (1183-5) was noted for his

---

[1] Sargent, p. 183.
[2] Most of this paragraph is based on W. Keller, *Sh.Jb.* 74 (1938), 137-62; see also R. A. Law, *S.P.* 40 (1943), 145-53, where, amongst other things, it is suggested that the play is indebted to Plutarch's Life of Scipio Africanus, which contains a large number of the play's Roman names.
[3] See *Cambridge Bibliography of English Literature*, I. 661.
[4] Miss F. A. Yates (see note on IV. iii. 4) suggests that the name connotes " the evil opposite of the golden age of Saturn," and cites IV. iii. 56.

cruelty.   He was eventually mutilated (his right hand being cut off) and killed by the mob.   The pronunciation "Andrónicus," instead of " Andronícus," may be an example of the tendency to treat the Greek tonic accent as a stress accent: see P. Simpson on " The Elizabethan Pronunciation of Accented Greek Words," *M.L.R.* 45 (1950), 509-10, and Baldwin, II. 391.

The resemblances to the story of Tereus and Philomela in Ovid, which is referred to several times in the play, are already in the chap-book version, except that the outraged female does not in the chap-book take an active part in in the revenge, as she does in *Titus* and in Ovid: cf. H. Baker quoted below.   Keller (pp. 139, 157) unconvincingly suggests that Shakespeare also used the version in Chaucer's *Legend of Good Women.*   I think a better case can be made out for his having read Gower's version in the *Confessio Amantis*: see note on v. ii. 59.

The most interesting analogue is the novella by Bandello (III. 21), which tells of the rape and murder by a revengeful Moorish slave of the wife of his master, and of the murder of their sons.   The Moor promises his master to spare the sons if he will cut off his nose, and he breaks his promise like the Moor in the prose story and Aaron in the play. The story was translated into French by Belleforest (*Histoires Tragiques*, vol. 2, Paris, 1570) and there is an English ballad version (*Roxburghe Ballads*, vol. 2, Hertford, 1874, pp. 49-55). The parallel was first pointed out by E. Koeppel, *Englische Studien* 16 (1891), 365-71, and though it is no longer necessary to suppose it a main source if the chap-book version was accessible to Shakespeare, it gives us a Moor with a more Aaron-like character and power of initiative, especially in the delight he takes in his villainy.   This is not prominent in the chap-book, though when the Moor cut off Titus's hand he " inwardly laugh'd at the Villainy." [1]

The relative importance for the play of Ovid's story of Tereus and Philomel and Seneca's of Thyestes has been much discussed, and the wider question of Ovid and Seneca as influences is raised in the last section of this Introduction. Where Shakespeare's version corresponds to the chap-book,

[1] Sargent, p. 178.

it would be rash to read any particular significance into the fact that it also agrees with Ovid against Seneca, or *vice versa*, but a few remarks may be made. It is the Ovidian story alone that is referred to in the play itself,[1] and it is in some ways the closer analogue. The banquet is related to the other events as in Ovid: "revenge for a rape followed by the cutting out of the victim's tongue. The further mutilation of the victim—amputation of her hands—is, according to the text (II. iv. 40), a device intended directly to prevent her from using Philomel's method of revealing the crime." [2] Titus and Lavinia prepare the banquet together as in Ovid: in *Thyestes*, Atreus works alone. "For a deflowered and peculiarly mutilated woman to assist in contriving a peculiar gruesome revenge—this is what connects *Titus Andronicus* with Ovid and probably with Ovid alone." [3] There are, on the other hand, points in which *Titus* is closer to *Thyestes*.[4] The summoning of Revenge from below (IV. iii. 38; v. ii. 3) recalls Seneca's apparitions from the underworld; two sons are served up at the banquet in both Seneca and *Titus*, and one has been guilty of ambition, whereas in Ovid there is one—innocent—victim; the mother is not the slayer either in Seneca or in *Titus*, as she is in Ovid; In Seneca as in *Titus*, there are elaborate preparations for the killing, the killer is also the cook (this is at most implied in Ovid), the feast is public, and the head is not shown (this last may reflect a difference between drama and narrative: but heads were not uncommon on the Elizabethan stage, and, indeed, figure in III. i. of *Titus*). On balance, the resemblances to Ovid seem to me decidedly the more important, though most of them are already present in the prose story. There seems no strong evidence for any direct consultation of *Thyestes*, except perhaps in IV. iii (see note on line 64), and conceivably in the treatment of the figures supposed to have risen from the underworld.[5]

---

[1] Such a reference, however, is itself a Senecan parallel: Atreus appeals to the story of Philomel and Progne in *Thyestes* 275-6.

[2] H. Baker, *Induction to Tragedy*, p. 121.   [3] *Ibid.*, p. 122.

[4] All these are taken from A. Brandl, *Göttingische Gelehrte Anzeiger*, 1891, 723-4.

[5] I have noted also a not very striking verbal parallel in v. iii. 72.

4. The Play

The evaluation of *Titus Andronicus* has been intimately bound up with the question of its authorship. I have already indicated my conviction that the play is through and through Shakespearian in its planning, though there are strong indications that another hand, that of Peele, was responsible for the writing of Act i. But its inferiority to all Shakespeare's other tragedies remains to be discussed. It would help if a date about 1589, rather than the 1592-3 of many recent scholars, were to be accepted; but the whole *genre* to which the play belongs is one which it requires a special effort of imagination to appreciate, and a label such as " tragedy of blood " is not really very helpful.

To my mind the most useful recent discussions [1] are in the following three books: M. C. Bradbrook, *Themes and Conventions of Elizabethan Tragedy* (1935), E. M. W. Tillyard, *Shakespeare's History Plays* (1944) and, most fully, Howard Baker, *Induction to Tragedy* (1939). Tillyard (pp. 137-8) writes:

This play has exactly the same qualities as the *Comedy of Errors*: it is academic, ambitious and masterfully planned. Miss Bradbrook [2] sees the academicism very plainly :

> *Titus Andronicus* is a Senecal exercise; the horrors are all classical and quite unfelt, so that the violent tragedy is contradicted by the decorous imagery. The tone is cool and cultured in its effect.

Actually there is just as much Ovid in the play as there is Seneca. The rape and mutilation of Lavinia comes from Ovid's story of Procne and Philomela, though the culminating scene of Tamora eating her son's [3] flesh in a pasty comes from Seneca's most popular play, the *Thyestes*.

In view of the chap-book version, " comes from " may be too unqualified, but Shakespeare certainly did everything in

---

[1] Two earlier accounts may be mentioned: The Introduction to the first Arden edition, which is diffuse and wayward but has some perceptive comments; and the Introduction to the Praetorius facsimile of Q 2 by Arthur Symons (1885). I mention the latter because it has recently been praised by Wilson (p. xvii), but I cannot share his high opinion of it.

[2] Pp. 98-9; Miss Bradbrook has now given a fuller account of the play in *Shakespeare and Elizabethan Poetry* (1951), pp. 104-10.

[3] A slip for " sons' "; a few lines below Tillyard again writes " son " for " sons."

his power to remind his audience of the classical analogue (esp. IV. i. 41 ff.), and it is Ovid that is uppermost in his mind. The relevance of this to the gruesome elements in the play is well brought out by Baker (p. 124), who calls attention to the difficulties of transferring such a story, familiar in narrative form, to the stage.[1] He points out that almost any "metrical tragedy" of the *Mirror for Magistrates* type (whose importance in the rise of Elizabethan drama he makes clear) likewise contains more gruesome details than does a play of Seneca. Whether the problems are as successfully solved as Miss Bradbrook suggests by the " cool tone " she mentions is perhaps open to doubt, but it is interesting that the detachment of treatment was noted by Coleridge in those poems which provide so many parallels to *Titus*. Of *Venus and Adonis* Coleridge says: " Shakespeare writes in this poem as if he were of another planet." [2]

The considerations I have mentioned seem to me to tell very strongly against Dover Wilson's suggestion than many of the most gruesome passages in *Titus* are written with a burlesque intention. Our usual critical vocabulary is perhaps not entirely adequate to discussing these questions, and it would be rash to say that a uniform attitude of deadly seriousness is presupposed. Certainly Aaron seems to owe much to Marlowe's Barabas, and *The Jew of Malta* is a play whose nature is notoriously difficult to define. When T. S. Eliot in 1918 [3] described it as a farce, he was for long regarded as putting forward a paradox;[4] but professional scholarship has now caught up, and P. H. Kocher in a valuable analysis describes the play as " more a malicious comedy than anything else." [5] Yet no account

[1] The problems involved were already familiar to Aristotle: " The epic affords more opening [than Tragedy] for the improbable, the chief factor in the marvellous, because in it the agents are not visibly before one. The scene of the pursuit of Hector would be ridiculous on the stage . . . but in the poem the absurdity is overlooked " (*Poetics*, tr. Bywater, rev. Fyfe, ch. 24).

[2] *Lectures on Shakespeare and Other Dramatists* (World's Classics), p. 47.

[3] *The Sacred Wood* (4th ed., 1934), p. 92.

[4] See, e.g., H. S. Bennett's edition (1931), p. 17. Wilson too, in his comparison of Barabas and Aaron (pp. lxii-iii), assumes without question that Barabas is to be taken entirely seriously. Marlowe, I believe, has done exactly what Wilson here says he can *not* do, viz. " create a vivacious villain."

[5] *Christopher Marlowe* (1946), p. 279.

that denied that it was also a melodrama would be adequate. More recently still, Miss Agnes Latham has ably argued for a strong burlesque element in the horrors of Nashe's *Unfortunate Traveller.*[1] All this goes to show the capacity of an Elizabethan audience for a mixed response—and Wilson's description [2] of Aaron as " a humorous villain," comparable to " humorous heroes and humorous lovers " such as the Bastard in *King John* and Berowne, may gladly be accepted—yet I cannot feel that in its broad outlines *Titus* is anything but a tragedy in intention. It is, of course, precisely the " broad outlines " that Wilson denies to Shakespeare : his view is more plausible in the context of his own theory of Shakespeare revising a Peele play.

It is, then, to those outlines that we must now turn. From Ravenscroft in 1687 (" rather a heap of Rubbish then a Structure ") to Wilson in 1947 (" like some broken-down cart, laden with bleeding corpses from an Elizabethan scaffold, and driven by an executioner from Bedlam dressed in cap and bells ") the structure of the play has been severely criticized. But judged by the standards of its own day, not those of Shakespeare's maturity, it is a well-planned play. Most of the modifications made in the chap-book version (if that indeed represents the source) are purposeful, and such new difficulties as the dramatist involves himself in, like the relations of the Goths to Tamora on the one hand and to Lucius on the other, are easily accounted for by inexperience, combined with an ambition to treat political themes seriously.[3]

All this does not make *Titus* a good play, but it does make it a play that we can believe Shakespeare to have written seriously. I should like to look, as an example, at one of Wilson's objections, which is not, I think, so much wrong as over-stated. He remarks (p. x) that Tamora " takes a leading part in Act i, and is referred to in the rest of the play as an able schemer. But it is Aaron . . . who . . . afterwards contrives all the outrages against the family of the Andronici, not only without consulting Tamora, but professedly out of sheer devilry." There is admittedly lack

[1] *English Studies, 1948* (ed. F. P. Wilson), pp. 85-100.
[2] P. lxiv: cf. Tillyard, p. 138.   [3] See especially Tillyard, pp. 139-40.

of skill and uncertainty of purpose here, but surely not of a kind surprising in an inexperienced dramatist, whose imagination has been caught by the potentialities of a character which occupies only a subordinate position in his source. The liaison between Aaron and Tamora, too, forms a much more satisfactory sub-plot than Wilson admits, and oddly points forward, as do so many things in this play, to *King Lear* and the intrigue between Edmund and the wicked sisters. What *Titus* here lacks is spiritual depth and imaginative significance, not (or at least not so much) constructional competence.

But it is clearly not enough to show that some criticisms of the play have been too strongly put. Its positive claims to be in any sense a tragedy depend on whether Titus himself has any of the qualities of a tragic hero. I think he has, but that he is much less interesting in himself than as foreshadowing several of Shakespeare's mature tragedies. The best discussion of this topic, and indeed of the play as a whole, is that of H. T. Price,[1] who sees hints especially of Othello and Lear. I should like to look at those in turn, after glancing at the more obvious but perhaps more superficial parallel with Hamlet. In both *Hamlet* and *Titus* we have a combination of feigned madness with some degree of real mental unbalance. In both plays, Shakespeare has clearly learnt from Kyd, and I doubt whether a development to *Hamlet* through *Titus* can be convincingly claimed. In the main, the two plays would seem to belong to different lines of development from Kyd. At any rate, the figure of Titus surely owes something to Kyd's Hieronymo in *The Spanish Tragedy*, just as Hamlet probably does to Kyd's own *Hamlet*. Even in *Titus* there is something more than the alternate presentation of real madness and of cunning revenge under the guise of madness which we find in *The Spanish Tragedy*, but, of course, nothing approaching the subtlety of Hamlet's " antic disposition."

[1] *J.E.G.P.* 42 (1943), esp. pp. 70-80; t is to this essay that I would refer those interested in comparing the structure of *Titus* with that of Shakespeare's other tragedies. Professor Price has returned to the subject in *Construction in Shakespeare* (Ann Arbor, 1951), of which pp. 37-41 are devoted to *Titus*. Some similarities have, I hope, emerged from the discussion of the play and the chapbook in the section on *Source* in this Introduction.

The comparison with Othello is more illuminating. Titus, writes Price,[1] " has something of the simplicity of Othello; although he can estimate a man's capacity in the field, he is hopeless in the hands of a dishonest schemer at home." Further resemblances can be detected.[2] His idealism leads him to kill his daughter as a tribute to the ideal of purity, as he has earlier killed his son in the name of honour. He is, like Othello, essentially an isolated figure, though Shakespeare has not yet devised an adequate presentation of this: the feigned madness is the best he can do at the culminating point. The resemblance between Aaron and Iago is obvious, and Chiron and Demetrius are somewhat analogous to Roderigo as at once crude villains and dupes.

The resemblance to Lear is even more striking. The errors and crimes into which Titus's anger and inflexibility betray him in Act I have the same function in the play as those of Lear. The sense that errors and crimes alike spring from the same personality strikes me as already particularly Shakespearian. The man who slays his virtuous son in a bad quarrel (I. i. 342) is the same man who, when called upon to arbitrate on the rival claims for the empire, makes the fatal decision of accepting the invidious role, and then comes down on the side of the principle of primogeniture without reference to the merits of the case. Where he diverges from Lear is that he " never arrives at healing self-knowledge." [3] Price, from whom I take this phrase, acutely remarks that Marcus represents the moderation which Titus rejects, and that " roughly speaking, Lear is a Titus who becomes a Marcus, but a revenge-play necessarily precluded this type of development." [4] Later in the play, too, suggestions of *King Lear* are frequent: notably the sub-plot turning on the lust of a principal female character for a flamboyant villain, and the calling in of foreign aid to re-establish internal order.[5] Some affinities between *Titus* and *Lear* were noted by P. Allen, *Shakespeare, Jonson and Wilkins as Borrowers* (1928), pp. 13-18. The gulf

[1] *J.E.G.P.* 42 (1943), 74.
[2] I am here indebted to some notes given me by Mr. E. Honigmann.
[3] Price, p. 73.   [4] *Ibid.*
[5] The former motif, but not the latter, is in the chap-book.

between the plays is about as great as there could be between any two works by the same author, but at any rate one already sees Shakespeare in *Titus* planning on the grand scale, and achieving a result that, however little it may appeal to us, is beyond the powers of any other dramatist writing at the time.

To assign to *Titus* a definite place in Shakespeare's development is difficult, especially in view of the conflicting theories about its dating (absolute and relative); but I should like to conclude with a few remarks, made on the assumption of early date and serious (i.e. non-burlesque) intention.

It is, I think, the one play of Shakespeare which could have left an intelligent contemporary in some doubt whether the author's truest bent was for the stage, and this in spite of its superiority in sheer competence over most contemporary drama. It is true that the drama of the time had, as a whole, close connections with non-dramatic poetry,[1] but even when allowances have been made for that, we may still feel with Miss Bradbrook that *Titus* is " more like a pageant than a play." [2] What is not yet present is any sustained power of building up to a climax: as W. H. Clemen puts it, " instead of preparing us for *one* great event, for *one* climax, and leading us through all the stages of development up to this peak, Shakespeare overwhelms us from the first act on with ' climaxes,' with a multiplicity of fearful events and high-sounding words." [3] Professor Clemen, in the discussion from which this extract is taken, is specially concerned with Shakespeare's failure to make the imagery of the play subserve a genuinely dramatic purpose, and I have nothing to add to his account. But in concentrating on Shakespeare's failure to do what he does with increasing mastery in his mature plays, there is a danger of overlooking how far he has already got. He has a sense of the play as a whole, and a sense of the individual episode. It is principally in bringing the two into relation that he is still deficient. So too on the side of language:

[1] Two books already mentioned are relevant here: H. Baker, *Induction to Tragedy*, and M. C. Bradbrook, *Shakespeare and Elizabethan Poetry*.

[2] *Op. cit.* p. 110.

[3] *The Development of Shakespeare's Imagery* (1951), p. 25.

the individual phrase or line, and the rhetorical outline of a speech, are often successful; what is lacking is commonly the sense of appropriateness of speech to situation and character, and above all the power to convey a real impression of dramatic interchange:[1] " the characters are not yet talking with *each other*, but are delivering pompous orations to the audience." [2]

Yet the very fact that we can point to so many things that are wrong with *Titus* is itself evidence of dramatic life: no one dwells on defects, and suggests improvements, in the irremediably dull and worthless. And even if the things in *Titus* which look forward to the later tragedies derive most of their interest from what becomes of them in those tragedies, they have some impressiveness in their inchoate state. *Romeo and Juliet* is on almost every count a vastly superior play to *Titus*, but it could be maintained that *Titus* is strictly speaking more *promising*. The author of *Romeo and Juliet* could conceivably have gone in that play as far as he was destined to go in tragedy—and indeed Shakespeare's tragic development does not exactly proceed through *Romeo and Juliet*—but the author of *Titus* was obviously going *somewhere*: though it was not yet certain whether he would steer clear of violent episodic melodrama on the one hand and exaggeratedly Ovidian narrative in dialogue on the other.

5. RECENT WORK ON *TITUS*

Since my 1953 edition was published, a number of important scholarly and critical contributions to the study of *Titus* have appeared.

On the bibliographical side, there are Sir Walter Greg's last words on the play in *The Shakespeare First Folio* (1955). I discuss some of his views in the Additional Note on III. i. 36. Fredson Bowers, *Studies in Bibliography*, 9 (1957), 3-20, has

---

[1] But the scenes involving Aaron, Chiron and Demetrius seem to me to represent a tolerable level of achievement in this respect.

[2] Clemen, *op. cit.* p. 29; so in his *Die Tragödie vor Shakespeare* (1955) he discusses the process " wie sich aus dem starren und beziehungslosen Nebeneinanderstehen und Aneinandervorbeireden der Redepartner ein beziehungsreiches Zueinanderreden entwickelt " (p. 12).

argued that the Folio *Titus*, like *Romeo and Juliet*, was set up not, as has generally been believed, by one of the two principal compositors (B), but, except for the first page, by a less skilled workman whom he has renamed E. He notes on p. 7 that Dr. Alice Walker continues to attribute *Romeo and Juliet* to B. The press-variants in F which he records Dr. Hinman as having discovered (p. 12, n. 13) have not yet been published.

Two important new editions have appeared: that of C. J. Sisson, supplemented by his *New Readings in Shakespeare* (1956), in which I have found some welcome confirmation, some arguments that have convinced me, and some others which leave me still of my original opinion; and the post-humously published *London Shakespeare* of John Munro (1958).

The book which discusses *Titus* at greatest length is T. W. Baldwin's *On the Literary Genetics of Shakspere's Plays 1592-1594* (1959). I have given my views on this book as a whole in *Notes and Queries* 205 (1960), 354-5. Baldwin believes, largely on grounds of its structure and " casting-pattern," that *Titus* " was first written for the Admiral's men around 1588 or 1589 " (p. 234), not by Shakespeare (p. 445), and that the existing version represents a 1594 revision by Peele and Shakespeare (p. 420), but that " the *Old Titus* ran in much the same fashion as the *Titus* of 1954." He re-examines the Peele links, notably the " palliament " (pp. xxvii-viii above). The fact that " pallium " was the recognized term for the Garter mantle gives some weight to his contention that the poem precedes the passage in the play (p. 412), and his whole discussion (ch. XXII) strengthens the case for Peele's hand in *Titus*. He emphasizes that at II. iii. 129-30 (see note) it is easier to see Nashe as the source than as the debtor (pp. 416-18). A claim for the priority of *Venus and Adonis* to II. iii. 17-20 (see note on l. 17) is less persuasive to me (pp. 418-20). Baldwin also examines the Dutch and German versions, which I ignored in my earlier edition because I could see no reason to dissent from E. K. Chambers's view (*William Shakespeare*, I. 319) that " the facts are quite consistent with the natural hypothesis of divergence from a common source in an adaptation of [the surviving] *Titus Andronicus* for continental travel." Baldwin's claims for a debt to the *Old Titus* are not far-reaching, but modest as they are, they have not persuaded me that Chambers was wrong. The hypothesis of revision has its attractions—it does some justice to Henslow's " ne," and accounts for certain 1593-4 links (p. xxvi above)—but I find it hard to believe in a completely non-Shakespearian *Old Titus* which yet resembled the existing play in structure as closely as Baldwin holds that it did.

Shakespeare Survey, vol. 10 (1957), contained three excellent articles relevant to *Titus*. Terence Spencer's brilliant " Shakespeare and the Elizabethan Romans " brings out the way in which *Titus* must have been less un-Roman to the Elizabethans than it is to us: " One could almost say without paradox that, in many respects, *Titus Andronicus* is a more typical Roman play, a more characteristic piece of Roman history, than the three great plays of Shakespeare which are generally grouped under that name " (p. 32). He also emphasizes the oddly eclectic treatment of Roman institutions of all periods: " The author seems anxious, not to get it all right, but to get it all in " (*ibid.*). R. F. Hill, in " The Composition of *Titus Andronicus*," is studiedly agnostic on the authorship question. He still leans towards crediting it all to Shakespeare as his first play, but his analysis of the use of certain rhetorical devices shows marked divergence between *Titus* and any of the other ten early plays chosen for comparison. I think he has established beyond all reasonable doubt that " to contend for sole Shakespearian authorship of *Titus* and composition in 1593-4 is nonsense " (p. 68). His acute analysis (p. 63) of the play's structural weaknesses is a corrective to more indulgent accounts, including that on pp. xxxviii-ix above, though I would still hold (and Hill does not deny) that it is beyond the ascertained power of any contemporary dramatist except Kyd (Marlowe's whole approach to drama being radically different). Finally, E. M. Waith in " The Metamorphosis of Violence in *Titus Andronicus* " follows out some of the implications of Shakespeare's Ovidianism, concluding (p. 48) that " in taking over certain Ovidian forms Shakespeare takes over part of an Ovidian conception which cannot be fully realized by the techniques of drama " (cf. p. xxxvii above).

He also notes how the play answers to the Renaissance demand for " admiration " as one main effect of a tragedy. In a paper in *Essays in Criticism*, vol. 10 (1960), 275-89, "Wilderness of Tigers: Structure and Symbol in *Titus Andronicus*", Mr. Alan Sommers discusses the conflict between Rome and " the barbarism of primitive, original nature " (p. 276) embodied in Tamora and Aaron.

ADDITIONAL NOTES

p. xii, l. 1. *comma at end of the line.* On this, see A. C. Baugh, " A Medieval Survival in Elizabethan Punctuation " (*Studies in the English Renaissance Drama in Memory of Karl Julius Holzknecht* (1959), pp. 1-15).

pp. xv-vi. On the Longleat drawing, see Oppel, ch. viii, who persuasively develops Munro's views, and concludes (p.115) that no single occasion is depicted but " drei Hauptgestalten zu einem repräsentativen Gesamtbild vereinigt werden."

p. xxii, *A Knack to Know a Knave.* Mr. P. E. Bennett (*Notes and Queries*, 200 (1955), 422-4, 462-3) has argued that *A Knack to Know a Knave* is a Bad Quarto, that " Goths " is a reporter's substitution, under the influence of *Titus*, for "Jews," and that the " Titus " in question is the Flavian Emperor. The contamination, he thinks, took place about the end of 1593, when some of Strange's men were rehearsing *Titus*, which he believes really was " new " on 24 Jan. 1594. (He interprets the Q 1 title-page as referring to this production by " a mixed company of actors, mostly Sussex's, as Henslowe notes, but also with a few of Derby's [Strange's] and Pembroke's.") I think the other evidence against such a late date remains strong, but I agree that caution is advisable in using the lines from *A Knack.* The passage is inept as a reference to the Titus of our play (but then, much of *A Knack* is inept, and it can scarcely all be the reporter's fault). Mr Bennett certainly goes much too far in holding that, with the substitution of " Jews " for " Goths," we have a perfectly normal reference to the emperor Titus. To say of the senators that they

in requitall of his service done
Did offer him the imperiale Diademe

would be a most confused way of referring to the fact that, as Mr. Bennett himself puts it, " Titus Vespasianus was welcomed back from Jerusalem by the senators and by them made co-emperor with his father, virtually on the spot." It is certainly not so much more apt than a reference to the Titus of our play as to entitle us to accept Mr. Bennett's restoration with confidence, though I should myself be prepared to refrain from making any use at all of *A Knack* in view of the uncertain nature of its text. If its author did write " Goths," his mind may have been in a state of glorious confusion about the two Tituses.

pp. xxvii-viii *palliament.* See the elaborate discussion in Baldwin (1959), pp. 404 ff., briefly referred to on p. xliii above.

Shakespeare Survey 14 (1961) includes two articles bearing on *Titus*. Gustav Ungerer prints and discusses an account of a performance on New Year's Day, 1596, for Sir John Harington at Burley-on-the-Hill; the critical comment is worth quoting : " la monstre a plus valeu q̃ le suiect." Nicholas Brooke, writing on " Marlowe as Provocative Agent in Shakespeare's Early Plays ", deals with Titus on pp. 35-7.

D

TITUS ANDRONICUS

DRAMATIS PERSONÆ [1]

SATURNINUS, *son to the late Emperor of Rome and afterwards Emperor.*

BASSIANUS, *brother to Saturninus.*

TITUS ANDRONICUS, *a noble Roman, general against the Goths.*

MARCUS ANDRONICUS, *tribune of the People, and brother to Titus.*

LUCIUS,
QUINTUS,
MARTIUS, }*sons to Titus Andronicus.*
MUTIUS,

Young LUCIUS, *a boy, son to Lucius.*

PUBLIUS, *son to Marcus Andronicus.*

SEMPRONIUS,
CAIUS, }*kinsmen to Titus.*
VALENTINE,

ÆMILIUS, *a noble Roman.*

ALARBUS,
DEMETRIUS, }*sons to Tamora.*
CHIRON,

AARON, *a Moor, beloved by Tamora.*

Messenger, and Clown.

Goths and Romans.

TAMORA, *Queen of the Goths.*

LAVINIA, *daughter to Titus Andronicus.*

A Nurse, and a black Child.

Kinsmen of Titus, Senators, Tribunes, Officers, Soldiers, and Attendants.

Scene : *Rome, and the Country near it.*

[1] First given imperfectly by Rowe.

2

TITUS ANDRONICUS

ACT I

SCENE I

Enter the Tribunes and Senators aloft ; and then enter SATURNINUS
and his followers at one door, and BASSIANUS *and his followers
at the other, with drums and trumpets.*

Sat. Noble patricians, patrons of my right,
Defend the justice of my cause with arms;
And, countrymen, my loving followers,

ACT I

Scene 1

Actus Primus. Scæna Prima. F;   om. Qq.   Enter] Flourish.
Enter F.   at the other] om. Qq.   drums] Drum Q 3, F.   trumpets]
Colours F.

Scene 1] Except for scene division, and a few F and editorial supplements, I have throughout gone right back to Q stage-directions. Such additional information as " Rome " or " the Capitol " is evident from the text when it is of any importance.

Enter . . . aloft] This does not mean that we see them coming on, but that they are " discovered " by drawing back the curtains of the upper stage: G. F. Reynolds, *The Staging of Elizabethan Plays*, p. 48, quotes for this use of *Enter* from *George a Greene* sc. xi: " Enter a Shoemaker sitting upon the stage at worke." The staging of the play is throughout very simple and any standard account, e.g. the brief one by C. J. Sisson in *Companion to Shakespeare Studies*, ed. Granville-Barker and Harrison, will give the necessary information.

at one door . . . at the other] The specification of " at one door " in Q 1 makes it clear that the contrasting " at the other," supplied

by F, is required. On this form of expression in stage directions cf. W. Archer and W. J. Lawrence in *Shakespeare's England* II. 304-5: " Though there were in fact three doors opening upon the stage, two of them were so much more prominent and more frequently used, that playwrights often expressed themselves as though they alone existed. They would, indeed, be the only doors visible when the curtains of the Rear Stage were closed "—as they would be in this scene.

Flourish] trumpet-call. F has a number of additional directions of this kind, originating in the prompt-book with which the copy of Q 3 used by the printer has been very roughly collated.

1. Sat.] this (unabbreviated) and the speech prefixes at ll. 9, 18, 46, 47 and 56, and also at v. i. 121-4, are centred in Qq. At I. i. 64, 157, II. iii. 192, II. iv. 11, a centred entry serves instead of a speech heading. For I. i. 358, 360 see critical apparatus.

3

Plead my successive title with your swords:
I am his first-born son that was the last   5
That ware the imperial diadem of Rome;
Then let my father's honours live in me,
Nor wrong mine age with this indignity.

Bass. Romans, friends, followers, favourers of my right,
If ever Bassianus, Cæsar's son,   10
Were gracious in the eyes of royal Rome,
Keep then this passage to the Capitol,
And suffer not dishonour to approach
The imperial seat, to virtue consecrate,
To justice, continence, and nobility;   15
But let desert in pure election shine,
And, Romans, fight for freedom in your choice.

Marc. [*holding the crown*] Princes, that strive by factions and
        by friends
Ambitiously for rule and empery,
Know that the people of Rome, for whom we stand   20
A special party, have by common voice,

5. *am his*] *was the* F.   6. *ware*] *wore* F.   14. *virtue consecrate,*] Rowe
(2nd ed.) ; *vertue, consecrate* Qq; *Vertue: consecrate* F.   18. Marc. [holding the
crown]] Bolton ; Marcus Andronicus with the Crowne Qq. (centred) ; Enter
Marcus Andronicus aloft with the Crowne F (centred).

4. *successive title*] title to the succession. Cf. *2H6* III. i. 49: "successive heir."
5. *his . . . that*] of him who. Q I
gives a comma after *son*. This is in
keeping with the practice of Shakespeare's time (cf. Simpson, p. 42),
but I omit the comma, here and in
ll. 39-40, 122, to make the construction clearer to the modern reader.
For the possible bearing of the
frequency of this construction on the
authorship of Act I, see Introduction,
pp. xxvi-xxvii.
8. *mine age*] the fact that I am the
elder. Delius's view that *age* virtually means "youth", and that
Shakespeare means he is too young
to enforce recognition of his rights,
is less plausible.
10-13. *If . . . And*] Wilson, pp.
xxvii-viii, notes the identity of
structure with ll. 428-31.

11. *gracious*] acceptable: so ll. 170,
381 (graciously), 429, II. i. 32.
15. *continence*] self-restraint, with
special reference to the use of power.
16. *pure election*] in contrast to
Saturninus's claim from primogeniture.
18. Marc. [holding the crown]]
Bolton's interpretation of the Q I
direction (*Modern Language Notes*, 45
(1930), 139-40) is undoubtedly correct. Marcus has been on stage with
the other Tribunes from the beginning
of the scene. Q I centres the
speech-heading of the two speeches
that precede this and of the three
that follow.
19. *empery*] status of emperor, as
in ll. 22, 201, and *empire* in l. 183.
20-1. *people . . . party*] The very
vaguely conceived Rome of this
play is divided into patricians and
plebeians ("people"), the latter

In election for the Roman empery,
Chosen Andronicus, surnamed Pius
For many good and great deserts to Rome.
A nobler man, a braver warrior,   25
Lives not this day within the city walls:
He by the senate is accited home
From weary wars against the barbarous Goths,
That with his sons, a terror to our foes,
Hath yok'd a nation strong, train'd up in arms.   30
Ten years are spent since first he undertook
This cause of Rome, and chastised with arms
Our enemies' pride: five times he hath return'd
Bleeding to Rome, bearing his valiant sons
In coffins from the field, and at this day   35
To the monument of the Andronici   35a
Done sacrifice of expiation,   35b
And slain the noblest prisoner of the Goths.   35c
And now at last, laden with honour's spoils,
Returns the good Andronicus to Rome,
Renowned Titus, flourishing in arms.

---

23. *Pius*] Pious F.   35-35c. *and . . . Goths*] om. Q 2-3, F.
35a. *the Andronici*] Chambers; *that* Andronicy Q 1.

---

being represented by tribunes as
in republican Rome (and, as a
nominal survival, under the empire).
The *factions* of l. 18 are both
patrician.

23. *Pius*] Q 1's colon after this
word, if it is not a sheer blunder,
may be analogous to the use of the
colon to introduce reported speech,
cf. Simpson, pp. 77-8. The next
line, as it were, quotes the grounds
for the assignment of the "sur-
name." Q 2 (more normally) prints
a comma (and a colon at the end of
l. 24 where Q 1 has a comma).

27. *accited*] summoned.

30. *yok'd*] brought under the yoke:
the symbol of conquest by Rome,
cf. l. 69.

32. *chastised*] Seven times in Shakespeare with this stress, against two
with "chastíse" (On.).

35-35c. *and . . . Goths*] These lines,
omitted in Q 2, conflict with the rest
of the scene. But it is doubtful
whether they belong to an earlier
version. The general account of
Titus's return in ll. 36 ff. reads very
oddly after the more specific account
in these lines of what he has done
on his return. L. 36 sounds like a
fresh start, made after the preceding
lines had already been, in intention,
deleted. The whole speech may never
have been reduced to a satisfactory
state by the author.

35a. *the Andronici*] The MS. presumably had "yᵉ," which could
easily be misread as "yᵗ" by a compositor who did not realize (note his
spelling of it) that *Andronici* was
plural. The correction by Chambers
appears in his "Red Letter" edition,
1907.

Let us entreat, by honour of his name
Whom worthily you would have now succeed,   40
And in the Capitol and senate's right,
Whom you pretend to honour and adore,
That you withdraw you and abate your strength,
Dismiss your followers, and, as suitors should,
Plead your deserts in peace and humbleness.   45
Sat. How fair the tribune speaks to calm my thoughts!
Bass. Marcus Andronicus, so I do affy
In thy uprightness and integrity,
And so I love and honour thee and thine,
Thy noble brother Titus and his sons,   50
And her to whom my thoughts are humbled all,
Gracious Lavinia, Rome's rich ornament,
That I will here dismiss my loving friends,
And to my fortune's and the people's favour
Commit my cause in balance to be weigh'd.   55
                    [*Exeunt the followers of Bassianus.*
Sat. Friends, that have been thus forward in my right,
I thank you all and here dismiss you all,
And to the love and favour of my country
Commit myself, my person, and the cause.
                    [*Exeunt the followers of Saturninus.*
Rome, be as just and gracious unto me   60
As I am confident and kind to thee.

---

40. *succeed*] succeeded Capell.   41. *Capitol*] Capitall Q 1-2.   54. *fortune's*]
Delius; *fortunes* Qq; *Fortunes* F.   55. Exeunt . . . Bassianus] Capell;
Exit Soldiers Qq, F.   59. Exeunt . . . Saturninus] Capell; om. Qq, F,

---

39-40. *by honour . . . succeed*] The
ground of Marcus's appeal to the
factions seems to be the respect each
of them feels for its own candidate.
This is a little odd, but not sufficiently
to make acceptable Capell's ingenious
emendation, according to which *his* . . .
whom would refer to the late emperor.
41. *Capitol . . . right*] the right
of the Capitol and the senate.
The omission of inflection after the
first of two co-ordinate possessive
nouns is common (Abbott § 397;
Franz § 684d, quoting *Mac.* v. vii. 16:

" my wife and children's ghosts ").
as indeed it is in colloquial modern
English. The whole phrase seems
to mean " with due respect for the
rightful claims of the Capitol and
the senate ": cf. On. *right* sb.¹, 2.
42. *pretend*] claim.
47. *affy*] trust.
54. *fortune's*] Delius's interpretation of the ambiguous *fortunes* seems
preferable to treating it as plural.
61. *confident and kind*] a trusting and
loving son: *kind* = possessed of
natural affection.

Open the gates and let me in.

Bass. Tribunes, and me, a poor competitor.

[*They go up into the Senate-house.*

Enter a Captain.

Cap. Romans, make way, the good Andronicus,
Patron of virtue, Rome's best champion,   65
Successful in the battles that he fights,
With honour and with fortune is return'd
From where he circumscribed with his sword,
And brought to yoke, the enemies of Rome.

Sound drums and trumpets, and then enter two of Titus' *sons,
and then two Men bearing a coffin covered with black; then
two other sons; then* Titus Andronicus; *and then* Tamora,
the Queen of Goths, and her sons, Alarbus, Chiron, *and*
Demetrius, *with* Aaron *the Moor, and others as many as
can be; then set down the coffin, and* Titus *speaks.*

63. They] Flourish. They F.   65 *Patron*] *Pattern* Anon. conj. (in Camb.).
68. *where*] *whence* F.   69. and then two] After them, two F. then
Titus] After them, Titus F. her . . . *ALARBUS*] Rowe; her two . . . Qq, F.
then set] They set F.

65. *Patron*] Up to the sixteenth century, this spelling represented both the meanings now differentiated as patron and pattern (see *N.E.D.*, "pattern"), as still in French "patron." By Shakespeare's time the two had become fairly distinct, but there are a few instances from Spenser which suggest the earlier undifferentiated stage. In *F.Q.*, Argument to I. i. "the Patron of true Holinesse" and *Letter to Raleigh* "of the xii. other vertues, I make xii. other knights the patrones," the appropriate gloss might be "representative," which looks towards both the modern words. Lodowick Bryskett in his account of Spenser's plan stresses the "patron" aspect: "assigning to every vertue, a Knight to be the patron and defender of the same" (*Discourse of Civill Life*, 1606, p. 27). In the present passage, "representative" gives good sense. Another survival of the original identity of the two words is recorded in *English Dialect Dictionary*, "patron *sb.*¹," where the form "pattern" is quoted as current in Ireland for "a fair in honour of a patron saint."

68. *circumscribed*] brought within bounds.

69. S.D. There is no entrance for Alarbus (Rowe added one), though he has an exit at l. 129. Since he has not a speaking part, and since Q 1 was set up from author's "foul papers" and not from prompt-copy, the omission need not indicate revision. J. Munro (*T.L.S.*, 10 June 1949, p. 388) holds that Alarbus was never on the stage at all, and that the mention of him at l. 129 S.D. is an erroneous addition by "somebody" unspecified. The book-keeper could have made a jotting on the MS. (cf. v. i., initial S.D.), but there is no reason to think he would have done so without justification.

others . . . be] a typical S.D. from author's MS. At *2H6* IV. ii. 33, F

Tit. Hail, Rome, victorious in thy mourning weeds ! 70
 Lo, as the bark that hath discharg'd his fraught
 Returns with precious lading to the bay
 From whence at first she weigh'd her anchorage,
 Cometh Andronicus, bound with laurel boughs,
 To re-salute his country with his tears, 75
 Tears of true joy for his return to Rome.
 Thou great defender of this Capitol,
 Stand gracious to the rites that we intend.
 Romans, of five and twenty valiant sons,
 Half of the number that King Priam had, 80
 Behold the poor remains, alive and dead.
 These that survive, let Rome reward with love;
 These that I bring unto their latest home,
 With burial amongst their ancestors. 84
 Here Goths have given me leave to sheathe my sword.
 Titus, unkind, and careless of thine own,
 Why suffer'st thou thy sons, unburied yet,
 To hover on the dreadful shore of Styx ?

71. *his*] F 4. 76. *Rome.*] Rowe (Ravenscroft); *Rome,* Qq, F. 78. *rites*] *rights* Q 1-2.

has, less modestly, "Enter Cade . . . with infinite numbers."

S.D. the coffin] The singular is surprising, as A. Koszul, *English Studies* 31 (1950), 182, points out, since ll. 84, 89, 94 call for a number of corpses. But this is probably how the author envisaged the staging and we cannot safely emend. At l. 149, but not elsewhere, F emends to "coffins."

71. *his*] The alteration to *her* is, in the light of l. 73, an obvious one, but the irregularity may well go back to author's MS. In the 1609 text of *Sonnet* 102 ll. 8 and 10 we have the same sequence of "his . . . her."

73. *anchorage*] "set of anchors" (On.); but it seems to be scarcely more than a rhetorical variation for "anchors."

77. *Thou . . . defender*] Jupiter Capitolinus.

78. *rites*] The spelling of Q 1-2 is not uncommon, cf. l. 143, v. iii. 196, *Ham.* (Q 2) v. ii. 413.

80. *Half . . . had*] Priam's fifty sons are so well known that a specific source need not be sought. The total of Titus's sons actually adds up to twenty-six, cf. III. i. 10. This may (C. Crawford cited by Baildon) be because Mutius was an afterthought: see Oppel, pp. 22-3.

83. *latest home*] ultimately from *Ecclesiastes* XII. 5, "long home." *O.D.E.P.* p. 381 cites Brunne (1303): "And thy traueyle shalt thou sone ende, | For to thy long home sone shalt thou wende"; Tilley, H533, Lyly's *Euphues and his England* (1580) : "Shal. . . a trauailer that hath sustained harm. . . disswade al Gentlemen to rest at their own home till they come to their long home ?"

87-8. *Why . . . Styx ?*] Lee quotes Virgil, *Aen.* VI. 325-9: "haec omnis, quam cernis, inops inhumataque turba est . . . volitantque haec litora circum." The closeness of *hover* to *volitant* suggests an actual echo.

Make way to lay them by their brethren.

[*They open the tomb.*

There greet in silence, as the dead are wont,   90
And sleep in peace, slain in your country's wars.
O sacred receptacle of my joys,
Sweet cell of virtue and nobility,
How many sons hast thou of mine in store,
That thou wilt never render to me more!   95

Luc. Give us the proudest prisoner of the Goths,
That we may hew his limbs, and on a pile
Ad manes fratrum sacrifice his flesh
Before this earthy prison of their bones,
That so the shadows be not unappeas'd,   100
Nor we disturb'd with prodigies on earth.

Tit. I give him you, the noblest that survives,
The eldest son of this distressed queen.

Tam. Stay, Roman brethren! Gracious conqueror,
Victorious Titus, rue the tears I shed,   105
A mother's tears in passion for her son:

89. *brethren*] *bretheren* Q 3, F (so 123, 160, 357).   90. *the*] om. Q 2.
94. *hast thou of mine*] *of mine hast thou* Q 3, F.   98. *manes*] F 3;
manus Qq, F.   *flesh* Stoll; *flesh:* Qq, F.   99. *earthy*] *earthly* F.   103. *this*]
his Q 3.

89. *brethren*] Q 1 varies between the
spellings *brethren* and *bretheren* (and
similarly between *empress* and *em-
peress*). Since it never uses the longer
form except where a trisyllabic scansion is appropriate, it is tempting to
follow Wilson and Alexander in
varying the spelling throughout according to scansion ; but on balance
it seems best to use the present-day
spelling consistently. I have, however, recorded in the apparatus all
occurrences of the longer form in Q 1.
In the history plays the name
" Henry " is constantly varying between a disyllabic and a trisyllabic
pronunciation without any variation
of spelling. This fact makes it ex-
tremely unlikely that the variations
in *Titus* " may point to difference of
authorship " (Wilson on l. 240).
On the allied question of divergent
spellings of proper names as a clue
to divergent authorship, cf. P.

Alexander, *Shakespeare's* Henry VI *and*
Richard III (Cambridge, 1929),
pp. 178-84, whose conclusions are
entirely negative.

92. *receptacle*]   Stressed   " ré-
ceptácle " as in *Rom.* iv. iii. 40, and
as late as Wordsworth (*Prel.* x. 170,
and two other passages: the only ones
in which he uses the word). Wilson
glosses " sepulchre, vault," which is
too specific, though the word can
be used, as here and in the *Rom.*
passage, with reference to a sepulchre. The word is now more
prosaic and more exclusively used
of a *small* container.

98. Ad manes fratrum] to the
shades of (our) brethren.

101. *prodigies*] ominous events.

106. *passion*] grief; this word has a
wide range of meanings in Shakespeare's English; for others, cf. II. i.
36, III. i. 217.

And if thy sons were ever dear to thee,
O, think my son to be as dear to me.
Sufficeth not that we are brought to Rome,
To beautify thy triumphs, and return   110
Captive to thee and to thy Roman yoke;
But must my sons be slaughtered in the streets
For valiant doings in their country's cause?
O, if to fight for king and commonweal
Were piety in thine, it is in these.   115
Andronicus, stain not thy tomb with blood:
Wilt thou draw near the nature of the gods?
Draw near them then in being merciful;
Sweet mercy is nobility's true badge:
Thrice-noble Titus, spare my first-born son.   120

Tit. Patient yourself, madam, and pardon me.
These are their brethren whom your Goths beheld
Alive and dead, and for their brethren slain
Religiously they ask a sacrifice:
To this your son is mark'd, and die he must,   125
T' appease their groaning shadows that are gone.

Luc. Away with him, and make a fire straight,
And with our swords, upon a pile of wood,
Let's hew his limbs till they be clean consum'd.

                        [Exit Titus' sons, with Alarbus.

Tam. O cruel, irreligious piety!   130
Chi. Was never Scythia half so barbarous!

---

108. *son*] *sonnes* F.   110. *triumphs, and return*] *triumphs and return,* Theobald (see Add. Notes).   112. *slaughtered*] *slaughtred* F.   122. *their*] *the* F. *your*] *you* Q 2-3, F.   129. *Titus'*] om. F.   131. *never . . . barbarous!*] *neuer . . barbarous.* Q 1 ; *euer . . . barbarous?* Q 2-3, F.

112. *slaughtered*] I have throughout followed the Q spelling for words of this kind, except where rhythm tells strongly against it. Here the extra unstressed syllable is quite unobjectionable.

116. *thy tomb*] thy family tomb.

117-18. *Wilt . . . merciful*] No specific source need be sought for this commonplace. Steevens quoted Cicero, *pro Ligario* xii. 38. Mr. G. K. Hunter refers me to *England's*

Parnassus (ed. C. Crawford), Nos. 1157, 1158.

121. *Patient yourself*] calm down; so in *Arden of Feversham* (*Shakespeare Apocrypha*, ed. Tucker Brooke), v. i. 86 (Steevens).

127. *fire*] Disyllabic, as often with similar words : the best-known example is *R2* i. iii. 294: " O, who can hold a fire in his hand."

129. S.D. Exit . . . Alarbus] See on l. 69 S.D.

Dem. Oppose not Scythia to ambitious Rome.
Alarbus goes to rest, and we survive
To tremble under Titus' threat'ning look.
Then, madam, stand resolv'd, but hope withal   135
The self-same gods that arm'd the Queen of Troy
With opportunity of sharp revenge
Upon the Thracian tyrant in his tent
May favour Tamora, the Queen of Goths,
(When Goths were Goths, and Tamora was queen) 140
To quit the bloody wrongs upon her foes.

Enter the sons of Andronicus again.

Luc. See, lord and father, how we have perform'd
Our Roman rites: Alarbus' limbs are lopp'd,
And entrails feed the sacrificing fire,
Whose smoke like incense doth perfume the sky.   145
Remaineth nought but to inter our brethren,
And with loud 'larums welcome them to Rome.

Tit. Let it be so; and let Andronicus
Make this his latest farewell to their souls.

[Sound trumpets, and lay the coffin in the tomb.

In peace and honour rest you here, my sons;   150
Rome's readiest champions, repose you here in rest,

132. *not*] *me* F.   134. *look*] *lookes* F.   138. *his*] *her* Theobald.
141. *the*] *her* Rowe; *these* Capell conj.   143. *rites*] F 2; *right(e)s* Qq, F.
149. Sound] Flourish. Then Sound F. Coffin] Coffins F.   151. *Rome's*]
Roomes Q 1 (so 164, 186, 193).

132. *Oppose*] compare: a Latinism,
for which *N.E.D.* has no exact
parallel; but its 5 is fairly close.

136-8. *Queen . . . tent*] Hecuba,
who killed the sons of Polymnestor
in revenge for the murder of her son
Polydorus. If the author knew
the version in the *Hecuba* of Euripides,
the emendation *her* for *his* is probable.
But Steevens remarked that he
"might have been misled by the
passage in Ovid: ' vadit ad *artificem* '
(*Met.* XIII. 551), and therefore took
it for granted that she found him in
his tent."

141. *the*] Capell's conjecture may
well be right.

143. *rites*] See on l. 78.

143-4. *Alarbus' . . . entrails*] The
possessive can, I think, carry over the
intervening phrase in a way that is
not possible in modern English,
though I can find no close parallel
for this usage.

147. *'larums*] trumpet calls (lit.
" calls to arms "). Or (On.) the
sense may be more general: " tumul-
tuous noises."

151. *Rome*] For the Q 1 spelling,
representing the pronunciation, see
Wyld, p. 239, and cf. *John* III. i. 180:
" That I have room with Rome to
curse awhile." This, and the more
normal spelling, alternate in what
seems quite a random fashion in
Titus.

Secure from worldly chances and mishaps.
Here lurks no treason, here no envy swells,
Here grow no damned drugs, here are no storms,
No noise, but silence and eternal sleep.   155
In peace and honour rest you here, my sons.

Enter LAVINIA.

Lav. In peace and honour live Lord Titus long;
My noble lord and father live in fame.
Lo, at this tomb my tributary tears
I render for my brethren's obsequies;   160
And at thy feet I kneel, with tears of joy
Shed on this earth for thy return to Rome.
O, bless me here with thy victorious hand,
Whose fortunes Rome's best citizens applaud.

Tit. Kind Rome, that hast thus lovingly reserv'd   165
The cordial of mine age to glad my heart.
Lavinia, live; outlive thy father's days,
And fame's eternal date, for virtue's praise.

Enter MARCUS ANDRONICUS *and Tribunes; re-enter*
SATURNINUS, BASSIANUS, *and others.*

Marc. Long live Lord Titus, my beloved brother,
Gracious triumpher in the eyes of Rome.   170

---

154. *drugs] drugges* Q 1-2 ; *grudgges* Q 3 ; *grudges* F.   157. Lav.] om. Q 1.
158 *father] Father,* F.   162. *this] the* Q 2-3, F.   164. *fortunes] Fortune* F.
168. Enter . . . others] Dyce (substantially) ; om. Qq, F.

154. *drugs*] plants which produce poisons: " poisons " is the commonest Shakespearian sense. For the absence of poisonous plants as an item in the praise of a country, Prof. R. A. B. Mynors refers me to the praise of Italy in Virgil, *Georg.* II. 152: " nec miseros fallunt aconita legentes." Seneca, *Troades* 145 ff., has been quoted as a source for this whole speech—not, I think, very convincingly.

156. S.D.] Wilson places Lavinia's entry after l. 155, in order to indicate that she has heard the last line of Titus's speech.

158. *live*] Probably third person (" let him live ") rather than ordinary imperative. The absence of punctuation after *father* in Qq is not conclusive in favour of this, since they do not habitually place commas after nouns in the vocative (cf. Simpson, pp. 21-2), but it is natural to take ll. 157 and 158 as parallel in construction.

166. *cordial*] comfort; cf. *R3* II. i. 41-2: " a pleasing cordial . . . Is this thy vow."

168. S.D. Enter . . . others] As Wilson says, F's S.D. at l. 233 shows that this entry is on the upper stage.

Tit. Thanks, gentle tribune, noble brother Marcus.

Marc. And welcome, nephews, from successful wars,
  You that survive, and you that sleep in fame.
  Fair lords, your fortunes are alike in all
  That in your country's service drew your swords;   175
  But safer triumph is this funeral pomp
  That hath aspir'd to Solon's happiness
  And triumphs over chance in honour's bed.
  Titus Andronicus, the people of Rome,
  Whose friend in justice thou hast ever been,   180
  Send thee by me, their tribune and their trust,
  This palliament of white and spotless hue,
  And name thee in election for the empire,
  With these our late-deceased emperor's sons:
  Be *candidatus* then, and put it on,   185
  And help to set a head on headless Rome.

Tit. A better head her glorious body fits
  Than his that shakes for age and feebleness.
  What should I don this robe, and trouble you?
  Be chosen with proclamations to-day,   190
  To-morrow yield up rule, resign my life,
  And set abroad new business for you all?
  Rome, I have been thy soldier forty years,
  And led my country's strength successfully,
  And buried one and twenty valiant sons,   195
  Knighted in field, slain manfully in arms,
  In right and service of their noble country.

174. *alike*] *all alike* F.   184. *late-deceased*] Theobald; *late deceased* Qq, F.
189.*What*] *What!* Theobald.   *you?*] Q 1 (F 3); *you*, Q 2-3, F.   192. *abroad*]
abroach F 3.   *all?*] Pope; *all*. Qq, F.

177. *aspir'd*] risen, implying (in
contrast to modern English) that
the end has been attained. But the
modern sense was also common in
Shakespeare's time.
  Solon's happiness] A reference to the
saying (first in Herodotus, I. 32)
" call no man happy until he is
dead."
  181. *trust*] trusted one.
  182. *palliament*] See Introduction,
pp. xxvii-viii.
  183. *in election*] i.e. as a candidate.

185. candidatus] lit. " clad in a
white robe."
  189. *What*] why; but Theob. may
be right.
  190. *proclamations*] Five syllables.
  192. *set abroad*] Not recorded elsewhere. F 3's emendation, which
was accepted by Dyce, is tempting,
and restores a very common expression, meaning " set on foot."
  197. *In . . . of*] in support of the
just claims of, and in service to.

Give me a staff of honour for mine age,
But not a sceptre to control the world:
Upright he held it, lords, that held it last.   200
Marc. Titus, thou shalt obtain and ask the empery.
Sat. Proud and ambitious tribune, canst thou tell?
Tit. Patience, Prince Saturninus.
Sat.   Romans, do me right:
Patricians, draw your swords, and sheathe them not
Till Saturninus be Rome's emperor.   205
Andronicus, would thou were shipp'd to hell,
Rather than rob me of the people's hearts!
Luc. Proud Saturnine, interrupter of the good
That noble-minded Titus means to thee!
Tit. Content thee, prince; I will restore to thee   210
The people's hearts, and wean them from themselves.
Bass. Andronicus, I do not flatter thee,
But honour thee, and will do till I die:
My faction if thou strengthen with thy friends,
I will most thankful be; and thanks to men   215
Of noble minds is honourable meed.
Tit. People of Rome, and people's tribunes here,
I ask your voices and your suffrages:
Will ye bestow them friendly on Andronicus?
Tribunes. To gratify the good Andronicus,   220
And gratulate his safe return to Rome,
The people will accept whom he admits.
Tit. Tribunes, I thank you; and this suit I make,

---

206. *were*] *wert* Q 3, F.   214. *friends*] Q 1 (F 3); *friend* Q 2-3, F.
217. *people's*] *Noble* F.   219. *ye*] *you* Q 2-3, F. *Andronicus?*] Andronicus. Q 1.
223. *suit*] *sute* Qq (F 3); *sure* F.

201. *obtain and ask*] obtain if only
you ask; perhaps (Baildon) to
indicate "the certainty of Titus'
election." Tilley A343 quotes "ask
and have" as a proverb from
Stewart's *Chronicle of Scotland* (1535).
202. *canst thou tell?*] For this
"defiant or evasive phrase" (On.)
cf. *Err.* III. i. 52, *1H4* II. i. 43. The
meaning of the latter passage, as here,
seems to be: "that's what *you* think,
is it?"
214. *friends*] The "s" is very

heavily inked in Q 1, and may
have been mistaken for a semicolon
by Q 2, which reads "friend,".
217. *people's*] F's "noble" is taken
up from the previous line.
219. *Will . . . Andronicus?*] The
Q 1 punctuation (comma at the
end of 218 and full stop after
Andronicus) could perhaps be defended as something more tentative
than a direct question: "I ask
them, if you feel inclined to give
them."

That you create our emperor's eldest son,
Lord Saturnine; whose virtues will, I hope,   225
Reflect on Rome as Titan's rays on earth,
And ripen justice in this commonweal :
Then, if you will elect by my advice,
Crown him, and say " Long live our emperor ! "
Marc. With voices and applause of every sort,   230
Patricians and plebeians, we create
Lord Saturninus Rome's great emperor,
And say " Long live our emperor Saturnine! "
Sat. Titus Andronicus, for thy favours done
To us in our election this day,   235
I give thee thanks in part of thy deserts,
And will with deeds requite thy gentleness:
And for an onset, Titus, to advance
Thy name and honourable family,
Lavinia will I make my empress,   240
Rome's royal mistress, mistress of my heart,
And in the sacred Pantheon her espouse.
Tell me, Andronicus, doth this motion please thee?
Tit. It doth, my worthy lord, and in this match
I hold me highly honoured of your grace: 245
And here in sight of Rome, to Saturnine,
King and commander of our commonweal,
The wide world's emperor, do I consecrate
My sword, my chariot, and my prisoners;
Presents well worthy Rome's imperious lord: 250

---

224. *our*] *your* Q 2-3, F.   226. *Titan's*] *Tytans* Q 2-3, F ; *Tytus* Q 1.
233. After this line F has: A long Flourish till they come downe.   242. *Pantheon*]
Panthæon F 2 ; *Pathan* Qq, F.   250. *imperious*] *imperiall* Q 3, F.

226. *Reflect*] shine. *Titan*] the god
of the sun.

231-3.] The first few letters of these
lines are torn away in the surviving
copy of Q 1, but the text is obviously
as in later editions.

236. *in part of*] as part of the reward
for.

238. *onset*] beginning; cf. *Gent.*
III. ii. 94: "give the onset to thy good
advice."

240. *empress*] See on l. 89.

242. *Pantheon*]   The   errors
" Pathan " here and " Tytus " in l.
226 suggest the writing of " n "
by a stroke above the preceding
vowel. The Pantheon was a temple
dedicated to all the gods in the reign
of Augustus.

243. *motion*] proposal.

250. *imperious*] imperial.

E

Receive them then, the tribute that I owe,
Mine honour's ensigns humbled at thy feet.
Sat. Thanks, noble Titus, father of my life.
How proud I am of thee and of thy gifts
Rome shall record, and when I do forget   255
The least of these unspeakable deserts,
Romans, forget your fealty to me.
Tit. Now, madam, are you prisoner to an emperor;
To him that for your honour and your state
Will use you nobly and your followers.   260
Sat. A goodly lady, trust me, of the hue
That I would choose, were I to choose anew.
Clear up, fair queen, that cloudy countenance:
Though chance of war hath wrought this change of cheer,
Thou com'st not to be made a scorn in Rome: 265
Princely shall be thy usage every way.
Rest on my word, and let not discontent
Daunt all your hopes: madam, he comforts you
Can make you greater than the Queen of Goths.
Lavinia, you are not displeas'd with this?   270
Lav. Not I, my lord, sith true nobility
Warrants these words in princely courtesy.
Sat. Thanks, sweet Lavinia.   Romans, let us go:
Ransomless here we set our prisoners free:
Proclaim our honours, lords, with trump and drum. 275
Bass. Lord Titus, by your leave, this maid is mine.
Tit. How, sir!   Are you in earnest then, my lord?
Bass. Ay, noble Titus; and resolv'd withal
To do myself this reason and this right.

252. *thy*] *my* F.   258. *you*] *your* F.   259. *for your*] *for you* F.   261.
me,] Rowe; *me* Qq, F.   261-2. [Aside] Capell.   264. *chance*] *change* Q 1.
266-7. *way. . . . discontent*] *waie . . . discontent.* Q 1; *way. . . . discontent,*
Q 2.   269. *you*] *your* F.   270. *this?*] *this.* Qq.

259. *for*] because of.
261. *trust me*] No punctuation
before or after this phrase in Qq, F.
I take it as a parenthesis and hence
put only a comma after it, and not
a semi-colon or an exclamation-
mark, as some editors have done.
264. *cheer*] countenance.   *chance of
war*] The commonplace that "the

chance of war is uncertain" is
quoted by Tilley C223 from a
variety of sources beginning with
Robinson's translation of the *Utopia*
(1551).
268-9. *he . . . Can*] the man who
comforts you is one who can.
271. *sith*] since.
272. *Warrants*] justifies.

Marc. *Suum cuique* is our Roman justice: 280
 This prince in justice seizeth but his own.
Luc. And that he will, and shall, if Lucius live.
Tit. Traitors, avaunt! Where is the emperor's guard?
 Treason, my lord! Lavinia is surpris'd.
Sat. Surpris'd! by whom?
Bass.   By him that justly may   285
 Bear his betroth'd from all the world away.
     [*Exeunt Marcus and Bassianus, with Lavinia.*
Mut. Brothers, help to convey her hence away,
 And with my sword I'll keep this door safe.
     [*Exeunt Lucius, Quintus, and Martius.*
Tit. Follow, my lord, and I'll soon bring her back.
Mut. My lord, you pass not here.
Tit.   What, villain boy, 290
 Barr'st me my way in Rome? [*He kills him.*
*During the fray, exeunt Saturninus, Tamora, Demetrius, Chiron
    and Aaron.*
Mut.   Help, Lucius, help!

Re-enter LUCIUS.

Luc. My lord, you are unjust, and, more than so,
 In wrongful quarrel you have slain your son.
Tit. Nor thou, nor he, are any sons of mine;
 My sons would never so dishonour me.   295
 Traitor, restore Lavinia to the emperor.

---

280. cuique] F 2 ; cuiqum Q 1-2 ; cuiquam Q 3, F. 286. Exeunt... Lavinia]
Malone (substantially) ; om Qq, F. 288. Exeunt . . . Martius] Malone ;
om. Qq, F. 290-1. *What . . . Rome?*] divided by Pope ; one line Qq, F.
291. He kills him] om. Q 1-2. During . . . Aaron] Camb. (substantially) ;
om. Qq, F. 292. Re-enter *LUCIUS*] Capell ; om. Qq, F.

280. Suum cuique] to each his
own (Tilley, M209).
288. *door*] Disyllabic, cf. l. 127.
290-1. *My . . . help!*] For convenience of lineation I retain the
traditional arrangement. But I find
it hard to believe that " What . . .
Rome? " is not intended as a single
line, as in Qq, F.

294. *Nor thou, nor he*] Wilson notes
the repetition in ll. 300, 344 and
425. It carries with it a repetition
of " dishonour " (ll. 303, 345, 425)
and ll. 303 and 344 are linked by the
word " confederates." I share
Wilson's reluctance to attribute these
mechanical recurrences to Shakespeare at any point of his career.

Luc. Dead, if you will; but not to be his wife,
   That is another's lawful-promis'd love.   [*Exit.*

Enter aloft the EMPEROR *with* TAMORA *and her two sons and*
   AARON *the Moor.*

Sat. No, Titus, no; the emperor needs her not,
   Nor her, nor thee, nor any of thy stock: 300
   I'll trust by leisure him that mocks me once;
   Thee never, nor thy traitorous haughty sons,
   Confederates all thus to dishonour me.
   Was none in Rome to make a stale
   But Saturnine?   Full well, Andronicus,   305
   Agree these deeds with that proud brag of thine
   That said'st I begg'd the empire at thy hands.
Tit. O monstrous! what reproachful words are these?
Sat. But go thy ways; go, give that changing piece
   To him that flourish'd for her with his sword.   310
   A valiant son-in-law thou shalt enjoy;

298. *lawful-promis'd*] W. S. Walker; *lawfull promist* Qq, F.   Exit] Capell;
om. Qq, F.   299. Sat.] Emperour. Qq; Empe. F.   304. *Was none*]
Was there none els F 2.

298. *That is*] Almost equivalent to "since she is."

299. Sat.] Q 1's "*Emperour*" is the first example of irregular speech-prefixes in this play. Cf. "*King*" in II. iii. 260, 262, 276, 281, 292, 299, IV. iv. 69, 79, 94, 104 (but not 113), and throughout v. iii, except for "*Emperour*" at l. 64. Oddly enough, at I. i. 459, 478, 482, Q 3 introduces an irregularity ("*King*" for "*Saturnine*") where Q 1 was normal. Such irregularities are characteristic of texts set up from author's "foul papers" as R. B. McKerrow pointed out (*R.E.S.* 11 (1935), 459-65).

301. *by leisure*] not in a hurry.

304. *stale*] laughing-stock. There is no obvious supplement to make this a complete line. The parallel passage in *3H6* III. iii. 260: "Had he none else to make a stale but me?" perhaps gives some support to the conjecture of F 2 (which how-

ever wrongly adds *of* at the end of the line, not omitted till Boswell, 1821).

306-7. *that . . . hands*] Titus had made no such boast, but Saturnine's jealousy of his influence over the people is an important factor in the play.

309. *changing piece*] Wilson quotes Peele, *Tale of Troy*, l. 288 for this phrase, applied to Cressida. The word "piece" is a treacherous one in Elizabethan English. It can, as here, be a somewhat derogatory term for a woman, but it often = "master-piece," as in *H8* v. v. 27 (which On. does not distinguish from the present passage), and *Lr.* IV. vi. 138: "O ruin'd piece of nature!". Though "changing-piece" is not recorded as a compound I am not sure that it is not one here and in the *Tale of Troy*, in the sense of "a piece of small change," passing from hand to hand.

310. *flourish'd . . . sword*] brandished his sword in order to win her.

    One fit to bandy with thy lawless sons,
    To ruffle in the commonwealth of Rome.
Tit. These words are razors to my wounded heart.
Sat. And therefore, lovely Tamora, Queen of Goths,   315
    That like the stately Phœbe 'mongst her nymphs
    Dost overshine the gallan'st dames of Rome,
    If thou be pleas'd with this my sudden choice,
    Behold, I choose thee, Tamora, for my bride,
    And will create thee Empress of Rome.   320
    Speak, Queen of Goths, dost thou applaud my
      choice?
    And here I swear by all the Roman gods,
    Sith priest and holy water are so near,
    And tapers burn so bright, and everything
    In readiness for Hymenæus stand,   325
    I will not re-salute the streets of Rome,
    Or climb my palace, till from forth this place
    I lead espous'd my bride along with me.
Tam. And here in sight of heaven to Rome I swear,
    If Saturnine advance the Queen of Goths,   330
    She will a handmaid be to his desires,
    A loving nurse, a mother to his youth.
Sat. Ascend, fair queen, Pantheon.   Lords, accompany

316. *Phœbe*] F 2; Thebe Qq, F.   317. *gallan'st*] gallanst Q 1; *gallant'st* Q 2-3, F.   320. *Empress*] *Emperesse* Qq 1, 3.   333. *queen, Pantheon.*] Pope; *Queene: Panthean* Qq, F; *queen, the Pantheon.* W. S. Walker.

312. *bandy*] brawl.
313. *ruffle*] swagger; "very common, *c.* 1540-1650" (*N.E.D.*).
316-17. *Phœbe . . . Rome*] Cf. Virgil, *Aen.* I. 498-501. The word "overshine" suggests, as Ritson noted, that the author used Phaer's translation (1558; I quote from the 1607 edition): "Most like vnto *Diana* bright when she to hunt goth out. . . . | Whom thousands of the lady Nimphes await to do her will, | She on her armes her quiuer beares, and all them ouershines."
317. *gallan'st*] The spelling is phonetic, to avoid the almost unpronounceable combination *ntst*: *gallant*

is "loosely used as a gen. epithet of praise" (On.).
325. *Hymenæus*] god of marriage: "Hymen" elsewhere in Shakespeare. *stand*] Plural because "everything" is plural in sense.
332. *a mother . . . youth*] Stresses the disparity of age between Tamora and Saturninus.
333. *Pantheon*] The correction of text and punctuation must be right as far as it goes, but since in l. 242 "Pantheon" is stressed on the first syllable, and since the corruption in Qq, F would in any case lead to the omission of "the," Walker's further emendation is very plausible.

Your noble emperor, and his lovely bride,
Sent by the heavens for Prince Saturnine,   335
Whose wisdom hath her fortune conquered.
There shall we consummate our spousal rites.

[Exeunt all but Titus.

Tit. I am not bid to wait upon this bride.
Titus, when wert thou wont to walk alone,
Dishonoured thus, and challenged of wrongs?   340

Re-enter MARCUS, LUCIUS, QUINTUS, *and* MARTIUS.

Marc. O Titus, see, O see what thou hast done,
In a bad quarrel slain a virtuous son.
Tit. No, foolish tribune, no; no son of mine,
Nor thou, nor these, confederates in the deed
That hath dishonoured all our family: 345
Unworthy brother, and unworthy sons!
Luc. But let us give him burial, as becomes;
Give Mutius burial with our brethren.
Tit. Traitors, away! he rests not in this tomb:
This monument five hundreth years hath stood,   350
Which I have sumptuously re-edified:
Here none but soldiers and Rome's servitors
Repose in fame; none basely slain in brawls.
Bury him where you can, he comes not here.
Marc. My lord, this is impiety in you.   355

337. Exeunt . . . Titus] Exeunt. Manet Titus Andronicus Theobald;
Exeunt Omnes Qq, F.   340. Re-enter . . . *MARTIUS*] Capell; Enter
Marcus and Titus sonnes Qq, F.   348. *Mutius*]Mucius Q 1-2 (but Mutius
at 356, 362).   358. Mart.] Bolton; Titus two sonnes speakes Qq, F
(centred); Quint. Mart. Capell.

336. *Whose wisdom*] The antecedent
is presumably " bride "—she has
shown her wisdom in accepting
Saturninus's advances—though Delius
takes it to be " heavens."
338. *bid*] invited.
340. *challenged*] accused.
347. *as becomes*] as is fitting ; a tag
used by Peele both in *Device of the
Pageant*, l. 35 (Wilson) and *Edw. I.* ix.
22.
348. *brethren*] See on l. 89.

350. *hundreth*] This form occurs in
the preface to the Authorised Version
of the Bible. In this line it was not
modernized until F 3.
354. *Bury . . . here*] Q 1 has no
punctuation after *can*. Probably a
telescoped way of saying at once
" bury him where you can," and
" wherever you bury him he comes
not here." Cf. *Rom.* III. v. 190 :
" Graze where you will, you shall
not house with me."

My nephew Mutius' deeds do plead for him;
He must be buried with his brethren.
Mart. And shall, or him we will accompany.
Tit. "And shall"! What villain was it spake that
    word?
Mart. He that would vouch it in any place but here.   360
Tit. What, would you bury him in my despite?
Marc. No, noble Titus, but entreat of thee
    To pardon Mutius and to bury him.
Tit. Marcus, even thou hast stroke upon my crest,
    And with these boys mine honour thou hast
      wounded: 365
    My foes I do repute you every one;
    So trouble me no more, but get you gone.
Quint. He is not with himself; let us withdraw.
Mart. Not I, till Mutius' bones be buried.

              [*The brother and the sons kneel.*

Marc. Brother, for in that name doth nature plead,—   370
Mart. Father, and in that name doth nature speak,—
Tit. Speak thou no more, if all the rest will speed.
Marc. Renowmed Titus, more than half my soul,—
Luc. Dear father, soul and substance of us all,—
Marc. Suffer thy brother Marcus to inter   375
    His noble nephew here in virtue's nest,

---

360. Mart.] Capell; Titus sonne speakes Qq, F (centred).   368. Quint.]
Capell; 3. Sonne. Qq; 1 Sonne. F; Luc. Rowe; Mart. Malone. *with*]
om. F.   369, 371. Mart.] Capell; 2. Sonne. Qq, F; Quint. Rowe.
373. *Renowmed*] Renowned Q 3, F.   379. *Ajax*] Ayax Q 1.

---

358. Mart.] Bolton's correction
assumes that "two sonnes" is an
error for "2. [i.e. second] sonne."
As he points out, Titus's reply suggests
that this line belongs to only one
speaker. The assignment of names
to the second and third sons must be
conjectural, but Bolton compares II.
iii. 251, 257, where Martius shows
somewhat more spirit than does his
companion, as the second son does
in the present passage. Bolton's
discussion is in *Modern Language Notes*
45 (1930), 140-1.
    360. *vouch it*] Rowe's *vouch't* no

doubt represents the way the line was
pronounced. "Vouch" = maintain.
    364. *stroke*] This variant of the past
participle (properly a past indicative
form) should not be modernized
to "struck." It occurs again at
II. i. 93.
    368. *not with*] beside.
    372. *if . . . speed*] Perhaps "if every-
thing else is to go well," but the future
tense is awkward and the whole expression vague. Wilson's "if the rest
of you wish to live" is unconvincing.
    373. *Renowmed*] A normal Eliza-
bethan spelling.

That died in honour and Lavinia's cause.
Thou art a Roman; be not barbarous:
The Greeks upon advice did bury Ajax
That slew himself; and wise Laertes' son   380
Did graciously plead for his funerals.
Let not young Mutius then, that was thy joy,
Be barr'd his entrance here.

Tit.   Rise, Marcus, rise;
The dismall'st day is this that e'er I saw,
To be dishonoured by my sons in Rome!   385
Well, bury him, and bury me the next.

                        [They put him in the tomb.

Luc. There lie thy bones, sweet Mutius, with thy friends,
Till we with trophies do adorn thy tomb.

---

380. *wise*] om. F.   389. All. [Kneeling.]] they all kneele and say,
Qq, F (centred).   390. Exit all but Marcus and Titus. Qq; Exit. F;
om. Rowe.

377. *in . . . cause*] See on l. 41.

379. *advice*] deliberation, as in modern "advisedly."

380-1. *wise . . . funerals*] "Laertes' son" is Ulysses, who persuaded Agamemnon to give honourable burial to Ajax when he had killed himself on recovering from a fit of insanity in which he had slaughtered sheep which he mistook for the Greek generals. He was angry with the latter because the arms of Achilles had been assigned to Ulysses instead of to him. The ultimate source of the story is the *Ajax* of Sophocles, and it has been thought that it was not accessible elsewhere. But all that is required for this reference could be got from Lambinus's note on Horace, *Sat.* II. iii. 187, which reads: "Vlysses clamore, & iurgio exaudito adueniens mitigatus iam, ac placatus in Aiacem mortuum, Agamemnonem quoque flexit, atque exorauit, vt Aiacem sineret sepeliri." For the wide currency of Lambinus' commentary in sixteenth-century English grammar

schools, see Baldwin, I. 422, II. 524: it is true that Baldwin thinks the *Satires* were less familiar to Shakespeare than the rest of Horace. Except for Euripides, the Greek tragedians were not very widely read in Shakespeare's time even by tolerable Greek scholars, and it is preferable to avoid assuming that the author of this scene knew Sophocles, even if that author should be Peele rather than Shakespeare. The most ardent champion of the view that Shakespeare had a good first-hand knowledge of Greek tragedy was J. Churton Collins, *Studies in Shakespeare* (1904), but his evidence has carried conviction to few. "Graciously" probably means "acceptably" rather than kindly : for "gracious" = "acceptable," cf. ll. 170, 429. "Funerals" plural also in *Caes.* v. iii. 105.

388. *trophies*] memorials. Not On. notes, used by Shakespeare in the definite sense of "spoil taken from the enemy." Cf. *Ham.* IV. v. 214: "No trophy, sword, or hatchment o'er his bones."

All. [*Kneeling.*] No man shed tears for noble Mutius;
    He lives in fame that died in virtue's cause.   390
Marc. My lord, to step out of these dreary dumps,
    How comes it that the subtle Queen of Goths
    Is of a sudden thus advanc'd in Rome?
Tit. I know not, Marcus, but I know it is:
    Whether by device or no, the heavens can tell.   395
    Is she not then beholding to the man
    That brought her for this high good turn so far?
    Yes, and will nobly him remunerate.

Enter the EMPEROR, TAMORA *and her two sons with the* Moor,
at one door. Enter at the other door BASSIANUS *and* LAVINIA,
with others.

Sat. So, Bassianus, you have play'd your prize:
    God give you joy, sir, of your gallant bride.   400
Bass. And you of yours, my lord: I say no more,
    Nor wish no less; and so I take my leave.
Sat. Traitor, if Rome have law or we have power,
    Thou and thy faction shall repent this rape.
Bass. Rape call you it, my lord, to seize my own,   405
    My true-betrothed love, and now my wife?

391. *dreary*] *dririe* (*dreary* Pope) Qq; *sudden* F.   398. om. Qq.; Malone
(conj.) attr. to Marcus.   398. S.D. Enter] Flourish. Enter F.   399.
Bassianus] Bascianus Q 1-2.   406. *true-betrothed*] Theobald; *true betrothed*
Qq, F.

390.] For the deletion of the exit given in Qq, F, see ll. 474-6, which belong to one of the sons. It is curious that the misattribution there should agree with a mistaken exit here.

391. *dumps*] melancholy, a common cliché in the third quarter of the sixteenth century, especially in alliterative phrases of this kind.

395. *Whether*] Presumably monosyllabic : often spelt *where* in Elizabethan texts, e.g. *Caes.* I. i. 65.
    device] scheming.

396. *beholding*] beholden; commoner than the latter in Elizabethan English.

398. *Yes . . . remunerate*] This line is probably genuine (see Introduction, p. xviii): it must have been added at the same time as the " Flourish " added to the following S.D. It may belong to Marcus, but it is equally possible that Titus answered his own rhetorical question.

398. S.D. (app. crit.) Flourish] See on S.D. before l. 1.

399. *play'd your prize*] won your bout. According to A. Forbes Sieveking in *Shakespeare's England*, II. 390, this was " the technical term for qualifying for the patent as a member of the fencing fraternity."

400. *gallant*] See on l. 137.

But let the laws of Rome determine all;
Meanwhile am I possess'd of that is mine.
Sat. 'Tis good, sir: you are very short with us;
But, if we live, we'll be as sharp with you.   410
Bass. My lord, what I have done, as best I may,
Answer I must, and shall do with my life.
Only thus much I give your grace to know:
By all the duties that I owe to Rome,
This noble gentleman, Lord Titus here,   415
Is in opinion and in honour wrong'd,
That, in the rescue of Lavinia,
With his own hand did slay his youngest son,
In zeal to you, and highly mov'd to wrath
To be controll'd in that he frankly gave: 420
Receive him then to favour, Saturnine,
That hath express'd himself in all his deeds
A father and a friend to thee and Rome.
Tit. Prince Bassianus, leave to plead my deeds:
'Tis thou, and those, that have dishonoured me.   425
Rome and the righteous heavens be my judge
How I have lov'd and honoured Saturnine.
Tam. My worthy lord, if ever Tamora
Were gracious in those princely eyes of thine,
Then hear me speak indifferently for all;   430
And at my suit, sweet, pardon what is past.
Sat. What, madam, be dishonoured openly,
And basely put it up without revenge?
Tam. Not so, my lord; the gods of Rome forfend
I should be author to dishonour you!   435
But on mine honour dare I undertake

408. *am I*] *I am* Q 3, F.

408. *that*] that which (very common
in Elizabethan English, cf. l. 420).

416. *opinion*] reputation: cf. *1H4*
v. iv. 48: "Thou hast redeem'd
thy lost opinion."

420. *controll'd*] thwarted.
frankly] generously, unreservedly.

422. *express'd*] shown: cf. *Ham.*
I. iii. 70-1: "Costly thy habit . . .
But not express'd in fancy."

428-31. *if ever . . . And*] See on
ll. 10-13.

430. *indifferently*] impartially.

433. *put it up*] submit to it (metaphor from sheathing a weapon).

434. *forfend*] forbid.

435. *be author . . . you*] countenance any action that would dishonour
you. *N.E.D. author* 1d. cites Hobbes:
"Author, is he which owneth an
action, or giveth a warrant for it."

436. *undertake*] vouch.

For good Lord Titus' innocence in all,
Whose fury not dissembled speaks his griefs:
Then, at my suit, look graciously on him;
Lose not so noble a friend on vain suppose,   440
Nor with sour looks afflict his gentle heart.
[*Aside to Sat.*] My lord, be rul'd by me, be won
    at last;
Dissemble all your griefs and discontents:
You are but newly planted in your throne;
Lest then the people, and patricians too,   445
Upon a just survey take Titus' part,
And so supplant you for ingratitude,
Which Rome reputes to be a heinous sin,
Yield at entreats, and then let me alone:
I'll find a day to massacre them all,   450
And race their faction and their family,
The cruel father, and his traitorous sons,
To whom I sued for my dear son's life;
And make them know what 'tis to let a queen
Kneel in the streets and beg for grace in vain.   455
[*Aloud.*] Come, come, sweet emperor; come,
    Andronicus;
Take up this good old man, and cheer the heart
That dies in tempest of thy angry frown.

442 [Aside to Sat.]] Rowe; om. Qq, F. 447. *you*] *vs* Q 3, F.   448.
sin,] Rowe; *sinne*. Qq, F.   456. [Aloud.]] Hanmer; om. Qq, F.

438. *Whose . . . griefs*] i.e. the
fact that he is not able to dissemble
his rage proves the genuineness of
his grievances.

440. *suppose*] supposition; for a
collection of nouns of this type see
Abbott § 451.

442. *My lord*] A new paragraph in
Qq indicates the aside.

449. *at entreats*] to entreaty.

let me alone] Very common for
" leave it to me," often, as here, with
a sinister implication.

451. *race*] I retain the Qq F
spelling since here and elsewhere the
sense seems to be " root out." There
is no etymological connection with
race = root (Latin *radix*) or *enrace* =

implant (used by Spenser), but there
is semantic influence. *N.E.D.* gives
two verbs, *race*³ as variant of *rase* and
*race*⁴ as aphetic form of *arace*, but the
dividing-line is clearly hard to draw,
as it admits in a note on *race*³, 3b.

457. *Take up*] Surely (cf. *R3* I. ii.
184-5: " Take up the sword again,
or take up me. | *Anne.* Arise, dis-
sembler ") " raise to his feet," i.e.
" bid him rise," as Saturninus
proceeds to do, rather than (Wilson)
" make friends with ": where " take
up " = " reconcile," as in IV. iii. 91,
the object is the quarrel, not the
enemy. The kneeling and rising
in this scene are somewhat complicated, as Professor Ellis-Fermor

Sat. Rise, Titus, rise; my empress hath prevail'd.

Tit. I thank your majesty, and her, my lord. 460
 These words, these looks, infuse new life in me.

Tam. Titus, I am incorporate in Rome,
 A Roman now adopted happily,
 And must advise the emperor for his good.
 This day all quarrels die, Andronicus; 465
 And let it be mine honour, good my lord,
 That I have reconcil'd your friends and you.
 For you, Prince Bassianus, I have pass'd
 My word and promise to the emperor
 That you will be more mild and tractable. 470
 And fear not, lords, and you, Lavinia;
 By my advice, all humbled on your knees,
 You shall ask pardon of his majesty.

Luc. We do, and vow to heaven and to his highness,
 That what we did was mildly as we might, 475
 Tend'ring our sister's honour and our own.

Marc. That on mine honour here do I protest.

Sat. Away, and talk not; trouble us no more.

Tam. Nay, nay, sweet emperor, we must all be friends:
 The tribune and his nephews kneel for grace; 480
 I will not be denied: sweet heart, look back.

---

459. Sat.] King. Q 3, F (so 478, 482).   467. *reconcil'd*] *reconciled* Q 1-2.
474. Luc.] Rowe; Q 1 continues to Tamora; Q 2 indents but without new
prefix; All. Q 3; Son. F.   477. *do I*] *I doe* Q 2-3, F.

points out to me. There are never
any S.D.'s to say when the characters
rise, and here there is none for Titus's
kneeling either. He and Marcus must
have risen at l. 391. I suppose he
kneels again as soon as the Emperor
enters. It would seem dramatically
more effective for him to be in the
same posture right from l. 415, when
he is first mentioned, up to l. 459.

462. *incorporate*] On Latinate past
participles of this kind, often adopted
into English in this form earlier than
as ordinary verbs, see H. Bradley in
Shakespeare's England II. 561-3, and
Abbott § 342. They seemed natural
because of the existence of many
common native English verbs in

which the past participle had come
to be identical with the stem, e.g.
cast, cut, hit, put.

465. *die*] i.e. let them die, cf. *lie* in
l. 387.

475-6. *mildly . . . Tend'ring*] done as
mildly as we could, consistently
with our concern for. For " mildly "
when an adjective would be more
normal (or, put another way, for
the ellipse of " done ") cf. iv. iv. 76:
" That Lucius' banishment was
wrongfully."

481. *sweet heart*] Normally spelt as
two words, even when, as here, the
sense is much the same as that of the
modern *sweetheart.* The old spelling
is a better guide to the rhythm here.

Sat. Marcus, for thy sake, and thy brother's here,
　　And at my lovely Tamora's entreats,
　　I do remit these young men's heinous faults:
　　Stand up.　　　　　　　　　　　　　　　485
　　Lavinia, though you left me like a churl,
　　I found a friend, and sure as death I swore
　　I would not part a bachelor from the priest.
　　Come, if the emperor's court can feast two brides,
　　You are my guest, Lavinia, and your friends.　　490
　　This day shall be a love-day, Tamora.
Tit. To-morrow, and it please your majesty
　　To hunt the panther and the hart with me,
　　With horn and hound we'll give your grace bonjour.
Sat. Be it so, Titus, and gramercy too.　　　　495

[Sound trumpets. Exeunt all but Aaron.

485-6. *Stand . . . churl*] divided by Capell; one line Qq, F; Pope makes
"Stand up" S.D.　　　487. *swore*] sware F.　　　495. Sound . . . Aaron]
Exeunt. | sound trumpets, manet *Moore.* Qq; Exeunt F.

485. *Stand up*] Pope's conjecture is
very plausible.

487. *sure as death*] This is the earliest
occurrence of this expression known
to Tilley D136.

488. *part*] depart.

491. *love-day*] a day appointed to
settle disputes, no doubt (Wilson)
with a quibble on the sense " a day
given up to love."

494. *bonjour*] good-day (Fr.).

495. *gramercy*] thanks (Fr. *grand
merci*).

495. S.D. Sound . . . Aaron] The Q
S.D. shows that II. i. is continuous in
action with Act I. F's " Flourish,"
after " Actus Secunda " [*sic*] is
clearly misplaced from the end of
Act I.

ACT II

SCENE I

AARON *alone.*

Aar. Now climbeth Tamora Olympus' top,
Safe out of fortune's shot, and sits aloft,
Secure of thunder's crack or lightning flash,
Advanc'd above pale envy's threat'ning reach.
As when the golden sun salutes the morn,   5
And, having gilt the ocean with his beams,
Gallops the zodiac in his glistering coach,
And overlooks the highest-peering hills;
So Tamora.
Upon her wit doth earthly honour wait,   10
And virtue stoops and trembles at her frown.
Then, Aaron, arm thy heart, and fit thy thoughts,
To mount aloft with thy imperial mistress,
And mount her pitch whom thou in triumph long
Hast prisoner held, fett'red in amorous chains,   15
And faster bound to Aaron's charming eyes

ACT II

Scene 1

Act II. *Scene* 1.] Rowe; Actus Secunda. Flourish. F. *AARON* alone.] Enter Aaron alone. F; om. Qq. 4. *above] about* F. *reach.] reach,* Qq; *reach:* F.
8. *highest-peering]* Theobald; *highest piering* Qq, F. *hills;] hills.* Qq; *hills:* F.
9. Centred in Qq. 13. *mount] soar* W. S. Walker.

3. *of*] from.
4. *reach.*] I have with some hesitation adopted the usual modern punctuation, based on F. Qq make ll. 5-8 subordinate to ll. 1-4. This can scarcely be right, as *As* in l. 5 must surely be answered by *So* in l. 9, but it is possible that ll. 5-8 look backwards as well as forwards. Similarly, though I have retained the full-stop in l. 9 after *Tamora,* I think that line (separated in Qq from what precedes as well as from what follows by full-stops) may look forward as well as backward, and should perhaps be followed by a colon, which Camb. prints.

7. *Gallops*] gallops through. Cf. Peele, *Anglorum Feriae* l. 24: " Gallops the zodiac in his fiery wain" (Verity).
8. *overlooks*] looks down upon from above.
14. *mount her pitch*] rise to the highest point of her flight (a technical term of falconry). Note that in l. 11 *stoop,* though not so used there, is a word technically used in falconry: a falcon " stoops " to strike its prey when it is at its " pitch." Such an associative link would be characteristic of Shakespeare.
16. *charming*] casting a spell. The modern enfeebled sense makes the line sound rather absurd.

28

Than is Prometheus tied to Caucasus.
Away with slavish weeds and servile thoughts!
I will be bright, and shine in pearl and gold,
To wait upon this new-made empress.   20
To wait, said I? to wanton with this queen,
This goddess, this Semiramis, this nymph,
This siren that will charm Rome's Saturnine,
And see his shipwrack and his commonweal's.
Holla! what storm is this?   25

Enter CHIRON *and* DEMETRIUS, *braving.*

Dem. Chiron, thy years wants wit, thy wits wants edge,
And manners, to intrude where I am grac'd,
And may, for aught thou knowest, affected be.
Chi. Demetrius, thou dost overween in all,
And so in this, to bear me down with braves.   30
'Tis not the difference of a year or two

---

18. *servile*] *idle* Q 3, F.   20. *empress*] *Emperesse* Qq.   22. *nymph*] *Queene*
Q 3, F.   26. *years wants*] *years want* F 2.   *wits*] *wit* Q 2-3, F.   *wants*]
want Wilson.   28. *knowest*] *know'st* F.

---

17. *Prometheus*] The resemblance of
ll. 16-17 to two separate lines in
Peele's *Edward I* is noteworthy: " To
tie Prometheus' limbs to Caucasus "
(iv. 21) and " Fast to those looks are
all my fancies tied " (x. 201). It is
certainly easiest to believe that
" Peele, writing the two plays about
the same time, used up his own
rhetoric twice over " (J. M. Robertson
*Introduction to the Study of the Shakespeare
Canon*, p. 178; cited by Baldwin
(1959), p. 413).
    19. *I . . . gold*] Adapted by Clown
in Heywood and Rowley, *Fortune by
Land and Sea* (c. 1607), III. iv. (*Sh. Soc.*
ed., 1845, p. 47): " he might go brave
and shine in pearl and gold "; Heywood has a less close echo in *Fair
Maid of the West* (a. 1631) Pt. II,
Act IV (*Sh. Soc.* ed., 1850, p. 148):
" That all our Court may shine in
gold and pearl."

22. *Semiramis*] a beautiful, ambitious and lustful (mythical)
Assyrian queen, wife of Ninus.

25. S.D. *braving*] swaggering de-
fiantly.

26. *wants*] It is never easy to
decide when to retain the inflection
" -s " with a plural subject. Its
occurrence twice in the one line
makes it rash to alter it here : moreover it seems appropriate in a jingling
phrase with a semi-proverbial ring
(cf. " as sure as eggs is eggs "). In
general, see Abbott §§ 333-7, Franz
§§ 155, 673, 679.

27. *grac'd*] received with favour.

28. *affected*] loved: this meaning
has survived in the noun " affection."

29. *overween*] be presumptuous.

30. *braves*] blustering threats: cf.
the verb in l. 25 S.D.

Makes me less gracious or thee more fortunate:
I am as able and as fit as thou
To serve, and to deserve my mistress' grace;
And that my sword upon thee shall approve,   35
And plead my passions for Lavinia's love.

Aar. Clubs, clubs! these lovers will not keep the peace.

Dem. Why, boy, although our mother, unadvis'd,
Gave you a dancing-rapier by your side,
Are you so desperate grown to threat your friends?   40
Go to; have your lath glued within your sheath
Till you know better how to handle it.

Chi. Meanwhile, sir, with the little skill I have,
Full well shalt thou perceive how much I dare.

Dem. Ay, boy, grow ye so brave?   [*They draw.*

Aar.   Why, how now, lords!   45
So near the emperor's palace dare ye draw,
And maintain such a quarrel openly?
Full well I wot the ground of all this grudge:
I would not for a million of gold
The cause were known to them it most concerns;   50
Nor would your noble mother for much more
Be so dishonoured in the court of Rome.
For shame, put up.

Dem.   Not I, till I have sheath'd
My rapier in his bosom, and withal

32. *or*] om. Hanmer.   37. Aar.] Moore. Qq (so 45, 60, 75, 90, 95, 97).
46. *ye*] *you* Q 2-3, F.

32. *gracious*] See on I. i. 11. The
word is here trisyllabic, and the
line an Alexandrine. Hanmer's emendation is unnecessary.

35. *approve*] prove.

36. *passions*] ardent desires.

37. *Clubs, clubs*] The cry raised at a
London brawl for the watch to come
and separate the combatants with
clubs, cf. *1H6* I. iii. 85: " I'll call for
clubs if you will not away." The
cry was in particularly frequent use
for calling out the London prentices:
so Dekker, *Shoemaker's Holiday* v. ii
(Mermaid edition, p. 71): " Cry
clubs for prentices! " In such passages

the purpose of the clubs does not
seem to be so much to restore the
peace as to take sides with one of the
contesting parties.

38. *unadvis'd*] unwisely.

39. *dancing-rapier*] " sword worn
only for ornament in dancing " (On.).

41. *lath*] " property sword "
(Ridley), perhaps with special re-
ference to the sword carried by the
Vice in the Morality plays (Wither-
spoon), cf. *Tw. N.* IV. ii. 138 ff.:
" Like to the old Vice, | Your need
to sustain; | Who with dagger of
lath, | In his rage and his wrath, |
Cries, Ah, ah! to the devil."

Thrust those reproachful speeches down his throat   55
That he hath breath'd in my dishonour here.

Chi. For that I am prepar'd and full resolv'd,
Foul-spoken coward, that thund'rest with thy tongue,
And with thy weapon nothing dar'st perform!

Aar. Away, I say!   60
Now, by the gods that warlike Goths adore,
This petty brabble will undo us all.
Why, lords, and think you not how dangerous
It is to jet upon a prince's right?
What, is Lavinia then become so loose,   65
Or Bassianus so degenerate,
That for her love such quarrels may be broach'd
Without controlment, justice, or revenge?
Young lords, beware, and should the empress know
This discord's ground, the music would not please.   70

Chi. I care not, I, knew she and all the world:
I love Lavinia more than all the world.

Dem. Youngling, learn thou to make some meaner choice:
Lavinia is thine elder brother's hope.

Aar. Why, are ye mad? or know ye not in Rome   75
How furious and impatient they be,

---

55. *those*] these Q 3, F.   62. *petty*] *pretty* F.   64. *jet*] set F.
66. *Bassianus*] Bascianus Q 1-2.   70. *discord's*] discord F.   75. *Why,*]
Theobald; *Why* Qq, F.   *Rome*] F3; *Rome,* Qq, F.

---

61. *Now . . . adore*] Add to Wilson's
quotations for Shakespeare's use of
now " as introductory flourish to a
mild oath " (p. xxiv) the even closer
parallel, *Lucr.* 1835: " Now, by the
Capitol that we adore."
62. *brabble*] quarrel.
64. *jet*] encroach.
68. *controlment*] check.
69. *and . . . know*] H. T. Price,
Papers of the Michigan Academy, 21
(1935), 505, argues that the usual
interpretation of *and* = " *if* " is
impossible, since the word-order
should . . . know already expresses the
condition. I think he is right. For
the " emphatic *and* " he compares l. 63
of this speech, to which add l. 99.

70. *ground*] reason, with a play on
the musical sense, " bass on which a
descant is ' raised ' " (On.).
71. *care . . . knew*] I do not care
if she knew—a natural mixture of
tenses.
72. *I . . . world*] Probably an echo
of Kyd, *Spanish Tragedy* II. vi. 5-6 :
" On whom I doted more then all
the world, | Because she lou'd me
more then all the world."
73. *Youngling*] A contemptuous
expression also in *Shr.* II. i. 331:
" Youngling, thou canst not love
so dear as I," where the retort
is: " Greybeard, thy love doth
freeze " (Delius).
75. *in Rome*] With *be* in l. 76.

F

And cannot brook competitors in love?
I tell you, lords, you do but plot your deaths
By this device.

Chi.   Aaron, a thousand deaths
Would I propose, to achieve her whom I love.   80

Aar. To achieve her! how?

Dem.   Why makes thou it so strange?
She is a woman, therefore may be woo'd;
She is a woman, therefore may be won;
She is Lavinia, therefore must be lov'd.
What, man! more water glideth by the mill   85
Than wots the miller of; and easy it is
Of a cut loaf to steal a shive, we know:
Though Bassianus be the emperor's brother,
Better than he have worn Vulcan's badge.

Aar. [*Aside.*] Ay, and as good as Saturninus may.   90

Dem. Then why should he despair that knows to court it

79-80. *Aaron . . . love*] divided by Hanmer; Qq, F give two lines, divided after *propose*.   80. *love*] do loue Q 3, F.   81. *her! how?*] her how? Qq ; her, how? F.   *makes*] mak'st F.   90. [*Aside.*]] Theobald ; om. Qq, F.   *Saturninus*] Saturnine Q 3 ; Saturnius F.

---

80. *propose*] " be ready to meet " (Schmidt, On.) rather than " propose to carry out " (Wilson).

81. *To . . . how?*] Takes up the previous speaker's word, as in I. i. 285. This being so, I retain the usual editorial punctuation (Alexander has *her*—) rather than return to Qq with Wilson. Qq spell *atchiue*, which could be cited in support of *griude* against my emendation in II. iii. 260.

81. *makes . . . strange*] *makes* is phonetically easier than *mak'st*, especially as the next word begins with *th*. See Franz § 152. The whole phrase means " seem to be surprised or shocked " (On.). Cf. Lyly, *Euphues* (ed. R. W. Bond, I. 231): "loue hath as well inueigled me as others, which make it as straunge as I."

82-3. *She . . . won*] See *O.D.E.P.*, p. 723, where the earliest quotation

is from Greene's *Perimedes* (1588): " Melissa was a woman and therefore to be woone." Tilley W 681 quotes " there is no woeman but shee will yeelde in time " from Lyly's *Euphues* (1578). Cf. also *1H6* v. iii. 78-9.

85-6. *more . . . of*] See *O.D.E.P.* p. 694, and Tilley W 99, where the earliest quotation is from Heywood's *Dialogue* (1546).

86-7. *easy . . . shive*] This is the earliest quotation in *O.D.E.P.*, p. 582, and in Tilley T 34. *Shive* = slice.

89. *worn . . . badge*] been cuckolded (as Vulcan by Venus). *Worn* is disyllabic, cf. on I. i. 127.

91. *court it*] play the suitor. For this use of *it* cf. Abbott § 226, Franz § 295, who compares modern colloquial phrases like " do it in style."

With words, fair looks, and liberality?
What, hast not thou full often stroke a doe,
And borne her cleanly by the keeper's nose?

Aar. Why, then, it seems some certain snatch or so   95
Would serve your turns.

Chi.   Ay, so the turn were served.

Dem. Aaron, thou hast hit it.

Aar.   Would you had hit it too!
Then should not we be tir'd with this ado.
Why, hark ye, hark ye, and are you such fools
To square for this? would it offend you then   100
That both should speed?

Chi. Faith, not me.

Dem.   Nor me, so I were one.

Aar. For shame, be friends, and join for that you jar:
'Tis policy and stratagem must do
That you affect; and so must you resolve,   105
That what you cannot, as you would, achieve,
You must perforce accomplish as you may.

---

93. *What,*] Pope; *What* Qq, F.   *stroke*] *strooke* Q 2; *strucke* Q 3, F.
101. om. F.

---

93. *stroke*] Cf. I. i. 364.

95. *snatch*] swift catch. Wilson compares *N.E.D.* 6b for the specifically sexual sense, subordinate to the meaning "hasty meal, snack." A. Forbes Sieveking, *Shakespeare's England*, II. 369, sees in it a coursing metaphor, comparing *H5* I. ii. 143: "the coursing snatchers," and referring to "the sudden snatch of the greyhound as he comes up with the quarry." Tilley S 587 quotes "a snatche and to go" as a proverbial phrase from Bale's *Three Laws* (1547), and from Heywood's *If You Know Not Me*, Part II (1605): "cannot a snatch and away serve your turn" (*Sh. Soc.* ed., 1851, p. 129), which, unless it echoes our passage, suggests that the whole phrase is proverbial.

96. *serve . . . turns*] "serve the turn" (cf. *Ant.* II. v. 59: "the best turn i' the bed") and "hit" are both common in bawdy word-play.

100. *square*] quarrel.

102. *so*] provided that (as in l. 96); very common from early times, and still occasionally used. *So that* and (rarer) *so as* are also found.

103. *for . . . jar*] for what you quarrel for. A common type of ellipse, cf. *3H6* II. v. 39: "Pass'd over to the end they were created."

104. *policy*] With the usual Elizabethan sense of "Machiavellian" unscrupulousness.

105. *That*] See on I. i. 408.
affect] aim at.

106-7. *That . . . may*] See *O.D.E.P.*, p. 148, where the earliest quotation is from Heywood (1546). The ultimate source is Terence, *Andria*, IV. vi. 10: "ut quimus, aiunt, quando ut volumus non licet,"

Take this of me: Lucrece was not more chaste
Than this Lavinia, Bassianus' love.
A speedier course than ling'ring languishment   110
Must we pursue, and I have found the path.
My lords, a solemn hunting is in hand;
There will the lovely Roman ladies troop:
The forest walks are wide and spacious,
And many unfrequented plots there are   115
Fitted by kind for rape and villainy:
Single you thither then this dainty doe,
And strike her home by force, if not by words:
This way, or not at all, stand you in hope.
Come, come, our empress, with her sacred wit   120
To villainy and vengeance consecrate,
Will we acquaint withal what we intend;
And she shall file our engines with advice,
That will not suffer you to square yourselves,
But to your wishes' height advance you both.   125

110. *than*] Rowe; *this* Qq, F.   122. *withal*] *withall* Q 1; *with all* Q 2-3, F.
what] *that* Q 2-3, F.

whose form shows it was already proverbial.

108. *Lucrece*] Killed herself after being raped by Tarquin. The story, which has obvious analogies with this play, is told at length by Shakespeare in *The Rape of Lucrece*.

110. *than*] This emendation is probably correct, *this* having crept in from the previous line. *Lingering languishment* then means "a long sentimental courtship" (Baildon). But Steevens's interpretation of the original text is perhaps just possible: "we must pursue by a speedier course *this coy laughing dame, this piece of reluctant softness.*"

112. *solemn*] ceremonial; cf. (Wilson) *Mac.* III. i. 14: "a solemn supper." The phrase *a solemn hunting* occurs also in Chapman, *The Gentleman Usher* (*Comedies*, ed. Parrott) III. ii. 297.

115. *plots*] spots. The other sense of *plot* may have contributed to its use in this context.

116. *kind*] nature: cf. II. iii. 281.

117. *Single*] a hunting term for selecting an animal from the herd in order to hunt it, cf. II. iii. 69.

120. *sacred*] Whether or not this is (Wilson, comparing *Arraignment of Paris* IV. i. 285) "a Peele automatism," one may agree that it is something of a cliché here: certainly not (Malone) "accursed."

122. *acquaint withal*] inform; cf. *All's* I. iii. 126 (Munro). So Sisson; *with all what*, which I read in 1953, is unobjectionable, but unnecessary.

123. *file our engines*] sharpen our wits.

124. *square yourselves*] quarrel with each other. But the reflexive is not found elsewhere. Wilson suggests as an alternative "settle matters with each other," which is equally without parallel and gives less appropriate sense. The context seems to demand something like "thwart yourselves, and each other, by quarrelling."

The emperor's court is like the house of Fame,
The palace full of tongues, of eyes and ears:
The woods are ruthless, dreadful, deaf, and dull:
There speak, and strike, brave boys, and take your
     turns;
There serve your lust, shadowed from heaven's eye, 130
And revel in Lavinia's treasury.
Chi. Thy counsel, lad, smells of no cowardice.
Dem. Sit fas aut nefas, till I find the stream
     To cool this heat, a charm to calm these fits,
     Per Stygia, per manes vehor.   [*Exeunt.* 135

127. and] *of* Q 3, F.   130. lust] lusts F.   shadowed] shadow'd F.
133. stream] streames F.   134. these] their Q 3, F.   135. Stygia]
Styga F 4.

126. *house of Fame*] Perhaps a direct allusion to Chaucer's poem, but J. A. K. Thomson, *Shakespeare and the Classics* (1952), p. 54, suggests Ovid, *Met.* XII. 39 ff. as more relevant. In any case, *Fame* has the Chaucerian sense of *rumour*, personified also in *Ado* II. i. 223: " Lady Fame."

133. sit . . . nefas] be it right or wrong.

135. Per . . . vehor] I am borne through the Stygian (i.e. infernal) regions, i.e. I am in hell: cf. *3H6* I. iii. 32-3: " And till I root out their accursed line, | And leave not one alive, I live in hell." The words are an adaptation of Seneca, *Phaedra* 1180: " per Styga, per amnes igneos amens sequar," i.e. " I [Phaedra] as a demented spirit will follow thee [Hippolytus] over Styx and over the fiery rivers." The context and the detailed meaning are thus quite

different from Shakespeare's. Editors have (*a*) read *Styga* with F 4; (*b*) interpreted " I am ready for anything." Against (*a*) it may be argued that the original text gives perfectly good sense and that the emendation introduces a metrical anomaly (against which Horace, *Ars Poetica* 257-8 gives a warning; this precept is also to be found in Fabricius, *De Re Poetica* (1560): G. Gregory Smith, *Elizabethan Critical Essays*, quotes the Latin text (I. 419) and Webbe's version of it (I. 294)): a resolved spondee (*Stÿgă per*) in an even foot of a senarius, where only an iamb is admitted—it was for this " smal faulte " that, according to Ascham (Gregory Smith, I. 24) " M. Watson . . . would neuer suffer yet his *Absalon* to go abroad "; against (*b*) that it makes much less apt sense than the interpretation given above.

SCENE II.

Enter TITUS ANDRONICUS, *and his three sons, making a noise with hounds and horns, and* MARCUS.

Tit. The hunt is up, the morn is bright and grey,
The fields are fragrant and the woods are green.
Uncouple here and let us make a bay,
And wake the emperor and his lovely bride,
And rouse the prince, and ring a hunter's peal,   5
That all the court may echo with the noise.
Sons, let it be your charge, as it is ours,
To attend the emperor's person carefully:
I have been troubled in my sleep this night,
But dawning day new comfort hath inspir'd.   10

Here a cry of hounds, and wind horns in a peal, then enter
SATURNINUS, TAMORA, BASSIANUS, LAVINIA, CHIRON,
DEMETRIUS, *and their Attendants.*

Many good morrows to your majesty;
Madam, to you as many and as good:
I promised your grace a hunter's peal.

Scene II

Scene II.] Rowe; om. Qq, F.   and Marcus] om. Qq.   1. *morn*]
Moone Q 1-2.   11. *Many*] Qq, F repeat speech-heading.

Scene II

and Marcus] An alternative to this addition by F would be to read *Martius* for *Marcus* at l. 20. But since Marcus takes part in the hunt (sc. iv), F is probably right.

1. *up*] on foot.

grey] Cf. " grey-ey'd morn " in *Rom.* II. iii. 1. On.'s statement that this, and the substantival use of *grey* to mean " the cold sunless light of early morning," are not pre-Shakespearian is misleading. The normal *adjectival* use of *grey* in this sense goes back to the fourteenth century (*N.E.D.* 5; and cf. J. M. Robertson, *Introduction to the Study of the Shakespeare Canon,* p. 95). But though the phrase is not specifically Shakespearian,

the " exact duplication of rhythm and structure " (Robertson) in Peele's *Old Wife's Tale,* 350-1: " The day is clear, the welkin bright and grey, | The lark is merry and records her notes " may be due to imitation of *Titus* by Peele, or, indeed, by the reporter of that sadly mangled text, which is dated between Jan. 1593 and May 1594 by T. Larsen, *Modern Philology* 30 (1932-33), 28.

3. *bay*] deep prolonged barking.

5. *hunter's peal*] " horn-blowing which set the hounds' tongues into activity, and produced a pleasing din " (J.W. Fortescue in *Shakespeare's England,* II. 347).

10. S.D. *cry*] deep barking in unison.

Sat. And you have rung it lustily, my lords;
    Somewhat too early for new-married ladies.   15
Bass. Lavinia, how say you?
Lav.   I say, no;
    I have been broad awake two hours and more.
Sat. Come on then; horse and chariots let us have,
    And to our sport.   Madam, now shall ye see
    Our Roman hunting.
Marc.   I have dogs, my lord,   20
    Will rouse the proudest panther in the chase,
    And climb the highest promontory top.
Tit. And I have horse will follow where the game
    Makes way, and run like swallows o'er the plain.
Dem. Chiron, we hunt not, we, with horse nor hound,   25
    But hope to pluck a dainty doe to ground. [*Exeunt.*

SCENE III

Enter AARON, *alone.*

Aar. He that had wit would think that I had none,
    To bury so much gold under a tree,
    And never after to inherit it.
    Let him that thinks of me so abjectly
    Know that this gold must coin a stratagem,   5
    Which, cunningly effected, will beget
    A very excellent piece of villainy:

14. *lords*] *lord* Dyce.   16-17. So F; *I . . . more* one line in Qq.
17. *broad*] om. F.   24. *run*] F 2; *runnes* Qq, F. *like*] *likes* F.

Scene III

Scene III.] Capell; om. Qq, F.

Scene III

18. *horse*] An archaic plural here and in l. 23: a use to be distinguished from the collective sense (*horse and foot*), cf. Franz § 191.

21. *chase*] hunting-ground.

24. *run*] In 1953 I retained *runs*, but it is better to emend; *runs* could have arisen from *makes*.

3. *inherit*] enjoy the possession of.
4. *thinks . . . abjectly*] thinks of me as contemptible; cf. N. Field, *Woman is a Weathercock* II. i. 273-4, "Ile thinke | As abjectly of thee," and *Tim.* III. iii. 18, "think so backwardly of me," with my *New Shakespeare* note.

And so repose, sweet gold, for their unrest
That have their alms out of the empress' chest.

Enter TAMORA *alone to the Moor.*

Tam. My lovely Aaron, wherefore look'st thou sad   10
When everything doth make a gleeful boast?
The birds chant melody on every bush,
The snake lies rolled in the cheerful sun,
The green leaves quiver with the cooling wind,
And make a chequer'd shadow on the ground;   15
Under their sweet shade, Aaron, let us sit,
And, whilst the babbling echo mocks the hounds,
Replying shrilly to the well-tun'd horns,
As if a double hunt were heard at once,
Let us sit down and mark their yellowing noise;   20
And after conflict, such as was suppos'd
The wand'ring prince and Dido once enjoyed,
When with a happy storm they were surpris'd,
And curtain'd with a counsel-keeping cave,
We may, each wreathed in the other's arms,   25
Our pastimes done, possess a golden slumber,
Whiles hounds and horns and sweet melodious birds

9. alone om. F.   13. *snake*] *snakes* Q 1-2.   20. *yellowing*] *yelping* F.
22. *enjoyed*] *enioy'd* F.

8. *repose . . . unrest*] The original
source of expressions of this type
(cf. IV. ii. 31 and *R3* IV. iv. 29 :
" Rest thy unrest on England's
lawful earth ") seems to be Kyd,
Spanish Tragedy, I. iii. 5 : " Then
rest we heere a while in our unrest."
9. *That . . . chest*] " who are to
come at this gold " (Johnson).
11. *boast*] display (Wilson).
13. *snake lies*] I do not think *snakes
lies* can be right (but see on II. i. 26).
If the Q 3 correction is accepted, the
Q 1 compositor must be supposed to
have set up *snakes* for *snake* under the
influence of *birds* and *leaves*.
17. *babbling echo*] Echo is " the
babbling gossip of the air " in *Tw. N.*
I. v. 294, and the two passages are
linked by IV. ii. 152 below, where

" babbling gossip " occurs in another
connection. Wilson quotes Sidney,
Arcadia I. x as a source for the whole
passage, and for other hunting
passages in Shakespeare. The resemblance is not striking. The closest
parallel in Shakespeare to the present
passage is (as Parrott, p. 27, noted)
Ven. 695-6: " Thus do they spend
their mouths : Echo replies, | As if
another chase were in the skies."
20. *yellowing*] " app. extension of *yell*
on the analogy of *bell, bellow*" (*N.E.D.*).
21-4. *And . . . cave*] On Dido and
Aeneas, see Virgil, *Aen.* IV.
23. *with*] by: Abbott § 193,
Franz § 535. So in l. 78.
27-9. *Whiles . . . asleep*] Parrott
(p. 28) compares *Ven.* 973-4: " By
this, far off she hears some huntsman

Be unto us as is a nurse's song
Of lullaby to bring her babe asleep.
Aar. Madam, though Venus govern your desires,   30
Saturn is dominator over mine:
What signifies my deadly-standing eye,
My silence and my cloudy melancholy,
My fleece of woolly hair that now uncurls
Even as an adder when she doth unroll   35
To do some fatal execution?
No, madam, these are no venereal signs:
Vengeance is in my heart, death in my hand,
Blood and revenge are hammering in my head.
Hark, Tamora, the empress of my soul,   40
Which never hopes more heaven than rests in thee,
This is the day of doom for Bassianus;
His Philomel must lose her tongue to-day,
Thy sons make pillage of her chastity,
And wash their hands in Bassianus' blood.   45
Seest thou this letter? take it up, I pray thee,
And give the king this fatal-plotted scroll.
Now question me no more; we are espied;

32. *deadly-standing*] Theobald; *deadlie standing* Qq, F.   34. *woolly*] *wollie*
Q 1.   47. *fatal-plotted*] Theobald; *fatall plotted* Qq, F.   48. *more;*] *more*
Q 1; *more,* Q 2-3, F.

hollo; | A nurse's song ne'er pleas'd
her babe so well."
    31. *dominator*] " a planet or sign
supposed [in astrology] to dominate
a particular person " (*N.E.D.*). For
the influence of Saturn, see *N.E.D.*,
saturnine, defined as " sluggish, cold
and gloomy in temperament," and
D. C. Allen, *The Star-crossed Renaissance*
(1941), p. 172. Oppel (p. 24) notes
the contrast between Aaron's cold
plans for revenge and Tamora's hot
love.
    32. *deadly-standing*] fixed in a death-
dealing—rather than a deathly (On.)
or deathlike (Wilson)—stare. Cf.
2H6 v. ii. 9, where " deadly-
handed " means murderous. (Wilson
quotes this, though it tells against his
interpretation, as does *R3* i. iii. 225:
" No sleep close up that deadly eye
of thine.") The implied comparison

is with the basilisk or cockatrice, cf. *R3*
iv. i. 54-5: " A cockatrice hast thou
hatch'd to the world, | Whose un-
avoided eye is murderous " (quoted
by P. Robinson, *Contemporary Review*
(1894), 406).
    37. *venereal*] connected with love
(Venus).
    39. *Blood . . . head*] Apparently
echoed by Giles Fletcher (the elder)
in " The Rising to the Crowne of
Richard the Third," printed in *Licia*
(?1593), Sig. M3ᵛ (p. 158 of Grosart's
edition, 1871): " Blood and revenge
did hammer in my head, | Vnquiet
thoughts did gallop in my braine."
As the preface *To the Reader* is dated
Sept. 8, 1593, Shakespeare could just
be the debtor on a very late dating
of *Titus*. I owe this reference to
Mr. E. Honigmann.

Here comes a parcel of our hopeful booty,
Which dreads not yet their lives' destruction.   50

Enter BASSIANUS *and* LAVINIA.

Tam. Ah, my sweet Moor, sweeter to me than life.
Aar. No more, great empress; Bassianus comes:
    Be cross with him; and I'll go fetch thy sons
    To back thy quarrels, whatsoe'er they be.   [*Exit.*
Bass. Who have we here? Rome's royal empress,   55
    Unfurnish'd of her well-beseeming troop?
    Or is it Dian, habited like her,
    Who hath abandoned her holy groves
    To see the general hunting in this forest?
Tam. Saucy controller of my private steps!   60
    Had I the pow'r that some say Dian had,
    Thy temples should be planted presently
    With horns, as was Actæon's; and the hounds
    Should drive upon thy new-transformed limbs,
    Unmannerly intruder as thou art.   65
Lav. Under your patience, gentle empress,
    'Tis thought you have a goodly gift in horning,
    And to be doubted that your Moor and you

---

50. Enter . . . *LAVINIA*] after 54 Pope.   52. *Bassianus*] Bascianus Q 1-2.
(and in 50 S.D.)   54. *quarrels*] quarrell Q 3, F.   55. *Who*] Whom F.
56. *her*] *our* Q 3, F.   60. *my*] *our* Q 3, F.   61. *pow'r*] Alexander; powre
Q 1; *power* Q 2-3, F.   64. *drive*] dine Collier (2nd ed.).   *thy*] his Q 3, F.

---

49. *parcel . . . booty*] part of the victims we expect.

50. Enter . . . *LAVINIA*] Wilson rightly restores the Qq F placing of this entrance, which Pope had postponed till after l. 54. He writes that " Bassianus and Lavinia are clearly intended to overhear Tamora's endearments."

53. *Be cross*] pick a quarrel.

55. *empress*] See on I. i. 89.

60. *controller*] " censorious critic " (On.).

62. *presently*] immediately : a frequent Elizabethan use.

63. *Actæon's*] He was transformed into a stag and killed by his own hounds, as a punishment for seeing Diana and her nymphs bathing. The point here is, of course, to lead up to the never-failing joke about the cuckold's horns in l. 67. The cuckold's horns are called " *Actæons* ornament " by Sidney, *Arcadia*, Bk. III (*Works*, ed. Feuillerat, II. 70), and " Actaeon's badge " in *The Batchelars Banquet* (1603), ed. F. P. Wilson, p. 51.

64. *drive*] rush.

66. *empress*] See on I. i. 89.

67. *gift in*] So always in Shakespeare (e.g. *MND.* III. ii. 301) where modern English would have " gift for." *N.E.D.* gives an instance as late as 1710.

Are singled forth to try experiments.
Jove shield your husband from his hounds to-day!   70
'Tis pity they should take him for a stag.

Bass. Believe me, queen, your swart Cimmerian
Doth make your honour of his body's hue,
Spotted, detested, and abominable.
Why are you sequest'red from all your train,   75
Dismounted from your snow-white goodly steed,
And wand'red hither to an obscure plot,
Accompanied but with a barbarous Moor,
If foul desire had not conducted you?

Lav. And, being intercepted in your sport,   80
Great reason that my noble lord be rated
For sauciness.   I pray you, let us hence,
And let her joy her raven-coloured love;
This valley fits the purpose passing well.

Bass. The king my brother shall have note of this.   85

Lav. Ay, for these slips have made him noted long:
Good king, to be so mightily abused!

Tam. Why, I have patience to endure all this.

---

69. *try experiments*] *trie thy experimens* Q 1.   72. *swart*] Capell; *swartie*
Q 1-2; *swarty* Q 3; *swarth* F.   78. *but*] om. Q 3, F.   85. *note*] Pope;
notice Qq, F.   88. *Why, I have . . . this.*] Alexander; *Why I haue . . . this.*
Qq; *Why I haue . . . this?* F; *Why haue I . . . this?* F 2.

---

69. *singled*] See on II. i. 117.

to try experiments] to experiment.
Cf. *to try conclusions* in *Ham.* III. iv.
195. For the spelling *experimens* (if
not a misprint) cf. Wyld, p. 302.

72. *swart*] Closer to the Q spelling
(probably *swarte* misread) than F's
swarth.

Cimmerian] A people thought to
live away from the light of the sun:
hence " Cimmerian darkness."

75. *sequest'red*] Stressed on the first
syllable, as in *Oth.* III. iv. 41 : " a
sequester from liberty."

78. *with*] See on l. 23.

79. *had*] A mixed construction, as
if " why would you have been
sequestered " had preceded; so
R3 II. ii. 5-7 (Folio): " Why do you
look on us, and shake your head, |

And call us orphans, wretches,
castaways, | If that our noble father
were alive?"

83. *joy*] enjoy: a parallel, not a
shortened, form.

86. *long*] Johnson noted the incongruity of this when " he had been
married but one night." In its
rudimentary way, this line suggests
the " double time " which is cus-
tomarily attributed to *Othello*.

88. *Why . . . this*] I take it that
Tamora is claiming to be unmoved
by the taunts hurled at her, in order
to deceive Bassianus and Lavinia.
This makes her change of attitude
in l. 91 more dramatic. This interpretation makes it unnecessary to
accept the emendation of F 2, as
Alexander, Sisson and Munro agree.

Enter CHIRON *and* DEMETRIUS.

Dem. How now, dear sovereign, and our gracious mother!
      Why doth your highness look so pale and wan?   90
Tam. Have I not reason, think you, to look pale?
      These two have tic'd me hither to this place:
      A barren detested vale you see it is;
      The trees, though summer, yet forlorn and lean,
      Overcome with moss and baleful mistletoe: 95
      Here never shines the sun: here nothing breeds,
      Unless the nightly owl or fatal raven:
      And when they show'd me this abhorred pit,
      They told me, here, at dead time of the night,
      A thousand fiends, a thousand hissing snakes,   100
      Ten thousand swelling toads, as many urchins,
      Would make such fearful and confused cries,

92. *tic'd*] *ticed* Qq.   95. *Overcome*] *Orecome* Q 2-3, F.

92. *tic'd*] enticed.
93. *barren*] monosyllabic, cf. *2H6*
II. iv. 3 : "Barren winter, with his
wrathful nipping cold." R. A. Law,
S.P. 40 (1943), 149, suggests that this
whole description is indebted to
Virgil, *Aen.* VII. 561-71. The resemblance does not seem to me very
close. In its rather melodramatic
horror it has some likeness to Seneca,
Thyestes 650 ff., as Kittredge notes
(p. 972).
95. *Overcome*] overgrown. The Q 1
spelling probably goes back to the
MS., and is quite compatible with
normal scansion : monosyllabic *never*
is common in Shakespeare.
97. *fatal*] ominous, cf. *Mac.* I. v.
39-40 : "The raven himself is
hoarse | That croaks the fatal entrance
of Duncan." The earliest quotation
given by Tilley R33 for the ominous
character of the raven is Marlowe,
Jew of Malta 640-1 (II. i. 1-2):
"the sad presaging Rauen that tolls |
The sicke mans passeport in her
hollow beake." The equally ominous
night-raven, or night-crow, is a
different species of bird : see *N.E.D.*

99. *dead . . . night*] The meaning
seems to be exactly that of present-
day *at dead of night*. I think the
basic meaning is "a time at which
nothing is going on," though Shake-
spear exploits contextual suggestions
here, as in *Ham.* I. i. 65 : "jump at
this dead hour," and *R2* IV. i. 10 :
"In that dead time when Gloucester's
death was plotted," where Wilson's
note "fatal (or 'gloomy') period"
concentrates on the suggestion at the
expense of the primary meaning.
Professor Ellis-Fermor compares
"dead water" (between two tides),
and suggests that the "dead time"
is when time itself seems to stand still.

101. *urchins*] "hedgehogs" or "gob-
lins"? Wilson gives the former
meaning, but notes "gen. associated
with witchcraft or devils," and compares *Tp.* I. ii. 326 (which On.
glosses *goblin*) and *hedge-pig* in *Mac.*
IV. i. 2. P. Robinson, *Contemporary
Review* (1894), 397-9, argues strongly
that "goblin" is the only Shakespearian sense for the word and its
compounds.

As any mortal body hearing it
Should straight fall mad, or else die suddenly.
No sooner had they told this hellish tale   105
But straight they told me they would bind me here
Unto the body of a dismal yew,
And leave me to this miserable death.
And then they called me foul adulteress,
Lascivious Goth, and all the bitterest terms   110
That ever ear did hear to such effect;
And had you not by wondrous fortune come,
This vengeance on me had they executed.
Revenge it, as you love your mother's life,
Or be ye not henceforth call'd my children.   115
Dem. This is a witness that I am thy son.

                    [*Stab him.*

Chi. And this for me, struck home to show my strength.
Lav. Ay, come, Semiramis, nay, barbarous Tamora,
For no name fits thy nature but thy own.
Tam. Give me the poniard; you shall know, my boys, 120
Your mother's hand shall right your mother's
          wrong.
Dem. Stay, madam, here is more belongs to her:
First thrash the corn, then after burn the straw.
This minion stood upon her chastity,
Upon her nuptial vow, her loyalty,   125

---

110. *Lascivious*] *Lauicious* Q 1-2.   115. *ye*] om. Capell. *henceforth*] *from*
henceforth Pope.   *call'd my children*] *my children call'd* Wilson.   118. *Ay,*]
Hanmer; *I,* Theobald; *I* Qq, F.   120. *the*] *thy* Q 3, F.

---

104. *Should*] would. The modern
" Standard " distinctions had not yet
been established in Shakespeare's
day, cf. Abbott § 322, Franz § 612.
straight] immediately, so in l. 106.
110. *lascivious   Goth*] Possibly
(though not necessarily), as Herford
suggests, with the same pun on *Goth*
and *goat* as in *A.Y.L.* III. iii. 7-9 :
" I am here with thee and thy
goats as the most capricious poet,
honest Ovid. was among the Goths."

Goats are proverbially lustful, cf.
Oth. III. iii. 404 : " as prime as
goats."
115. *Or . . . children*] Best read
as a headless line with a strong stress
on *Or*. Iı any alteration is required,
Capell's is the best (with *children*
trisyllabic).   Wilson's transposition
is arbitrary.
118. *Semiramis*] See on II. i. 22.
124. *minion stood upon*] saucy
creature made much of.

And with that painted hope braves your mightiness:
And shall she carry this unto her grave?
Chi. And if she do, I would I were an eunuch.
   Drag hence her husband to some secret hole,
And make his dead trunk pillow to our lust.   130
Tam. But when ye have the honey we desire,
Let not this wasp outlive, us both to sting.
Chi. I warrant you, madam, we will make that sure.
   Come, mistress, now perforce we will enjoy
That nice-preserved honesty of yours.   135
Lav. O Tamora, thou bearest a woman's face,—
Tam. I will not hear her speak; away with her!
Lav. Sweet lords, entreat her hear me but a word.

---

126. *painted*] *pall'd* A. Walker conj.   *braves*] *she braves* F 2.   131. *we*]
ye F 2.   132. *outlive, us*] Theobald; *out liue us* Q 1; *out-liue vs* Q 2-3, F;
outlive ye Dyce (2nd ed.); *o'erlive, us* Maxwell conj.   135. *nice-preserved*]
nice preserued Qq.   136. *bearest*] *bear'st* F. *woman's*] *woman* F.

126. *painted hope*] Metre and sense awkward. A. Walker's *pall'd* = " weakened " (*R.E.S.* n.s. 6, 1955, 81) implies a misreading of " pauled "; cf. *Ant.* II. vii. 87, " Thy paul'd Fortunes."

129-30. *Drag . . . lust*] J. D. Ebbs, *Modern Language Notes* 66 (1951), 480-1, notes the resemblance of this to Nashe, *Unfortunate Traveller* (in *Works*, ed. McKerrow, II. 226) : " Her husbands dead bodie he made a pillow to his abhomination." Nashe's novel was completed 27 June 1593, registered 17 September 1593, and printed 1594. Since Chiron and Demetrius do not in fact do what they here propose, it might be argued that these lines are a last-minute addition by Shakespeare to his text.

131. *we*] I retain this, with some hesitation, but encouraged by the example of Alexander, on the hypothesis that Tamora is entering whole-heartedly into her sons' plans, so that the desire is hers as well as theirs.

132. *outlive . . . sting*] A very awkward line. Theobald's punctuation seems to be the only way to make sense of it, but *outlive* intransitively in the sense of survive is unparalleled. *O'erlive* would be easier, and if Shakespeare spelt monosyllabic *over* as *our* the corruption would not be difficult (admittedly *ore* is the normal spelling but we have the spelling *moreour* at *Tw. N.* I. iii. 39). There is one other passage where a similar corruption is not unlikely : at *2H6* IV. viii. 27 *given out* occurs in the unparalleled sense of " surrendered " or " abandoned," and Walker's conjecture *given over* is attractive. In the present passage it is tempting to accept Dyce's *outlive ye* (= survive your attack).

133. *make that sure*] make sure of that, with the special implication of rendering harmless, cf. l. 187. The phrase is used in *1H4* v. iii. 47-8 : " I have paid Percy, I have made him sure," leading to a play in the retort on *sure* = *safe*.

138. *entreat . . . hear*] The infinitive without *to* after verbs of asking is commoner in Shakespeare than in modern English, cf. Abbott §§ 349-50, Franz § 650.

Dem. Listen, fair madam: let it be your glory
  To see her tears; but be your heart to them 140
  As unrelenting flint to drops of rain.
Lav. When did the tiger's young ones teach the dam?
  O, do not learn her wrath; she taught it thee;
  The milk thou suck'st from her did turn to marble;
  Even at thy teat thou hadst thy tyranny. 145
  Yet every mother breeds not sons alike:
  Do thou entreat her show a woman's pity.
Chi. What, would'st thou have me prove myself a bastard?
Lav. 'Tis true the raven doth not hatch a lark:
  Yet have I heard—O, could I find it now!— 150
  The lion mov'd with pity did endure
  To have his princely paws par'd all away.
  Some say that ravens foster forlorn children,
  The whilst their own birds famish in their nests:

---

144. *suck'st*] ⌐*suck'dst* Rowe (3rd ed.) (Ravenscroft). 147. *woman's*]
woman Q 2-3, F. 151. *mov'd*] *moued* Qq.

---

143. *learn*] teach : acceptable Elizabethan English, though now a vulgarism.

144. *suck'st*] instead of the unpronounceable *suckdst* : so in *1H6* v. iv. 28, *Cor.* III. ii. 129 : see on I. i. 317. Tilley E198 cites from Elyot's *Governour* (1531) : " often times the childe soukethe the vice of his nouryse with the milk of her pappe;" so Lyly, *Euphues*, ed. Bond, I. 266; and, for more detail about the belief, Burton, *Anatomy of Melancholy* 1, 2, 4, 1. Shakespeare alludes to the notion again in *R3* II. ii. 30 : " Yet from my dugs he drew not this deceit."

148. *What . . . bastard?*] The logic of this leaves something to be desired. Grant White asks : " how was he to prove himself a *bastard* by being unlike *his mother?*" But the whole line is only a rhetorical way of asking : " would you have me false to my parentage?"

149. *raven . . . lark*] Verity compares Horace, *Odes*, IV. iv. 31-2 :

" neque imbellem feroces | progenerant aquilae columbam " (" nor do fierce eagles bring forth an unwarlike dove.")   The earliest English quotation in Tilley E2 is from Pettie's *Civile Conversation* (1581).

151-2. *The lion . . . away*] The fable is that of the Lion as Suitor. The Latin version of Camerarius (1573) and Bullokar's English (1584) are quoted by A. Yoder, *Animal Analogy in Shakespeare's Character Portrayal* (1947), pp. 82-3, and Camerarius also in Baldwin I. 631-2. Camerarius's *ungues praecidi . . . patitur* might seem to support the emendation *claws* for *paws*, but the corruption would not be easy, and Shakespeare is no doubt " hunting the letter." Cf., moreover, Marlowe *I Tamb.* I. ii. 52-3 : " As princely lions when they rouse themselves, | Stretching their paws," which Shakespeare may be echoing.

154. *birds*] young ones (the original sense, and still in dialect).

O, be to me, though thy hard heart say no,   155
Nothing so kind, but something pitiful.
Tam. I know not what it means ; away with her !
Lav. O, let me teach thee! for my father's sake,
That gave thee life when well he might have slain
        thee,
Be not obdurate, open thy deaf ears.   160
Tam. Hadst thou in person ne'er offended me,
Even for his sake am I pitiless.
Remember, boys, I pour'd forth tears in vain
To save your brother from the sacrifice,
But fierce Andronicus would not relent: 165
Therefore away with her, and use her as you will:
The worse to her, the better lov'd of me.
Lav. O Tamora, be call'd a gentle queen,
And with thine own hands kill me in this place,
For 'tis not life that I have begg'd so long;   170
Poor I was slain when Bassianus died.
Tam. What begg'st thou then, fond woman? let me go.
Lav. 'Tis present death I beg; and one thing more
That womanhood denies my tongue to tell.
O, keep me from their worse than killing lust,   175
And tumble me into some loathsome pit,
Where never man's eye may behold my body:
Do this, and be a charitable murderer.
Tam. So should I rob my sweet sons of their fee:
No, let them satisfice their lust on thee.   180
Dem. Away! for thou hast stay'd us here too long.

---

158. *thee!*] *thee:* Theobald; *thee* Qq, F.   160. *ears*] *yeares* Q 1-2.
171. *Bassianus*] Bascianus Q 1-2 ; Bussianus Q 3.   172. *then, . . . woman?*
. . . go.] Chambers (1907); *then . . . woman . . . goe?* Qq; *then? . . . woman . . .*
go? F.   180. *satisfice*] satisfie Q 2-3, F.

---

156. *Nothing . . . pitiful*] not, indeed, as kind as the raven, but
showing some pity.
    157. *it*] the word " pity."
    160. *ears*] For the phonetic spelling
years cf. Wyld, p. 308. At *1H4* I. ii.
148 *Yedward* is a familiar form for
Edward ; *yer* for *ere* is regular in
Holinshed.
    172. *What . . . go?*]   A better

rhythm, I think, than the F punctuation usually adopted.
    174. *denies*] does not allow.
    179. *So*] if I did that.
    180. *satisfice*] Q 1 reads either this
or *satisfiee*. Even if it is the latter,
it is probably only a " foul case "
error for *satisfice*, a well-authenticated
sixteenth-century form, influenced by
the Latin, and by the analogy of *suffice*.

Lav. No grace? no womanhood? Ah, beastly creature,
  The blot and enemy to our general name!
  Confusion fall—
Chi. Nay, then I'll stop your mouth.   Bring thou her
      husband: 185
  This is the hole where Aaron bid us hide him.
    [*Exeunt* CHIRON *and* DEMETRIUS *with* LAVINIA.
Tam. Farewell, my sons: see that you make her sure.
  Ne'er let my heart know merry cheer indeed
  Till all the Andronici be made away.
  Now will I hence to seek my lovely Moor,   190
  And let my spleenful sons this trull deflower.   [*Exit.*

  Enter AARON, *with two of Titus' sons.*

Aar. Come on, my lords, the better foot before:
  Straight will I bring you to the loathsome pit
  Where I espied the panther fast asleep.
Quint. My sight is very dull, whate'er it bodes.   195
Mart. And mine, I promise you: were it not for shame,
  Well could I leave our sport to sleep awhile.
Quint. What, art thou fallen? What subtle hole is this,
  Whose mouth is covered with rude-growing briers,
  Upon whose leaves are drops of new-shed blood   200
  As fresh as morning dew distill'd on flowers?

184. *fall—*] Q 3, F ; *fall* Q 1; *fall.* Q 2.   186. Exeunt . . . *LAVINIA*]
om. Qq, F ; Exeunt F 2.   191. Exit] om. Qq.   198. *What,*] F 4 ;
What Qq, F.   199. *rude-growing*] Pope ; *rude growing* Qq, F.   201. *morning*]
mornings Q 3, F.

183. *our general name*] the name of
woman, which is common (general)
to our sex.
  184. *Confusion fall—*] Q 1's omission of punctuation after *fall* is a
customary way of indicating a
broken-off speech, cf. Simpson, p. 98.
  186. *bid*] An unusual but not unparalleled form of the past indicative
(it occurs at I. i. 338 and v. iii. 165
as a past participle), found as late as
Emily Brontë. See Wyld, p. 351, or
N.E.D., for the blending of two O.E.

verbs in *bid*, and the borrowing of
certain forms from O.E. Class I.
  187. *make her sure*] See on l. 133.
  189. *made away*] killed, cf. l. 208.
  191. *spleenful*] lustful. The spleen
was considered the seat of the passions
in general, cf. On. *trull*] harlot.
  192. *the . . . before*] Tilley F 570
quotes " set out the better leg " from
Medwall's *Nature* (*c.* 1500) and " set
forth the better foote " from Golding's
Abraham's Sacrifice (1577).

A very fatal place it seems to me.

Speak, brother, hast thou hurt thee with the fall?

Mart. O brother, with the dismall'st object hurt

That ever eye with sight made heart lament.   205

Aar. Now will I fetch the king to find them here,

That he thereby may have a likely guess

How these were they that made away his brother.

[*Exit.*

Mart. Why dost not comfort me, and help me out

From this unhallow'd and blood-stained hole?   210

Quint. I am surprised with an uncouth fear;

A chilling sweat o'er-runs my trembling joints:

My heart suspects more than mine eye can see.

Mart. To prove thou hast a true-divining heart,

Aaron and thou look down into this den,   215

And see a fearful sight of blood and death.

Quint. Aaron is gone, and my compassionate heart

Will not permit mine eyes once to behold

The thing whereat it trembles by surmise.

O, tell me who it is; for ne'er till now   220

Was I a child to fear I know not what.

Mart. Lord Bassianus lies beray'd in blood,

---

204. *hurt*] om. Q 3, F.   208 Exit] after 207 in Q 1; Exit Aaron F.
210. *unhallow'd*] *vnhollow* Qq.   214. *true-divining*] Theobald; *true diuining*
Qq, F.   220. *who*] *how* Q 3, F.   222. *beray'd* Wilson; *bereaud* Q1;
embrewed Q 2-3, F; *bedaub'd* or *bedew'd* Bolton conj. *in blood*] *heere* Q 2-3, F.

---

202. *fatal*] ill-omened. Cf. *Macb.*
I. v. 40: "the fatal entrance of
Duncan."

205. *That . . . lament*] that ever
eye made heart lament to see. On
the ellipse of *of* after *sight* see on II. i.
103.

208. *made away*] See on l. 189.

210. *unhallow'd*] Wilson suggests
that the MS. had *unhallowd* misread by the Q 1 compositor as
unhollowe. This is no doubt correct
for the *d* : *e* corruption, but the *o*
may represent a phonetic spelling by
Shakespeare, for whom *a* and *o*
(partly unrounded) were closer than

they are now : cf. Wyld, pp. 240-2.
In *Ham.* III. ii. 11, where F. reads
tatters, Q 2 (set up from Shakespeare's
MS.) and Q 1 (representing what
was heard on the stage) both read
totters.

211. *surprised*] bewildered.
uncouth] uncanny.

219. *by surmise*] when it only
imagines it.

222. *beray'd*] Probably, as Wilson
suggests, Q 1's text represents a misreading of *bereied* as *bereud*. Bolton's
conjectures are published in *P.M.L.A.*,
44 (1929), 769. *Bedew'd* (which
might have been spelt *bedeaud* in

All on a heap, like to a slaughtered lamb,
In this detested, dark, blood-drinking pit.

Quint. If it be dark, how dost thou know 'tis he?   225

Mart. Upon his bloody finger he doth wear
A precious ring, that lightens all this hole,
Which, like a taper in some monument,
Doth shine upon the dead man's earthy cheeks,
And shows the ragged entrails of this pit: 230
So pale did shine the moon on Pyramus
When he by night lay bath'd in maiden blood.
O brother, help me with thy fainting hand,
If fear hath made thee faint, as me it hath,
Out of this fell devouring receptacle,   235
As hateful as Cocytus' misty mouth.

Quint. Reach me thy hand, that I may help thee out,
Or, wanting strength to do thee so much good,

223. *to a*] *to the* F.   227. *this*] *the* Q 3, F.   229. *earthy*] *earthly* Q 3, F.
230. *this*] *the* F.   231. *Pyramus*] *Priamus* Q 1.   235. *fell devouring*] *fell-
devouring* W. S. Walker.   236. *Cocytus'*] F 2 (Cocitus) ; Ocitus Qq, F.

the MS.) is not impossible. If
Q 2's *embrewed* is a mere conjecture,
as it presumably is, it is odd that *in
blood* was altered, since *embrewde in
blood* would have restored both sense
and metre. An early owner of the
copy of Q 1 has emended to 'heere
reav'd of lyfe', perhaps with the help
of l. 282.

223. *on a heap*] prostrate, cf. *Tim.*
IV. iii. 101 : " laid proud Athens on a
heap."

227. *ring . . . hole*] An allusion to
the belief that carbuncles emitted
(Johnson) " not reflected but native
light." Johnson notes that Boyle, the
pioneer of modern chemistry, still
believed this. The same property is
attributed to the Moonstone of Wilkie
Collins's novel, First Period, ch. 9.

230. *ragged entrails*] rugged interior.

231. *Pyramus*] See *MND*. v. i.
for the story of Pyramus and Thisbe.
The Q 2 correction of *Priamus* to
Piramus shows some knowledge and
intelligence. There is always the
possibility (on which in general see

W. W. Greg, *The Editorial Problem in
Shakespeare*, p. 87, n. 4) that the
corrections had been made during
printing in the copy of Q 1 from
which Q 2 was printed; cf. v. i. 141.

235. *receptacle*] See on I. i. 92.

236. *Cocytus' misty mouth*] Probably
(Wilson) Cocytus, properly a river of
Hell, is here used generally for Hell,
and its mouth is simply the entrance to
Hell. Wilson's supposition that this
is a " confused memory " of *Locrine*
IV. v. 44-5 : " Backe will I post
to hell mouth *Taenarus*, | And
passe *Cocitus*, to the Elysian fields "
is more hazardous, but possible.
The mouth of Cocytus would more
strictly be the point at which it
flows into Acheron. They are the
first two rivers to be crossed in the
underworld—in which order, authorities are not agreed.

238-9. *Or . . . pluck'd*] or that,
if I want strength, I may be plucked.
This must be a subordinate clause
parallel to " that . . . out." It is

I may be pluck'd into the swallowing womb
Of this deep pit, poor Bassianus' grave.   240
I have no strength to pluck thee to the brink.
Mart. Nor I no strength to climb without thy help.
Quint. Thy hand once more; I will not loose again,
Till thou art here aloft, or I below.
Thou canst not come to me: I come to thee.   245

                                        [*Falls in.*

Enter the Emperor and AARON *the Moor.*

Sat. Along with me: I'll see what hole is here,
And what he is that now is leapt into it.
Say, who art thou that lately didst descend
Into this gaping hollow of the earth?   250
Mart. The unhappy sons of old Andronicus;
Brought hither in a most unlucky hour,
To find thy brother Bassianus dead.
Sat. My brother dead! I know thou dost but jest:
He and his lady both are at the lodge
Upon the north side of this pleasant chase;   255
'Tis not an hour since I left them there.
Mart. We know not where you left them all alive;
But, out alas! here have we found him dead.

---

243. *more;*] Theobald; *more,* Qq, F; *more* Pope.   245. Falls in] Pope;
Boths fall in F; om. Qq.   Emperor and] Emperour, Q 3, F.   251.
sons] *sonne* Q 2-3, F.   256. *them*] *him* Q 3, F.   257. *them*] *him* F.

---

not clear why Quintus should be so
gloomily resigned, but it is even
harder to make sense of the usual
editorial punctuation (contrary to
Qq F) with a semi-colon after *out*,
which presumably means that this is
a principal clause.

239. *swallowing womb*] Wilson (on
v. ii. 192 with a cross-reference from
this line) compares *Rom.* II. iii. 9 :
" The earth that's nature's mother is
her tomb," and *R2* II. i. 82-3 : " a
grave, | Whose hollow womb inherits
nought but bones."

244. *aloft*] Qq spell *a loft* (and Q 1
a liue in l. 257), as often. Here the
spelling corresponds to the deriva-
tion (*on* + *loft*) but it often occurs
without any such justification, as
in *a leauen* (= eleven), *Ham.* (Q 2)
I. ii. 251.

255. *chase*] See on II. ii. 21.

256. *hour*] Disyllabic, see on I. i.
127.

258. *out*] This interjection, " expressing abhorrence, reproach, or
indignation " (On.) here reinforces
alas.

Enter TAMORA, ANDRONICUS, *and* LUCIUS.

Tam. Where is my lord the king?

Sat. Here, Tamora; though grip'd with killing grief.　260

Tam. Where is thy brother Bassianus?

Sat. Now to the bottom dost thou search my wound:
　　　Poor Bassianus here lies murthered.

Tam. Then all too late I bring this fatal writ,
　　　The complot of this timeless tragedy;　265
　　　And wonder greatly that man's face can fold
　　　In pleasing smiles such murderous tyranny.

　　　　　　　[*She giveth Saturnine a letter.*

260. Sat.] King. Qq, F (and throughout scene).　*grip'd*] Maxwell;
griude Q 1 ; *greeu'd (-ie-)* Q 2-3, F ; *gnaw'd* W. S. Walker.

260. *grip'd*] seized, cf. *3H6* I. iv.
171 : "inly sorrow gripes his soul"
and *Rom.* IV. v. 129 : "griping grief."
Q 1's *griude* is not an inconceivable
spelling for *griev'd*, though Shakespeare
elsewhere has only *grieu'd* or *greeu'd*,
but "griev'd with grief" is surely
too careless for him to have written.
I cannot recall an instance of the
corruption *p : u*, but it would be
possible with the "stumpy *p*"
which occurs a number of times in the
Shakespearian three pages of *Sir
Thomas More* : see E. M. Thompson,
Shakespeare's Handwriting (Oxford,
1916), p. 49. In *Err.* v. i. 121 there
is an *a : p* error (*death* misread as
depth). The spelling *gripde* postu-
lated for the MS. would be possible,
though perhaps less usual than *gripte*,
as Dr. Alice Walker has pointed out
to me.

262. *search*] probe.

265. *complot*] This word is found in
most of the senses of plot, which is
(*N.E.D.*) perhaps an abbreviation
of it. Hence it seems to me probable
that there is here a pun on the
special theatrical sense of *plot* (or
plat) : "a skeleton outline of the
action" hung up at some convenient
place, perhaps "in the centre of
the tiring-house" (Chambers, I. 123-
4). The "writ" gives, as it were,

the outline of the tragedy. I think
this sense may be present in the rather
odd pun in Kyd's *Spanish Tragedy*
(ed. Boas) IV. ii. 12-13 : "No, not
an herb within this garden Plot— |
Accursed complot of my miserie" :
the garden where her son has been
hanged is, as it were, an epitome of
her misery. I doubt whether Boas's
suggestion of "part-plotter" covers
even part of the sense. The dramatic
implications of the word are more
evident in *Arden of Feversham* (in
Shakespeare Apocrypha, ed. Tucker
Brooke) v. i. 103-4 : "will you two
performe | The complot that I
laid?". For an extensive survey of
Shakespeare's imagery drawn from
the stage, see E. K. Chambers,
Shakespearean Gleanings (Oxford, 1944),
pp. 43-48. Sir Edmund quotes
the present passage. Among his
other quotations, the nearest parallel
is *2H6* III. i. 152-3 : "For thousands
more that yet suspect no peril | Will
not conclude their plotted tragedy."

timeless] untimely.

266. *fold*] conceal (Wilson). But
there is also surely, as Dr. B. L.
Joseph has pointed out to me, a
suggestion of the wrinkles of a false
smile. An interesting parallel is
Meas. v. i. 118-19 : "Unfold the evil
which is here wrapp'd up | In

Sat. *And if we miss to meet him handsomely,*
Sweet huntsman, Bassianus 'tis we mean,
Do thou so much as dig the grave for him: 270
Thou know'st our meaning; look for thy reward
Among the nettles at the elder-tree
Which overshades the mouth of that same pit
Where we decreed to bury Bassianus:
Do this, and purchase us thy lasting friends.   275
O Tamora, was ever heard the like?
This is the pit, and this the elder-tree.
Look, sirs, if you can find the huntsman out
That should have murthered Bassianus here.

Aar. My gracious lord, here is the bag of gold.   280

Sat. Two of thy whelps, fell curs of bloody kind,
Have here bereft my brother of his life.
Sirs, drag them from the pit unto the prison:
There let them bide until we have devis'd
Some never-heard-of torturing pain for them.   285

Tam. What, are they in this pit? O wondrous thing!
How easily murder is discovered!

Tit. High emperor, upon my feeble knee
I beg this boon, with tears not lightly shed,
That this fell fault of my accursed sons,   290
Accursed, if the fault be prov'd in them,—

268. Sat.] Saturninus reads the letter. Qq, F (centred).   271. meaning;]
meaning: Pope; meaning Q 1 ; meaning, Q 2-3, F.   reward] reward, Q 1-2 ;
reward. Q 3.   276. *O*] Theobald; King. *O* Qq, F.   285. *torturing*] F 3;
tortering Qq, F.   286. *What,*] Rowe(3rd ed.) ; *What* Qq, F.   291. *fault*]
Theobald (Ravenscroft) ; *faults* Qq, F.

countenance," where the primary
meaning of *countenance* is " authority "
or " worldly credit," but where the
literal sense of " face " is present—
the set, mask-like, false expression is
to be ironed out.
    268. handsomely] conveniently.
    272. elder-tree] An ill-omened tree :
" Judas was hanged on an elder "
(*LLL.* v. ii. 606-7).
    275. purchase] win.
    279. *should have*] was to have
(according to the " complot "), and
presumably has.

281. kind] natural disposition.
    285. torturing] Qq F's *tortering* is
phonetic, cf. *2H6* I. ii. 42 : " ill-
nurter'd," and Wyld, p. 265 and
(examples) p. 277.
    287. *easily*] Disyllabic; this com-
mon pronunciation is often in sixteenth-century English represented
by the spelling " easely."
    291-2. *Accursed . . . apparent*] Cf.
R3 III. iv. 72-3 : " *Hast.* If they have
done this thing my noble lord,— |
Glo. If! thou protector of this
damned strumpet."

Sat. If it be prov'd! you see it is apparent.
　　Who found this letter? Tamora, was it you?

Tam. Andronicus himself did take it up.

Tit. I did, my lord: yet let me be their bail;   295
　　For by my fathers' reverent tomb I vow
　　They shall be ready at your highness' will
　　To answer their suspicion with their lives.

Sat. Thou shalt not bail them: see thou follow me.
　　Some bring the murthered body, some the
　　　　murtherers: 300
　　Let them not speak a word; the guilt is plain;
　　For, by my soul, were there worse end than death,
　　That end upon them should be executed.

Tam. Andronicus, I will entreat the king:
　　Fear not thy sons, they shall do well enough.   305

Tit. Come, Lucius, come; stay not to talk with them.
　　　　　　　　　　　　　　　　　　[*Exeunt.*

SCENE IV.

Enter the empress' sons, with LAVINIA, *her hands cut off, and
her tongue cut out, and ravish'd.*

Dem. So, now go tell, and if thy tongue can speak,
　　Who 'twas that cut thy tongue and ravish'd thee.

Chi. Write down thy mind, bewray thy meaning so,
　　And if thy stumps will let thee play the scribe.

296. *fathers'*] Delius; *fathers* Qq, F; *father's* Rowe.　　306. Exeunt] om. Qq.

Scene IV

Scene IV.] Dyce; om. Qq, F.　　4. *thee*] thee, Rowe (Ravencroft).

292. *apparent*] manifest; more usual in Shakespeare than the modern sense in which the apparent is contrasted with the real.

296. *reverent*] Used interchangeably with *reverend*, cf. III. i. 23, v. iii. 137, and *1H6* III. i. 49-50: " *Win.* Unreverent Gloucester! *Glo.* Thou art reverent | Touching thy spiritual function, not thy life," where the word-play requires both identity of form and diversity of meaning.

298. *their suspicion*] the suspicion under which they lie. For this " objective genitive " cf. Franz § 322.

305. *Fear not*] do not be afraid for. Cf. *1H4* IV. i. 24 : " he was much fear'd by his physicians " (Delius).

Scene IV

3. *bewray*] make known.

4. *And if*] if, as in l. 1. To treat *And* as connective, and place a comma after *thee*, is much less satisfactory.

Dem. See how with signs and tokens she can scrowl. 5
Chi. Go home, call for sweet water, wash thy hands.
Dem. She hath no tongue to call, nor hands to wash;
And so let's leave her to her silent walks.
Chi. And 'twere my cause, I should go hang myself.
Dem. If thou hadst hands to help thee knit the cord. 10

[*Exeunt.*

Enter MARCUS, *from hunting.*

Marc. Who is this? my niece, that flies away so fast!
Cousin, a word; where is your husband?
If I do dream, would all my wealth would wake me!
If I do wake, some planet strike me down,
That I may slumber an eternal sleep! 15
Speak, gentle niece, what stern ungentle hands
Hath lopp'd and hew'd and made thy body bare
Of her two branches, those sweet ornaments,
Whose circling shadows kings have sought to sleep in,
And might not gain so great a happiness 20
As half thy love? Why dost not speak to me?

---

5. *scrowl*] scowle F. 10. *Dem.*] Dmet. Q 1. Exeunt] om. Qq.
Enter . . . hunting] Winde Hornes. Enter . . . hunting, to Lauinia F.
11. *this?* . . . *fast!*] *this,* . . . *fast,* Q 1-2; *this* . . . *fast?* Q 3; *this,* . . .
fast? F. 15. *an*] *in* Q 2-3, F. 21. *half*] *have* Theobald.

---

5. *See . . . scrowl*] An ironic anticipation of the final disclosure,
which Witherspoon compares with
the anticipation by Gloster (*Lr.* III.
vii. 56-7) of the torture he himself
undergoes immediately after. *Scrowl*
is apparently (On.) " a form of
' scrawl,' to gesticulate, with a play
on ' scroll,' to write down."

6. *sweet*] perfumed.

9. *cause*] case, perhaps with a
suggestion of the specific sense of
" disease."

10. S.D. from hunting] H.T. Price,
J.E.G.P. 42 (1943), 61, compares
Marcus's entry " in that mood of
hearty cheerfulness which is always
produced by a day's hunting in the
forest," only to find Lavinia in her

sorry plight, with Lear's entry from
hunting in *Lr.* I. iv, to face a comparable disaster.

12. *Cousin*] " collateral relative more
distant than brother or sister " (On.).

14. *some . . . down*] Cf. *Ham.* I. i.
162 : " The nights are wholesome;
then no planets strike." Shakespeare
refers to the astrological influence of
adverse planets also in *Oth.* II. iii. 184
and *Cor.* II. ii. 118-19 (Tilley P389).

17. *Hath*] Not uncommon with a
plural subject, cf. Abbott § 334, Franz
§ 156.

21. *half*] This makes tolerable sense
and the conjecture *have* is weak.
But *Lr.* I. i. 104, where the point of
half is much more obvious, does not
support it very strongly.

Alas, a crimson river of warm blood,
Like to a bubbling fountain stirr'd with wind,
Doth rise and fall between thy rosed lips,
Coming and going with thy honey breath.　　　25
But, sure, some Tereus hath deflow'red thee,
And, lest thou should'st detect him, cut thy tongue.
Ah, now thou turn'st away thy face for shame,
And, notwithstanding all this loss of blood,
As from a conduit with three issuing spouts,　　　30
Yet do thy cheeks look red as Titan's face
Blushing to be encount'red with a cloud.
Shall I speak for thee? shall I say 'tis so?
O, that I knew thy heart, and knew the beast,
That I might rail at him to ease my mind.　　　35

27. *him*] Rowe (Ravenscroft); *them* Qq, F.　　　30. *three*] Hanmer; *their* Qq,
F.　　33. *thee? . . . so? . . . so.*　Q 1-2; *thee, . . . so?* Q 3.

22-5. *Alas . . . breath*] Parrott, p.
29, compares *Lucr.* 1734-8 : " And
from the purple fountain Brutus
drew | The murderous knife, and as it
left the place, | Her blood, in poor
revenge, held it in chase; | And
bubbling from her breast, it doth
divide | In two slow rivers." Wilson
(p. liii-iv) holds, unconvincingly, it
seems to me, that Shakespeare is
here caricaturing what he had
treated seriously in *Lucr.*

26. *Tereus*] The story of Tereus is
constantly in Shakespeare's mind in
Titus. Tereus raped his wife's sister
Philomela, and cut out her tongue and
immured her in a tower. She
succeeded in depicting her fate in a
tapestry (l. 39), which she had
conveyed to her sister Progne, who
released her, and revenged her by
killing Itylus, her own son by Tereus,
and serving him to his father at a
meal. Philomela then threw the
head on the table. The gods then
changed Tereus to a hoopoe, Philomela to a nightingale, Progne to a
swallow and Itylus to a pheasant.

27. *him*] The reading *them* may have
been due to the compositor's belief
that *Tereus* was plural (for *hath* with
a plural subject see on l. 17). Plural

pronouns after *no, every, any,* are found
in sixteenth-century English (Franz
§ 353), but not after *some* with singular reference, as in mod. colloquial
English, and (after *another*) as early
as Bunyan (*Holy War*, Cambridge
English Classics, p. 217).

30. *three*] Hanmer's correction is
excellent. The MS. probably had
thre, misread as *ther*.

31. *Titan*] See on i. i. 226.

32. *Blushing . . . cloud*] Wilson (and
earlier E. Koeppel, *Englische Studien*
35 (1905), 124) compares the development of this image in *R2* iii. iii. 63-6 :
" As doth the blushing discontented
sun | From out the fiery portal of
the east, | When he perceives the
envious clouds are bent | To dim
his glory."

34. *heart*] Virtually, " what is in
your mind." The heart was the
seat of thought, not only of emotion ;
cf. T. Starkey, *Dialogue between Pole
and Lupset* (ed. K. M. Burton, 1948),
p. 57 : " all wit, reason and sense,
life and all other natural power
springeth out of the heart." Rolfe
cites *Ado* iii. ii. 13-14 : " what his
heart thinks his tongue speaks."
Failure to realize this led to the
conjecture *hurt* (W. S. Walker).

Sorrow concealed, like an oven stopp'd,
Doth burn the heart to cinders where it is.
Fair Philomel, why, she but lost her tongue,
And in a tedious sampler sew'd her mind:
But, lovely niece, that mean is cut from thee;   40
A craftier Tereus, cousin, hast thou met,
And he hath cut those pretty fingers off,
That could have better sew'd than Philomel.
O, had the monster seen those lily hands
Tremble like aspen-leaves upon a lute,   45
And make the silken strings delight to kiss them,
He would not then have touch'd them for his life.
Or had he heard the heavenly harmony
Which that sweet tongue hath made,
He would have dropp'd his knife, and fell asleep,   50
As Cerberus at the Thracian poet's feet.

38. *Philomel*] Camb.; Philomela Qq, F.   *why*] om. Q 3, F.   39. *sew'd*]
Pope; *sowed* Qq, F (so 43).   41. *cousin*] om. Q 3, F.   *met*] *met withall* F.

36-7. *Sorrow . . . is*] Particularly close (Parrott, p. 29) to *Ven.* 331-3 : " An oven that is stopp'd, or river stay'd, | Burneth more hotly, swelleth with more rage: | So of concealed sorrow may be said." Baldwin, II. 435-6, claims that the *Ven.* lines are the earlier, on grounds that are not clear to me. For the general notion cf. *Gorboduc* III. i. 101-2: " The fire not quenched, but kept in close restraint, | Fedde still within, breakes forth with double flame" (quoted Tilley F 265).

37. *where*] in which. This use is in modern English confined to compounds such as *wherein*, and even they are felt as stilted if not archaic.

38. *Philomel*] See on l. 26.

39. *tedious*] laboriously executed (Wilson).

45. *like aspen-leaves*] This comparison is found as early as Chaucer, *Troilus* III. 1200. There is a curious series of verbal resemblances between these lines and Spenser, *Amoretti* I. 1-4: " Happy ye leaues when as those lilly hands, | which hold my life in their

dead doing might, | shall handle you and hold in loues soft bands, | lyke captiues trembling at the victors sight." It is probably a coincidence; if not, Spenser must presumably have seen the printed text of *Titus*. *Amoretti* was entered on the Stationers' Register on 19 November, 1594, and published 1595, and this introductory sonnet might be expected to be among the last written. (Against the view that a version found in MS. in a copy of the *Faerie Queene*, 1590, represents an earlier draft, see A. C. Judson, *Modern Language Notes* 58 (1943), 548-50.)

48-51. *Or . . . feet*] Wilson, following Parrott, compares *Lucr.* 552-3 : " So his unhallowed haste her words delays, | And moody Pluto winks while Orpheus plays," and notes that nowhere but in these two passages is the story of Orpheus linked with a situation in which " a brutal ravisher is stayed by the charm of his victim's voice."

Come, let us go, and make thy father blind,
For such a sight will blind a father's eye:
One hour's storm will drown the fragrant meads;
What will whole months of tears thy father's eyes? 55
Do not draw back, for we will mourn with thee:
O, could our mourning ease thy misery!   [*Exeunt.*

50. *fell*] For the use of the past
indicative form for past participle
cf. Franz § 167.

51. *Cerberus*] the three-headed dog
that guarded the entrance to hell.
54. *hour's*] See on I. i. 127.

ACT III

SCENE I.

*Enter the Judges and Senators, with Titus' two sons, bound,
passing on the stage to the place of execution, and* TITUS
going before, pleading.

Tit. Hear me, grave fathers! noble tribunes, stay!
For pity of mine age, whose youth was spent
In dangerous wars, whilst you securely slept;
For all my blood in Rome's great quarrel shed,
For all the frosty nights that I have watch'd,   5
And for these bitter tears, which now you see
Filling the aged wrinkles in my cheeks,
Be pitiful to my condemned sons,
Whose souls is not corrupted as 'tis thought.
For two and twenty sons I never wept,   10
Because they died in honour's lofty bed:

    [*Andronicus lieth down, and the Judges pass by him.*

For these, tribunes, in the dust I write
My heart's deep languor and my soul's sad tears.
Let my tears staunch the earth's dry appetite;
My sons' sweet blood will make it shame and blush.   15
O earth, I will befriend thee more with rain,
That shall distil from these two ancient urns,

ACT III

Scene 1

ACT III. *Scene* 1.] Rowe; Actus Tertius. F; om. Qq.   4. *Rome's*] *Roomes*
Q 1.   9. *is*] are F 2.   12. *these,*] *these, these* F 2; *these, these,* F 4.
13. *tears*] *cares* Hudson.   17. *urns*] Hanmer; *ruines* Qq, F.

Scene 1

2. *mine . . . youth*] See on I. i. 5 :
the construction is not common in the
first and second persons.

9. *is*] See on II. i. 26.

10. *two and twenty*] See on I. i. 80.

12. *For . . . write*] A headless line:
but the F 2 supplement is plausible.

14. *staunch*] satisfy.

15. *shame*] be ashamed; cf. *AYL.*
IV. iii. 137 : "I do not shame |
To tell you what I was."

17. *urns*] water-jugs. An excellent
correction by Hanmer of a minim
error—*urnes* corrupted to *ruines.*

Than youthful April shall with all his show'rs:
In summer's drought I'll drop upon thee still;
In winter with warm tears I'll melt the snow,   20
And keep eternal spring-time on thy face,
So thou refuse to drink my dear sons' blood.

Enter LUCIUS, *with his weapon drawn.*

O reverent tribunes! O gentle aged men!
Unbind my sons, reverse the doom of death;
And let me say, that never wept before,   25
My tears are now prevailing orators.

Luc. O noble father, you lament in vain:
The tribunes hear you not, no man is by;
And you recount your sorrows to a stone.

Tit. Ah, Lucius, for thy brothers let me plead: 30
Grave tribunes, once more I entreat of you,—

Luc. My gracious Lord, no tribune hears you speak.

Tit. Why, 'tis no matter, man: if they did hear,
They would not mark me, or if they did mark,
They would not pity me, yet plead I must,   35
And bootless unto them.

22. *sons'*] Theobald (2nd ed.); *sonnes* Qq, F ; *Son's* F 4.   23. *gentle aged men*]
gentle-aged men W. S. Walker; *gentle-aged-men* Boswell.   28. *you*] om. F.
34. *or*] om. Q 1 ; *oh* F.   *did mark*] *did heare* F.   35. om. Q 3.   35-6.
yet . . . them] om. F.

19. *still*] all the time. Seldom used
by Shakespeare in the modern sense.
    22. *So*] on condition that. The
figure in this line is Biblical as Noble
points out, comparing *Hebrews* VI. 7
and *Genesis* IV. 11 : " the earth,
which hath opened her mouth to
receive thy brother's blood."
    23. *reverent*] See on II. iii. 296.
    36. *And . . . them*] Probably a
false start which Shakespeare omitted
to delete in his MS. Q 3 and F get
into curious tangles, of which the
only interest is that F restores part
of a line omitted altogether in Q 3,
and must therefore have consulted
some other source of information,
presumably the prompt-copy, which
would in all probability have elimina-
ted the unsatisfactory " And . . .
them." But why should " yet . . .
must " not have been in the prompt-
copy? And is it any more than
coincidence that F should here
introduce two new errors, " oh " for
" or " and " heare " (from the
previous line) for " marke "? It is
worth noting that " or " (though
almost certainly correct) does not
go back to Q 1, and " oh " may be
an alternative prompt-book reading,
independent of the later Quartos.
Bolton's suggestion of " a happy
guess on the part of the Folio editors "
(*P.M.L.A.* 44 (1929), 770 n. 14) does
not carry conviction, but the whole
passage raises problems which I
cannot solve. (See Add. Notes.)

Therefore I tell my sorrows to the stones,
Who, though they cannot answer my distress,
Yet in some sort they are better than the tribunes,
For that they will not intercept my tale.   40
When I do weep, they humbly at my feet
Receive my tears, and seem to weep with me;
And were they but attired in grave weeds,
Rome could afford no tribunes like to these.
A stone is soft as wax, tribunes more hard than
    stones;   45
A stone is silent, and offendeth not,
And tribunes with their tongues doom men to death.
But wherefore stand'st thou with thy weapon drawn?
Luc. To rescue my two brothers from their death;
For which attempt the judges have pronounc'd   50
My everlasting doom of banishment.
Tit. O happy man! they have befriended thee.
Why, foolish Lucius, dost thou not perceive
That Rome is but a wilderness of tigers?
Tigers must prey, and Rome affords no prey   55
But me and mine: how happy art thou then,
From these devourers to be banished!
But who comes with our brother Marcus here?

Enter MARCUS *with* LAVINIA.

Marc. Titus, prepare thy aged eyes to weep;
Or if not so, thy noble heart to break: 60
I bring consuming sorrow to thine age.
Tit. Will it consume me? let me see it then.
Marc. This was thy daughter.
Tit.   Why, Marcus, so she is.

37. *to*] *bootles to* Q 3, F.   44. *tribunes*] *Tribune* Q 2-3, F.   45. *soft as*]
as soft F.   58. with] and Q 3, F.   59. *aged*] *noble* Q 3, F.

40. *intercept*] interrupt; cf. *1H4*
I. iii. 150-1 : " his Irish expedition, |
From which he intercepted did
return."
54. *Rome . . . tigers*] Cf. *Tim.* IV.
i. 1-2 : " O thou wall | That girdles

in those wolves." Wilson justly
notes that " Shakespeare thought
of a wilderness or desert chiefly as a
place where neither law nor mercy
held sway," and quotes *Lucr.* 544 :
" a wilderness where are no laws."

Luc. Ay me, this object kills me!
Tit. Faint-hearted boy, arise, and look upon her.   65
　　Speak, Lavinia, what accursed hand
　　Hath made thee handless in thy father's sight?
　　What fool hath added water to the sea,
　　Or brought a faggot to bright-burning Troy?
　　My grief was at the height before thou cam'st,   70
　　And now like Nilus it disdaineth bounds.
　　Give me a sword, I'll chop off my hands too;
　　For they have fought for Rome, and all in vain;
　　And they have nurs'd this woe, in feeding life;
　　In bootless prayer have they been held up,   75
　　And they have serv'd me to effectless use.
　　Now all the service I require of them
　　Is that the one will help to cut the other.
　　'Tis well, Lavinia, that thou hast no hands,
　　For hands to do Rome service is but vain.   80
Luc. Speak, gentle sister, who hath mart'red thee?
Marc. O, that delightful engine of her thoughts,
　　That blabb'd them with such pleasing eloquence,
　　Is torn from forth that pretty hollow cage,
　　Where like a sweet melodious bird it sung   85
　　Sweet varied notes, enchanting every ear.
Luc. O, say thou for her, who hath done this deed?
Marc. O, thus I found her straying in the park,

---

69. *bright-burning*] F 3; *bright burning* Qq, F.   81. *mart'red*] *martred* Q 1-2;
marterd Q 3; *martyr'd* F(so 107).   86. *Sweet varied*] *Sweet-varied* W. S. Walker.

---

64. *Ay*] So spelt in the old editions
where the meaning is, as here, *alas.*
Contrast *ay* = yes, which is in-
variably spelt *I.*
　object] "spectacle. Lit. something presented to the sight"
(Wilson).
　66. *Speak . . . hand*] A headless
line.
　68. *What . . . sea*] See *O.D.E.P.*,
p. 695 and Tilley W106, where the
first quotation in approximately this
form is from Barclay's *Ship of Fools*
(1509).
　71. *disdaineth bounds*] Wilson quotes

from C. Spurgeon, *Shakespeare's
Imagery*, pp. 93-4, to the effect that
flood images are much commoner in
Shakespeare than in Peele, Greene,
Heywood or Kyd.
　76. *effectless*] fruitless. The whole
phrase is an oxymoron.
　80. *is*] See on II. i. 26. This
example is perhaps easier than
some, since the virtual subject is
"the doing of service to Rome by
hands."
　81. *mart'red*] disfigured.
　82. *engine*] instrument. The whole
phrase again in *Ven.* 367.

Seeking to hide herself, as doth the deer
That hath receiv'd some unrecuring wound.   90
Tit. It was my dear, and he that wounded her
Hath hurt me more than had he kill'd me dead:
For now I stand as one upon a rock
Environ'd with a wilderness of sea,
Who marks the waxing tide grow wave by wave,   95
Expecting ever when some envious surge
Will in his brinish bowels swallow him.
This way to death my wretched sons are gone;
Here stands my other son, a banish'd man,
And here my brother, weeping at my woes: 100
But that which gives my soul the greatest spurn
Is dear Lavinia, dearer than my soul.
Had I but seen thy picture in this plight
It would have madded me: what shall I do
Now I behold thy lively body so?   105
Thou hast no hands to wipe away thy tears,
Nor tongue to tell me who hath mart'red thee:
Thy husband he is dead, and for his death
Thy brothers are condemn'd, and dead by this.
Look, Marcus! ah, son Lucius, look on her!   110
When I did name her brothers, then fresh tears
Stood on her cheeks, as doth the honey-dew
Upon a gath'red lily almost withered.
Marc. Perchance she weeps because they kill'd her husband;
Perchance because she knows them innocent.   115
Tit. If they did kill thy husband, then be joyful,
Because the law hath ta'en revenge on them.
No, no, they would not do so foul a deed;

115. *them*] *him* Q 3, F.

89. *deer*] All the early editions spell *Deare* both here and in l. 91, thus emphasizing the pun. Tilley D189 quotes Surrey's *Faithful Lover* (*a.* 1547), l. 35 : " Then as the stricken deer withdraws him selfe alone."

90. *unrecuring*] incurable.

96. *Expecting . . . when*] waiting for the time when. Also Spenser, *F.Q.* III. xii. 1. 9 ; Jonson, *Cat.* III. 562 ; *N.E.D.* first in 1687, and as late as Godwin (1794). " Look . . . when " is recorded from 1568.

envious] malignant: " the most frequent Shakespearian sense " (On.).

101. *spurn*] contemptuous stroke or thrust (On.).

105. *lively*] living.

109. *by this*] by this time.

113. *Upon . . . withered*] An alexandrine.

Witness the sorrow that their sister makes.
Gentle Lavinia, let me kiss thy lips,   120
Or make some sign how I may do thee ease.
Shall thy good uncle, and thy brother Lucius,
And thou, and I, sit round about some fountain,
Looking all downwards to behold our cheeks
How they are stain'd, like meadows yet not dry,   125
With miry slime left on them by a flood?
And in the fountain shall we gaze so long
Till the fresh taste be taken from that clearness,
And made a brine-pit with our bitter tears?
Or shall we cut away our hands like thine?   130
Or shall we bite our tongues, and in dumb shows
Pass the remainder of our hateful days?
What shall we do? let us that have our tongues
Plot some device of further misery,
To make us wonder'd at in time to come.   135
Luc. Sweet father, cease your tears; for at your grief
See how my wretched sister sobs and weeps.
Marc. Patience, dear niece.   Good Titus, dry thine eyes.
Tit. Ah, Marcus, Marcus! brother, well I wot
Thy napkin cannot drink a tear of mine,   140
For thou, poor man, hast drown'd it with thine own.
Luc. Ah, my Lavinia, I will wipe thy cheeks.
Tit. Mark, Marcus, mark!   I understand her signs:
Had she a tongue to speak, now would she say
That to her brother which I said to thee: 145
His napkin, with his true tears all bewet,
Can do no service on her sorrowful cheeks.
O, what a sympathy of woe is this;
As far from help as limbo is from bliss.

121. *sign*] *signes* F.   125. *like*] Q 1 (Rowe) ; *in* Q 2-3, F.   134. *misery*]
miseries F.   146. *with his*] F 4 ; *with her* Qq, F.

121. *do thee ease*] help, or relieve, thee.
129. *And made*] i.e. and it (the
"clearness," or clear pool) made.
Cf. on v. iii. 101.
140. *napkin*] handkerchief.   The
form *napking*, which Q 1 prints at
l. 146, is probably Shakespeare's own.
Cf. Wyld, p. 290.

141. *drown'd*] saturated.
149. *As   far . . . bliss*]   Wilson
quotes *Err.* IV. ii. 32 :   " he's in
Tartar limbo,   worse   than hell,"
and notes that limbo, the abode of
the unbaptised, was further from
salvation than hell.   But the meaning
may be vaguer here.

H

Enter AARON *the Moor, alone.*

Aar. Titus Andronicus, my lord the emperor   150
    Sends thee this word: that, if thou love thy sons,
    Let Marcus, Lucius, or thyself, old Titus,
    Or any one of you, chop off your hand
    And send it to the king: he for the same
    Will send thee hither both thy sons alive,   155
    And that shall be the ransom for their fault.

Tit. O gracious emperor! O gentle Aaron!
    Did ever raven sing so like a lark
    That gives sweet tidings of the sun's uprise?
    With all my heart I'll send the emperor my hand. 160
    Good Aaron, wilt thou help to chop it off?

Luc. Stay, father, for that noble hand of thine,
    That hath thrown down so many enemies,
    Shall not be sent; my hand will serve the turn,
    My youth can better spare my blood than you,   165
    And therefore mine shall save my brothers' lives.

Marc. Which of your hands hath not defended Rome,
    And rear'd aloft the bloody battle-axe,
    Writing destruction on the enemy's castle?
    O, none of both but are of high desert: 170
    My hand hath been but idle; let it serve
    To ransom my two nephews from their death;
    Then have I kept it to a worthy end.

Aar. Nay, come, agree whose hand shall go along,
    For fear they die before their pardon come.   175

Marc. My hand shall go.

Luc.   By heaven, it shall not go!

150. Aar.] Moore. Qq, F (so 174). Theobald; *enemies* Qq, F.

151-2. *that . . . Let*] The same irregularity in *H5* IV. iii. 34-6 : " proclaim it . . . | That he which hath no stomach to this fight, | Let him depart." In the light of the present passage, the alternative explanation of the other becomes doubly improbable : that *that he* means " that man." Cf. Abbott § 415. Cf. also *Tim.* v. i. 206-8 : " Tell Athens . . . that whoso please | To stop affliction, let him take his haste."

169. *enemy's*] Capell conj. ; *enemies'*

160. *With . . . hand*] Many editors since Steevens have printed *my hand* as a separate line. But alexandrines are common in this play.

169. *castle*] There is no reason to think that this is corrupt, or that it has any but the normal meaning. Robertson aptly quotes Greene, *Orlando Furioso* I. ii. 370-1 : " on this Castle wall | Ile write my resolution with my blood."

Tit. Sirs, strive no more: such with'red herbs as these
Are meet for plucking up, and therefore mine.
Luc. Sweet father, if I shall be thought thy son,
Let me redeem my brothers both from death.   180
Marc. And for our father's sake, and mother's care,
Now let me show a brother's love to thee.
Tit. Agree between you; I will spare my hand.
Luc. Then I'll go fetch an axe.
Marc. But I will use the axe.   [*Exeunt.*   185
Tit. Come hither, Aaron; I'll deceive them both:
Lend me thy hand, and I will give thee mine.
Aar. [*Aside.*] If that be call'd deceit, I will be honest,
And never whilst I live deceive men so:
But I'll deceive you in another sort,   190
And that you'll say ere half an hour pass.
                                    [*He cuts off Titus' hand.*

Enter LUCIUS *and* MARCUS *again.*

Tit. Now stay your strife; what shall be is dispatch'd.
Good Aaron, give his majesty my hand:
Tell him it was a hand that warded him
From thousand dangers; bid him bury it;   195
More hath it merited; that let it have.
As for my sons, say I account of them
As jewels purchas'd at an easy price;
And yet dear too, because I bought mine own.
Aar. I go, Andronicus; and for thy hand   200
Look by and by to have thy sons with thee.
[*Aside.*] Their heads, I mean.   O, how this villainy
Doth fat me with the very thoughts of it!
Let fools do good, and fair men call for grace,
Aaron will have his soul black like his face.   205
                                    [*Exit.*

177. *with'red*] *withred* Qq; *withered* F.   188. [Aside.]] Rowe; om. Qq, F.
202. [Aside.]] Rowe; om. Qq, F.

179. *shall*] am to, cf. Abbott   203. *fat*] nourish, i.e. delight.
§ 315.   Comparable is *Mer. V.* i. iii. 48: " I
   191. *hour*] See on i. i. 127.   will feed fat the ancient grudge I
   201. *Look*] expect.   bear him."

Tit. O, here I lift this one hand up to heaven,
    And bow this feeble ruin to the earth:
    If any power pities wretched tears,
    To that I call. What, would'st thou kneel with me?
    Do then, dear heart; for heaven shall hear our
        prayers,   210
    Or with our sighs we'll breathe the welkin dim,
    And stain the sun with fog, as sometime clouds
    When they do hug him in their melting bosoms.
Marc. O brother, speak with possibility,
    And do not break into these deep extremes.   215
Tit. Is not my sorrows deep, having no bottom?
    Then be my passions bottomless with them.
Marc. But yet let reason govern thy lament.
Tit. If there were reason for these miseries,
    Then into limits could I bind my woes: 220
    When heaven doth weep, doth not the earth
        o'erflow?
    If the winds rage, doth not the sea wax mad,
    Threat'ning the welkin with his big-swol'n face?
    And wilt thou have a reason for this coil?
    I am the sea. Hark how her sighs doth blow;   225
    She is the weeping welkin, I the earth:
    Then must my sea be moved with her sighs;
    Then must my earth with her continual tears
    Become a deluge, overflow'd and drown'd;

---

209. *would'st*] *would* Q 2-3; *wilt* F.   214. *possibility*] *possibilities* Q 3, F.
216. *Is . . . sorrows*] Dyce (2nd ed.) conj.; *Is . . . sorrow* Qq, F;
Are . . . sorrows Heath.   225. *doth*] *doe* Q 2-3, F.   *blow*] F 2; *flow* Qq, F.
229. *overflow'd*] *ouerflowed* Qq. *drown'd*] *drowned* Q 2-3.

207. *ruin*] mutilated body. Wilson compares *Cymb.* IV. ii. 354, where *ruin* is used of Cloten's headless body.
    211. *breathe . . . dim*] Verity compares Marlowe's *Faustus* (ed. Boas), I. iii. 4 : " dims the welkin with her pitchy breath."
    212. *sometime*] Interchangeable in Shakespeare's English with *sometimes*.
    216. *Is . . . sorrows*] See on II. i. 26. A singular verb in a question before a plural subject is particularly common. This seems to me the easiest correction of the Qq, F reading if it is admitted, as I think it must be, that *them* in l. 217 makes *sorrows* necessary here.
    217. *passions*] passionate outbursts.
    220. *bind*] confine.
    221. *o'erflow*] become flooded.
    224. *coil*] ado; cf. *John* II. i. 165 : " I am not worth this coil that's made for me."
    225. *doth*] See on II. iv. 17.

For why my bowels cannot hide her woes,   230
But like a drunkard must I vomit them.
Then give me leave, for losers will have leave
To ease their stomachs with their bitter tongues.

Enter a Messenger with two heads and a hand.

Mess. Worthy Andronicus, ill art thou repaid
For that good hand thou sent'st the emperor.   235
Here are the heads of thy two noble sons,
And here's thy hand, in scorn to thee sent back:
Thy grief their sports, thy resolution mock'd;
That woe is me to think upon thy woes,
More than remembrance of my father's death.   240

             [Exit.

Marc. Now let hot Etna cool in Sicily,
And be my heart an ever-burning hell!
These miseries are more than may be borne.
To weep with them that weep doth ease some
  deal,
But sorrow flouted at is double death.   245
Luc. Ah, that this sight should make so deep a wound,
And yet detested life not shrink thereat;
That ever death should let life bear his name,
Where life hath no more interest but to breathe!

         [Lavinia kisses Titus.

---

230. *her*] *their* Theobald conj. 238. *grief*] *griefe*, Q 1-2; *griefes* Q 3;
griefes, F; *grief's* (and *sport* for *sports*) Pope. 240. Exit.] om. Q 1.
249. Lavinia . . . Titus.] Johnson; om. Qq, F.

230. *For why*] because.

232-3. *losers . . . tongues*] See
O.D.E.P. p. 386, and Tilley L 458,
where the first quotation is from
More (1533).

238. *grief*] I do not think this need
be changed to *griefs*. Titus's grief
is the sport of each one of them.
If a change were to be made I should
rather read *sport*.

239. *That*] so that, cf. *Mac.* II. ii. 6-7:
" I have drugg'd their possets, |

That death and nature do contend
about them."

woe is me] In such expressions,
me is originally a dative, cf. *methinks.*

244. *To . . . that weep*] Cf. *Romans*
XII. 15 : " weep with them that
weep."

245. *flouted at*] mocked.

247. *shrink*] slip away (*N.E.D.* 6),
rather than " wither away " (Wilson).

248. *bear his name*] i.e. still be
called " life."

Marc. Alas, poor heart, that kiss is comfortless   250
    As frozen water to a starved snake.
Tit. When will this fearful slumber have an end?
Marc. Now farewell, flatt'ry: die, Andronicus;
    Thou dost not slumber: see thy two sons' heads,
    Thy warlike hand, thy mangled daughter here;   255
    Thy other banish'd son, with this dear sight
    Struck pale and bloodless; and thy brother, I,
    Even like a stony image, cold and numb.
    Ah, now no more will I control thy griefs.
    Rent off thy silver hair, thy other hand   260
    Gnawing with thy teeth; and be this dismal sight
    The closing up of our most wretched eyes.
    Now is a time to storm; why art thou still?
Tit. Ha, ha, ha!
Marc. Why dost thou laugh? it fits not with this hour.   265
Tit. Why, I have not another tear to shed:
    Besides, this sorrow is an enemy,
    And would usurp upon my wat'ry eyes,
    And make them blind with tributary tears:
    Then which way shall I find Revenge's cave?   270
    For these two heads do seem to speak to me,
    And threat me I shall never come to bliss
    Till all these mischiefs be return'd again

253. *flatt'ry*] Kittredge; *flattrie* Q 1 ; *flattery (-ie)* Q 2-3, F.   255. *hand*]
hands F.   256. *son*] *sonnes* F.   259. *thy*] Q 1 (Theobald) ; *my* Q 2-3, F.

250 ff. *Alas . . .*] " The behaviour of all these personages upon this dreadful occasion is singularly proper, and the horrid ' laugh ' [l. 264] of the father has something great in it even for Shakespeare " (Capell).

251. *starved*] numbed, cf. *Cym.* I. iv. 187 : " catch cold and starve." The phrase " starved snake " is semi-proverbial : Parrott quotes *2H6* III. i. 343, to which add Jonson, *Poetaster* III. iv. 329.

256. *dear*] grievous. See On. on the distinction between this and the more common word *dear* (= beloved).

259. *control*] check : a slightly different sense from that of I. i. 420.

260. *Rent*] A common alternative form of *rend*.

263. *Now . . . still?*] With Titus's momentary silence at the supreme moment of grief, E. Wolff, *Die Antike* 20 (1944), 143-4, compares Hecuba's behaviour as described in Ovid, *Met.* XIII. esp. l. 538 : " Troades exclamant, obmutuit illa dolore." The resemblance is not very close, though both characters go on to plan revenge. The Hecuba story has already been referred to at I. i. 136-8 (see note).

264. *Ha, ha, ha!*] Wilson compares Hieronymo's laughter in *Spanish Tragedy* (ed. Boas) III. xi. 30.

Even in their throats that hath committed them.
Come, let me see what task I have to do.   275
You heavy people, circle me about,
That I may turn me to each one of you,
And swear unto my soul to right your wrongs.
The vow is made. Come, brother, take a head;
And in this hand the other will I bear.   280
†And, Lavinia, thou shalt be employ'd in these arms:†
Bear thou my hand, sweet wench, between thy teeth.
As for thee, boy, go get thee from my sight;
Thou art an exile, and thou must not stay:
Hie to the Goths, and raise an army there;   285
And if ye love me, as I think you do,
Let's kiss and part, for we have much to do.

                                    [*Exeunt.*

Luc. Farewell, Andronicus, my noble father;
The woefull'st man that ever liv'd in Rome.
Farewell, proud Rome, till Lucius come again;   290
He loves his pledges dearer than his life.

274. *hath*] *haue* Q 2-3, F.   281. *And*] om. F 2.   *arms*] *things* F.   *in these arms*] *in this* Lettsom conj.   286. *ye*] *you* Q 2-3, F.   287. Exeunt.] Exeunt. Manet Lucius F.   290. *Rome,* . . . *again;*] *Rome* . . . *againe,* Qq ; *Rome,* . . . *againe.* F; *Rome!* . . . *again,* Rowe.   291. *loves*] *leaves* Rowe; *loans* Ridley conj.

274. *hath*] See on II. iv. 17.

276. *heavy*] sorrowful.

281. *And* . . . *arms*] I leave this line as hopelessly corrupt. Lettsom's conjecture gives good sense, and could be used to modify a hypothesis of Camb. The latter suggests that *armes* was added above *teeth* as a substitute and was mistaken for the end of l. 281, and then assumes that *in these* was added by the printer to incorporate *armes* into the line, which it reconstructs in its original form as : *And thou, Lavinia, shalt be employ'd.* But equally easily *this* could have been corrupted to *these* with the same effect, as Lettsom's conjecture presupposes. The *And* at the beginning

of the line is metrically awkward, and may have been repeated from the previous line (Malone).

291. *loves*] I now (1961) accept the original text; l. 291 gives Lucius's ground for asserting that he is sure to return (Baildon): so Sisson, *New Readings in Shakespeare* (1956), II. 140, " I will carry out my vow and return even at the risk of my life." Rowe's correction, though graphically easy—*leues*: *loues* (cf. J. Dover Wilson, *The Manuscript of Shakespeare's Hamlet*, pp. 109-10)—is thus unnecessary; Ridley's is unduly commercial: *pledges* here corresponds to Latin *pignora* for " dear ones." Even with Rowe's emendation, his change of punctuation would be unnecessary.

Farewell, Lavinia, my noble sister;
O, would thou wert as thou tofore hast been!
But now nor Lucius nor Lavinia lives
But in oblivion and hateful griefs.   295
If Lucius live, he will requite your wrongs,
And make proud Saturnine and his empress
Beg at the gates like Tarquin and his queen.
Now will I to the Goths, and raise a pow'r,
To be reveng'd on Rome and Saturnine.   300
                                        [*Exit Lucius.*

SCENE II.—*A Banket.*

Enter ANDRONICUS, MARCUS, LAVINIA, *and the Boy.*

Tit. So, so; now sit; and look you eat no more
Than will preserve just so much strength in us
As will revenge these bitter woes of ours.
Marcus, unknit that sorrow-wreathen knot:
Thy niece and I, poor creatures, want our hands,   5
And cannot passionate our ten-fold grief
With folded arms. This poor right hand of mine

297. *empress*] *Emperesse* Q 1.   298. *like*] *likes* F.   299. *pow'r*] Kittredge;
powre Q 1 ; *power* Q 2-3, F.

Scene II

Scene II] Capell ; om. F (which first prints the scene).   Banket] Bnaket
F ; Banquet F 2.

293. *tofore*] formerly. Two words
in Qq, F.
297. *and his empress*] See on I. i. 89.
And his should be pronounced *and 's.*

Scene II

Scene II] Only in F; on whether it
belonged to the original text, see
Additional Notes.
Banket] A common sixteenth-
century form, also in Q 1, v. ii. 76,
194 and (Qq, F) 203.
Andronicus] So for *Titus* at S.D.
II. iii. 258. In this scene, and only
in it, the speech-prefix is *An.*

6. *passionate*] express with appropriate feeling : Steevens quotes
Spenser, *F.Q.* I. xii. 16. 1-2 : " Great
pleasure mixt with pittifull regard, |
That godly King and Queene did
passionate." B. L. Joseph, *Elizabethan Acting* (London, 1951), p. 73,
comments on this passage as an
example of the notion that folded
arms symbolize inexpressiveness :
" whilst they feel more than a dull
grief, their mutilations do not allow
the expression of what is really
within."

Is left to tyrannize upon my breast;
Who when my heart, all mad with misery,
Beats in this hollow prison of my flesh,　　　　10
Then thus I thump it down.
Thou map of woe, that thus dost talk in signs,
When thy poor heart beats with outrageous beating
Thou canst not strike it thus to make it still.
Wound it with sighing, girl, kill it with groans;　　15
Or get some little knife between thy teeth,
And just against thy heart make thou a hole,
That all the tears that thy poor eyes let fall
May run into that sink, and soaking in,
Drown the lamenting fool in sea-salt tears.　　　20
Marc. Fie, brother, fie! teach her not thus to lay
Such violent hands upon her tender life.
Tit. How now! has sorrow made thee dote already?
Why, Marcus, no man should be mad but I.
What violent hands can she lay on her life?　　　25
Ah, wherefore dost thou urge the name of hands,
To bid Æneas tell the tale twice o'er,
How Troy was burnt and he made miserable?
O, handle not the theme, to talk of hands,
Lest we remember still that we have none.　　　30
Fie, fie, how franticly I square my talk,

---

9. *Who*] *And* Rowe.　　　14. *still.*] *still?* F.

---

9. *Who*] Probably used for *which*
(Abbott § 264, Franz § 335), with
hand as antecedent. Then *I* is
substituted as subject in l. 11. Rowe's
emendation cuts the knot but does
not explain the F reading.

12. *map*] image, embodiment.

20. *fool*] This word often has an
affectionate implication, most notably
in *Lr.* v. iii. 307 : " my poor fool is
hang'd."

27-8. *To . . . miserable*] A reminiscence (Lee) of Virgil, *Aen.* ii. 2 :
" infandum, regina, iubes renovare
dolorem." This is such a commonplace that Wilson's parallel from
Troublesome Reign of King John, Part I,

x. 27-8 : " Must I discourse? let
Dido sigh and say | She weepes
againe to hear the wrack of Troy?"
is of no significance.

29-33. *handle . . . hands*] Here, as
in iv. i. 70 (see note), Shakespeare
may owe something to the story of
Io in Ovid, *Met.* i, where ll. 635-6
run " Illa etiam supplex Argo cum
bracchia vellet | Tendere, non habuit
quae bracchia tenderet Argo," which
Golding translates : " when she did
devise, | To *Argus* for to lift her hands
in meeke and humble wise, | She
saw she had no hands at all."

30. *still*] See on iii. i. 19.

31. *square*] regulate.

As if we should forget we had no hands,
If Marcus did not name the word of hands!
Come, let's fall to; and, gentle girl, eat this:
Here is no drink?   Hark, Marcus, what she says;   35
I can interpret all her martyr'd signs:
She says she drinks no other drink but tears,
Brew'd with her sorrow, mesh'd upon her cheeks.
Speechless complainer, I will learn thy thought;
In thy dumb action will I be as perfect   40
As begging hermits in their holy prayers:
Thou shalt not sigh, nor hold thy stumps to heaven,
Nor wink, nor nod, nor kneel, nor make a sign,
But I of these will wrest an alphabet,
And by still practice learn to know thy meaning.   45
Boy. Good grandsire, leave these bitter deep laments:
Make my aunt merry with some pleasing tale.
Marc. Alas, the tender boy, in passion mov'd,
Doth weep to see his grandsire's heaviness.
Tit. Peace, tender sapling; thou art made of tears,   50
And tears will quickly melt thy life away.
            [*Marcus strikes the dish with a knife.*
What dost thou strike at, Marcus, with thy knife?
Marc. At that that I have kill'd, my lord ; a fly.
Tit. Out on thee, murderer! thou kill'st my heart;
Mine eyes are cloy'd with view of tyranny: 55

38. *Brew'd*] *Breu'd* F.   39. *complainer, I*] Capell; *complainet, I* F; *complaint, O I* F 2.   52. *thy*] om. F.   54. *thee*] F 3; *the* F.   55. *are*] om. F.

36. *martyr'd signs*] " the signs the poor martyr makes " (Wilson). I doubt whether Wilson is right in seeing " an allusion to signs made by those burnt at the stake."

37. *drinks . . . tears*] Biblical, cf. Psalm LXXX. 5 : " and givest them plenteousness of tears to drink " (Prayer Book version).

38. *mesh'd*] Lit. " mixed with water to form wort" (On.); here a rhetorical variation of *brew'd*; cf. *mash* (tea).

40. *perfect*] as in " word-perfect." The epithet can be applied either (as here) to the person who knows a lesson perfectly, or to the lesson (" the lesson . . . once made perfect," *Ven.* 407-8), or to the knowledge (" a perfect thought," *John* v. vi. 6).

45. *still*] constant; cf. *Lucr.* 702 : " comprehend in still imagination."

48. *passion*] See on I. i. 106.

54. *thee, murderer*] The F 1 reading as an exclamation not directly addressed to Marcus, is perhaps defensible, but seems awkward after l. 52 and before the second half of this line. *The* for *thee* was a common sixteenth-century spelling, and sometimes leads to confusion.

A deed of death done on the innocent
Becomes not Titus' brother.　Get thee gone;
I see thou art not for my company.

Marc. Alas, my lord, I have but kill'd a fly.

Tit. " But "?　How if that fly had a father and mother?　60
How would he hang his slender gilded wings,
And buzz lamenting doings in the air!
Poor harmless fly,
That, with his pretty buzzing melody,
Came here to make us merry, and thou hast kill'd
　　him.　　　　　　　　　　　　　　　　　　　　65

Marc. Pardon me, sir;　it was a black ill-favour'd fly
Like to the empress' Moor;　therefore I kill'd him.

Tit. O, O, O!
Then pardon me for reprehending thee,
For thou hast done a charitable deed.　　　　　70
Give me thy knife, I will insult on him;
Flattering myself as if it were the Moor
Come hither purposely to poison me.
There's for thyself, and that's for Tamora.
Ah, sirrah!　　　　　　　　　　　　　　　　75
Yet, I think, we are not brought so low,
But that between us we can kill a fly
That comes in likeness of a coal-black Moor.

Marc. Alas, poor man! grief has so wrought on him,
He takes false shadows for true substances.　　80

60. " *But* "?] *But*? F.　*How if*] F 3;　*How: if* F.　　62. *doings*] *dolings*
Theobald.　　74. *Tamora*] Tamira F.　　75. as separate line Capell;　with
74 F;　with 76 Steevens (1778).

62. *lamenting doings*] An odd phrase, that seems to mean little more than " lamentations."

71. *insult on*] triumph over; cf. *R3* II. iv. 51 : " Insulting tyranny."

72. *as if*] with the thought that (perhaps following the similar use of *tamquam, quasi* in Silver Latin: see J. D. Duff on Juvenal III. 222). This usage is not uncommon in Shakespeare's time; Raleigh, *History of the World* (Selections ed. by G. E. Hadow, p. 139) ; " The *Illyrian* Queen was secure of the *Romans*, as if they would not dare to stirre against her " ; Sidney, *Arcadia* I. xiii. 1 (ed. Feuillerat, p. 85) : " thus did I flatter my selfe, as though my wound had bene no deeper " ; *ibid.* II. xx. 4 (p. 280) : " she founde meanes to have us accused to the King, as though we went about some practise to overthrowe him " ; Bunyan, *Holy War,* Advertisement to the Reader : " Insinuating as if I would shine." Cf. IV. iv. 53 n.; Milton, *Comus* 763.

Tit. Come, take away. Lavinia, go with me:
I'll to thy closet, and go read with thee
Sad stories chanced in the times of old.
Come, boy, and go with me: thy sight is young,
And thou shalt read when mine begin to dazzle.   85

[*Exeunt.*

85 *begin*] *begins* Rowe (3rd ed.).

81. *take away*] clear the table.
82-3. *read . . . old*] Cf. *R2* III. ii.
155-6 : " For God's sake, let us sit
upon the ground | And tell sad stories
of the death of kings." Parrott,
p. 32, notes that the parallel is more

than verbal : in both passages the
" sad stories " are a consolation for
present sorrow.

85. *begin*] If this is right, the
virtual subject is " eyes," understood
from *sight* (Dyce).

ACT IV

SCENE I.

Enter Lucius' son, and LAVINIA *running after him, and the boy flies from her with his books under his arm.* Enter TITUS *and* MARCUS.

Boy. Help, grandsire, help! my aunt Lavinia
Follows me everywhere, I know not why.
Good uncle Marcus, see how swift she comes:
Alas, sweet aunt, I know not what you mean.
Marc. Stand by me, Lucius; do not fear thine aunt.　　5
Tit. She loves thee, boy, too well to do thee harm.
Boy. Ay, when my father was in Rome she did.
Marc. What means my niece Lavinia by these signs?
Tit. Fear her not, Lucius: somewhat doth she mean.
Marc. See, Lucius, see how much she makes of thee;　　10
Somewhither would she have thee go with her.
Ah, boy, Cornelia never with more care
Read to her sons than she hath read to thee
Sweet poetry and Tully's *Orator.*
Canst thou not guess wherefore she plies thee thus?　　15
Boy. My lord, I know not, I, nor can I guess,
Unless some fit or frenzy do possess her;
For I have heard my grandsire say full oft,

ACT IV

Scene 1

ACT IV. *Scene* I.] Rowe; Actus Quartus. F; om. Qq.　　Lucius' son]
young Lucius F.　　1. Boy] Puer Qq (so throughout).　　5. *thine*] thy F.
9. *her*] om. F.　　10. Marc. *See*] W. S. Walker; *See* Qq, F.　　11. *Some-*
whither] *Some whither* Q 1; *Some whether* Q 2-3, F.　　12. *Ah,*] *A* Q 1-2.
15. *Canst*] Marc. *Canst* Capell.

Scene 1

10. Marc.] L. 18 shows that the boy's reply is addressed to Marcus, not to Titus. In view of the occurrence of *Lucius* both in l. 9 and in l. 10, it seems more likely that the change of speaker takes place here than at l. 15.

12. *Cornelia*] the mother of the Gracchi (second century B.C.).

Wilson's objection that " Cicero's *De Oratore* was not written until fifty years after their death " rests on a misinterpretation of l. 13, where *Read to* means " gave lessons to " (*N.E.D.* 12) and does not govern " Sweet . . . Orator."

14. *Tully's Orator*] Either Ciceros' *De Oratore* or, more probably, his *ad M. Brutum Orator.*

Extremity of griefs would make men mad;
And I have read that Hecuba of Troy   20
Ran mad for sorrow; that made me to fear,
Although, my lord, I know my noble aunt
Loves me as dear as e'er my mother did,
And would not, but in fury, fright my youth;
Which made me down to throw my books and fly, 25
Causeless perhaps, but pardon me, sweet aunt;
And, madam, if my uncle Marcus go,
I will most willingly attend your ladyship.

Marc. Lucius, I will.

Tit. How now, Lavinia! Marcus, what means this?   30
Some book there is that she desires to see.
Which is it, girl, of these? Open them, boy.
But thou art deeper read, and better skill'd;
Come, and take choice of all my library,
And so beguile thy sorrow, till the heavens   35
Reveal the damn'd contriver of this deed.
Why lifts she up her arms in sequence thus?

Marc. I think she means that there were more than one
Confederate in the fact: ay, more there was;
Or else to heaven she heaves them for revenge.   40

Tit. Lucius, what book is that she tosseth so?

Boy. Grandsire, 'tis Ovid's Metamorphosis;
My mother gave it me.

Marc.   For love of her that's gone,
Perhaps, she cull'd it from among the rest.

---

21. *for*] *through* Q 3, F.   36. F adds in separate line *What booke?*   38.
were] *was* Q 3, F.   40. *for*] *to* F.

20. *have   read*] Probably, as
J. A. K. Thomson, *Shakespeare and the
Classics* (1952), p. 54, suggests, in
Ovid, *Met.* XIII. 538 ff.

24. *but in fury*] except in a fit of
madness.

26. *causeless*] " without reasonable
cause " (Wilson).

33. *deeper*] i.e. than to read boys'
schoolbooks (Delius; Wilson).

36. app. crit. What booke?] The
insertion of this in F seems to be a
compositor's vagary. Professor Dover
Wilson tells me that he withdraws
the suggestion that it is a relic of
a partially deleted passage in the
MS.

39. *fact*] crime, as always in
Shakespeare.

41. *tosseth*] turns over the leaves of.

42. *Metamorphosis*] I retain this
spelling, which is, as Wilson notes,
that of Golding's translation.

Tit. Soft, so busily she turns the leaves!   45
Help her: what would she find? Lavinia, shall
I read?
This is the tragic tale of Philomel,
And treats of Tereus' treason and his rape;
And rape, I fear, was root of thy annoy.
Marc. See, brother, see! note how she quotes the leaves.   50
Tit. Lavinia, wert thou thus surpris'd, sweet girl,
Ravish'd and wrong'd, as Philomela was,
Forc'd in the ruthless, vast, and gloomy woods?
See, see!
Ay, such a place there is, where we did hunt,—   55
O, had we never, never hunted there,—
Pattern'd by that the poet here describes,
By nature made for murthers and for rapes.
Marc. O, why should nature build so foul a den,
Unless the gods delight in tragedies?   60
Tit. Give signs, sweet girl, for here are none but friends,
What Roman lord it was durst do the deed:
Or slunk not Saturnine, as Tarquin erst,
That left the camp to sin in Lucrece' bed?
Marc. Sit down, sweet niece: brother, sit down by me.   65
Apollo, Pallas, Jove, or Mercury,
Inspire me, that I may this treason find!

45. *so*] *see how* Rowe.   46. so Qq, F; two lines divided after *her* Capell.
Help her] S.D. Dyce conj.   49. *thy*] *thine* Q 2-3, F.   50. *quotes*] *coats* Q 1.
54-5. so Pope; one line in Qq, F.   63. *slunk*] *slonke* Q 1.

46. *Help her*] Very likely (Dyce) a
S.D.
47. *Philomel*] See on II. iv. 26.
50. *quotes*] marks, observes.
53. *vast*] desolate.
57. *pattern'd by*] on the pattern of;
cf. *Meas.* II. i. 30 : " Let mine own
judgment pattern out my death."
here] In *Met.* VI. 520-1 : " rex
Pandione natam | In stabula alta
trahit, silvis obscura vetustis." Golding translates : " king *Terew* tooke
the ladie by the hand, | And led hir
to a pelting grange that peakishly
did stand | In woods forgrowne."

62. *What Roman lord*] Wilson (on
l. 36) finds this inconsistent with ll.
38-40, which he therefore thinks
" perhaps a second-thought insertion." But (i) there might have been
" more than one | Confederate
in the fact " and yet only one actual
ravisher, (ii) in any case l. 40 offers
an alternative interpretation of
Lavinia's gestures.
63. *slunk*] Q 1's spelling *slonke* is
only graphic, to avoid a confusing
run of minims, as in *son*. Cf. v. i. 9,
where Q 1 has *sprong*, and v. iii. 163
(*Song*).

My lord, look here; look here, Lavinia:
This sandy plot is plain; guide, if thou canst,
This after me.

> [*He writes his name with his staff, and guides
> it with feet and mouth.*

I have writ my name   70
Without the help of any hand at all.
Curs'd be that heart that forc'd us to this shift!
Write thou, good niece, and here display at last
What God will have discovered for revenge.
Heaven guide thy pen to print thy sorrows plain,   75
That we may know the traitors and the truth!

> [*She takes the staff in her mouth, and guides
> it with her stumps, and writes.*

O, do ye read, my lord, what she hath writ?
Tit. Stuprum.   Chiron.   Demetrius.
Marc. What, what! the lustful sons of Tamora
Performers of this heinous, bloody deed?   80
Tit. Magni dominator poli,
  Tam lentus audis scelera? tam lentus vides?

70. [He . . . mouth.]] here Collier; after 68 Qq, F.   *me. I*] *me, I* Qq, F ;
me. See, I Keightley.   72. *this*] *that* F.   77. *O*] Titus.   *Oh* Q 3, F ;
Boy. *Oh* Capell conj.   78. Tit.] Maxwell; om. Qq, F.   81. Magni]
Magne Theobald.

70. *after me*] as I have done. Ovid
may have afforded a hint for the
writing of the name (which, however, is in the chap-book version).
When Io has been transformed into a
cow, she first tries to tell her father
who she is, but cannot any longer
speak; then "Littera pro verbis,
quam pes in pulvere duxit, | Corporis
indicium mutati triste peregit" (*Met.*
1. 649-50); Golding translates: "But
for because she could not speake
she printed in the sand | Two letters
with hir foot, whereby was given to
vnderstand | The sorrowfull changing
of hir shape." See also J. G.
McManaway, *R.E.S.* n.s. 9 (1958),
172-3.
    72. *forc'd . . . shift*] See on IV. ii. 177.
    78. Tit.] I think this is the best

solution of the problem of attribution
at this point. Q 1-2 continue ll. 77-8
to Marcus, but give a fresh prefix for
Marcus at l. 79. Q 3 transfers ll.
77-8 to Titus, but he never addresses
Marcus as " Lord " whereas Marcus
so addresses him several times (I. i.
355, 391, III. ii. 53, IV. i. 83, iii. 69).
It was to Capell's credit that, without
knowledge of Q 1-2, he proposed to
transfer both lines to the Boy, but
I think it is more dramatic to let
Titus himself read the fatal message.
" Stuprum " = rape.
    81-2. Magni . . . vides?] "Ruler
of the great heavens, art thou so slow
to hear and to see crimes?" From
Seneca, *Phaedra* 671-2, where the
first half-line reads *Magne regnator
deum.* At l. 1159, the beginning of

Marc. O, calm thee, gentle lord, although I know
There is enough written upon this earth
To stir a mutiny in the mildest thoughts   85
And arm the minds of infants to exclaims.
My lord, kneel down with me; Lavinia, kneel;
And kneel, sweet boy, the Roman Hector's hope;
And swear with me, as with the woeful fere
And father of that chaste dishonoured dame,   90
Lord Junius Brutus sware for Lucrece' rape,
That we will prosecute by good advice
Mortal revenge upon these traitorous Goths,
And see their blood, or die with this reproach.

Tit. 'Tis sure enough, and you knew how;   95
But if you hunt these bear-whelps, then beware:
The dam will wake, and if she wind ye once:
She's with the lion deeply still in league,
And lulls him whilst she playeth on her back,
And when he sleeps will she do what she list.   100
You are a young huntsman, Marcus, let alone;
And come, I will go get a leaf of brass,
And with a gad of steel will write these words,

88. *hope*] *hop* (or *l op*, slipping out of line) Q 1.   91. *sware*] F 3; *sweare*
Qq, F.   97. *wake,* . . . *once:*] Staunton; *wake* . . . *once*, Q 1; *wake,* . . .
once, Q 2-3, F; *wake;* . . . *once*, Theobald. *ye*] *you* Q 2-3, F.   101. *let*]
let it Q 3, F.

the speech echoed above at II. i. 135,
we have *saeve dominator freti.* J. A. K.
Thomson, *Shakespeare and the Classics*
(1952), p. 52, points out that Seneca,
Epistle 107, in a translation from
Cleanthes, has " parens celsique
dominator poli," and that the con-
flation suggests a good knowledge of
Seneca. I allow this parallel to
decide in favour of retaining
" Magni " instead of Theobald's
" Magne," though it is metrically
objectionable (see on II. i. 235).
    86. *exclaims*] outcries, protests; so
R2 I. ii. 2.
    89. *fere*] husband.
    92. *by good advice*] " by well-
considered means " (Hudson).
    96. *bear-whelps*] Noble notes that

" the ferocity of the she-bear bereft
of her whelps is a frequent figure in
the Old Testament. See *Hos.* XIII. 8,
2 Sam. XVII. 8, *Prov.* XVII. 12."
    97. *and if*] if. This seems better
than to take *and* as connective,
punctuate heavily after *wake* and
lightly after *once,* and make the *if*-
clause dependent on l. 99.
    wind] get wind of.
    98. *still*] See on III. i. 19.
    101. *let alone*] = let it alone. Cf.
Wint. II. ii. 53: " le't not be doubted "
and Furness's note on *Wint.* II. i. 18.
    102. *leaf of brass*] Recurs in *The
Welsh Embassador* (Malone Society
Reprint), l. 976, which quotes V.
ii. 9 (see note).
    103. *gad*] " sharp spike; applied
to a stylus " (On.).

I

And lay it by: the angry northen wind
Will blow these sands like Sibyl's leaves abroad,   105
And where's our lesson then?   Boy, what say you?

Boy. I say, my lord, that if I were a man
Their mother's bedchamber should not be safe
For these base bondmen to the yoke of Rome.

Marc. Ay, that's my boy! thy father hath full oft   110
For his ungrateful country done the like.

Boy. And, uncle, so will I and if I live.

Tit. Come, go with me into mine armoury:
Lucius, I'll fit thee; and withal, my boy,
Shalt carry from me to the empress' sons   115
Presents that I intend to send them both:
Come, come; thou'lt do my message, wilt thou not?

Boy. Ay, with my dagger in their bosoms, grandsire.

Tit. No, boy, not so: I'll teach thee another course.
Lavinia, come.   Marcus, look to my house;   120
Lucius and I'll go brave it at the court:
Ay, marry, will we, sir; and we'll be waited on.

[*Exeunt.*

---

104. *northen*] *Northerne* Q 3 ; *northern* F.   106. *our*] *you* Q 2 ; *your* Q 3, F.
109. *base*] *bad* Q 2-3, F.   114. *withal, . . . boy,*] Capell ; *withall . . . boy* Qq, F.
115. *Shalt*] Capell ; *Shall* Qq, F.   117. *my*] Q 1 (Rowe) ; *thy* Q 2-3, F.

---

104. *northen*] See *N.E.D.* for this
fairly common form.

105. *Sibyl's leaves*] The prophecies
of the Sibyl were written on leaves
which were frequently blown away
before there was time to collect them.
Steevens quotes Virgil, *Aen.* VI. 74-5 :
" Foliis tantum ne carmina manda, |
Ne turbata volent rapidis ludibria
ventis."—" But, oh! commit not
thy prophetic mind | To flitting leaves,
the sport of every wind, | Lest they
disperse in air our empty tale "
(Dryden).

114. *fit thee*] furnish you with what
you need.

114-15. *withal . . . Shalt*] Lucius is
the only boy in question, hence *my
boy* must be vocative, and should be
set off by commas. I also accept
Capell's *shalt*. It would easily be
corrupted when the construction was
misunderstood, and though *shall* for
shalt is sometimes found (Franz
§ 152) it would be very odd with
unexpressed subject. *Shalt* for *thou
shalt* is, on the other hand, common
(Franz § 306, Abbott § 401). Editors
except Capell seem to have gone to
sleep over this passage. It is true
that the third person can be used as
virtually equivalent to the second;
see *Lr.* I. i. 69 : " What says our
second daughter?" But I doubt
whether a parallel could be found
for a transition from the second to
the third person within the same
sentence, and then back again to
the second.

121. *brave it*] See on II. i. 91.

122. *be waited on*] " i.e. not ignored
as hitherto " (Wilson).

Marc. O, heavens, can you hear a good man groan
    And not relent, or not compassion him?
    Marcus, attend him in his ecstasy,   125
    That hath more scars of sorrow in his heart
    Than foemen's marks upon his batt'red shield,
    But yet so just that he will not revenge.
    Revenge the heavens for old Andronicus!   [*Exit.*

SCENE II.

Enter AARON, CHIRON *and* DEMETRIUS *at one door, and at the
    other door, young* LUCIUS *and another, with a bundle of
    weapons, and verses writ upon them.*

Chi. Demetrius, here's the son of Lucius;
    He hath some message to deliver us.
Aar. Ay, some mad message from his mad grandfather.
Boy. My lords, with all the humbleness I may,
    I greet your honours from Andronicus;   5
    [*Aside.*] And pray the Roman gods confound you
      both.
Dem. Gramercy, lovely Lucius: what's the news?
Boy. [*Aside.*] That you are both decipher'd, that's the
      news,

---

123. *good man*] goodman Q 1.   127. *batt'red*] battred Qq; *batter'd* F.   129. *the*]
ye Johnson conj.

Scene II

  Scene II.]   Pope; om. Qq, F.   the other] another Q 2-3, F.   6.
[*Aside.*]] Capell (so 8, 17); om. Qq, F.   7. *Gramercy*] Gramarcie Q 1-2.
8. om. F.

---

123. *good man*] Munro, *T.L.S.*,
10 June 1949, p. 385, would retain the
Q 1 spelling *goodman* and interpret " a
fellow being and a kinsman smitten
by suffering." I find this forced :
certainly *goodman* sometimes means
simply *good man*, as in the F text of *Lr.*
IV. iv. 18.
    125. *ecstasy*] fit of madness; cf.
Ham. II. i. 102 : " the very ecstasy
of love."
    129. *Revenge the heavens*] let the
heavens revenge. Marcus credits
Titus with adherence to the stock text

on this subject, *Romans*, XII. 19 :
" Vengeance is mine; I will repay,
saith the Lord."

Scene II

    7. *Gramercy*] The Q 1-2 spelling
represents the habitual pronunciation
of *e* before *r*, which has survived in a
few words like *clerk* : see Wyld, pp.
212-22.
    8. *decipher'd*] detected.   The F
omission results from the ending of ll.
7 and 8 with the same two words ;
cf. l. 76.

For villains mark'd with rape. [*Aloud.*] May it
   please you,
My grandsire, well-advis'd, hath sent by me   10
The goodliest weapons of his armoury
To gratify your honourable youth,
The hope of Rome, for so he bid me say;
And so I do, and with his gifts present
Your lordships, that, whenever you have need,   15
You may be armed and appointed well.
And so I leave you both, [*Aside.*] like bloody villains.

                   [*Exeunt Boy and Attendant.*

Dem. What's here?   a scroll; and written round about;
   Let's see:

        Integer vitae, scelerisque purus,   20
        Non eget Mauri iaculis, nec arcu.

Chi. O, 'tis a verse in Horace; I know it well:
   I read it in the grammar long ago.
Aar. Ay, just; a verse in Horace; right, you have it.
   [*Aside.*] Now, what a thing it is to be an ass!   25

---

13. *bid*] *bad* Q 3, F.   15. *that*] Pope; om. Qq, F.   17. Exeunt . . .
Attendant] Capell; Exit Qq, F.   18. *about;*] *about*, Qq; *about?* F.
20-21. one line in Qq; two lines (prose) in F.   arcu] Q 1 (F 2); arcus
Q 2-3, F.   25. [Aside.]] Johnson (so, unnecessarily, 48); om. Qq, F.

---

10. *well-advis'd*] in his right mind;
as Wilson says, this is meant to
contradict what Aaron has said in
l. 3. Cf. *Err.* II. ii. 217 : " mad or
well-advis'd."
  13. *bid*] See on II. iii. 186.
  14. *his gifts*] I cannot see what is
wrong with these words, for which
Wilson proposes *his gift.*
  17. *like . . . villains*] Q 1 indicates the aside by a capital for *Like,*
preceded by a rather long space
and a colon after *both.*
  18. *round about*] all round; appropriate for a scroll. Not quite the
same as v. ii. 98, with which Wilson
links it, glossing both " all over."
  20-1. Integer . . . arcu] Horace,

Odes I. xxii. 1-2 : " the man who is
upright in life and free from crime
does not need the javelins or bow of
the Moor." Possibly chosen in part
with a glance at Aaron the Moor.
  23. *grammar*] Lily's Latin Grammar,
the standard text book, in which the
quotation occurs twice, once with
Horace's name mentioned (H. R. D.
Anders, *Shakespeare's Books,* Berlin,
1904, p. 16). This second mention is
in the section on prosody, usually
begun (Baldwin, I. 579) in the fourth
form.
  24. *just*] precisely, as often in
expressions of assent, cf. *Meas.* III. i.
65-6 : " *Claud.* Perpetual durance? |
Isab. Ay, just; perpetual durance."

Here's no sound jest! the old man hath found their
    guilt,
And sends them weapons wrapp'd about with lines,
That wound, beyond their feeling, to the quick;
But were our witty empress well afoot,
She would applaud Andronicus' conceit: 30
But let her rest in her unrest awhile.—
And now, young lords, was't not a happy star
Led us to Rome, strangers, and more than so,
Captives, to be advanced to this height?
It did me good before the palace gate   35
To brave the tribune in his brother's hearing.

Dem. But me more good, to see so great a lord
Basely insinuate and send us gifts.

Aar. Had he not reason, Lord Demetrius?
Did you not use his daughter very friendly?   40

Dem. I would we had a thousand Roman dames
At such a bay, by turn to serve our lust.

Chi. A charitable wish and full of love.

Aar. Here lacks but your mother for to say amen.

Chi. And that would she for twenty thousand more.   45

Dem. Come, let us go and pray to all the gods
For our beloved mother in her pains.

Aar. Pray to the devils; the gods have given
    us over.   [*Trumpets sound.*

---

27. *them*] *the* Q 3, F.   48. Trumpets sound] Flourish F.

26. *no sound*] ironically for " excellent."

28. *wound . . . quick*] A deliberate
paradox: they are wounded to the
quick though, because of their
stupidity, they do not feel it.

29. *witty*] quick-witted.
afoot] up and about (On.).

31. *rest . . . unrest*] See on II. iii. 8.

35-36. This has not happened in
the play, as E. S. Brubaker notes in
Shakespeare Quarterly, 3 (1952), 140.
But it need not go back to an earlier
version, as he conjectures.

38. *insinuate*] curry favour.

42. *At . . . bay*] cornered like
that. A common metaphor from a
hunted animal turning to face its
pursuers.

43. *charitable . . . love*] Cf. *Romans*
XIII. 9-10. The collocation of *charitable* and *love* seems to reflect the
controversy on the relative merits
of *love* and *charity* to render the Greek
ἀγάπη. This is more clearly echoed
in *LLL.* IV. iii. 127 (" thy love
is far from charity ") and 365 (" who
can sever love from charity?"). Of
the main sixteenth-century versions,
only the Bishops' Bible read *charity*.
See Noble, pp. 140, 146.

45. *more*] i.e. more Roman dames.

Dem. Why do the emperor's trumpets flourish thus?
Chi. Belike for joy the emperor hath a son.   50
Dem. Soft, who comes here?

Enter Nurse, with a blackamoor Child.

Nurse.   God morrow, lords.
　　O, tell me, did you see Aaron the Moor?
Aar. Well, more or less, or ne'er a whit at all,
　　Here Aaron is; and what with Aaron now?
Nurse. O gentle Aaron, we are all undone!   55
　　Now help, or woe betide thee evermore!
Aar. Why, what a caterwauling dost thou keep!
　　What dost thou wrap and fumble in thy arms?
Nurse. O, that which I would hide from heaven's eye,
　　Our empress' shame, and stately Rome's disgrace.   60
　　She is delivered, lords, she is delivered.
Aar. To whom?
Nurse.   I mean she is brought a-bed.
Aar. Well, God give her good rest! What hath he sent
　　her?
Nurse. A devil.
Aar. Why, then she is the devil's dam: a joyful issue. 65
Nurse. A joyless, dismal, black, and sorrowful issue.
　　Here is the babe, as loathsome as a toad
　　Amongst the fair-fac'd breeders of our clime;
　　The empress sends it thee, thy stamp, thy seal,
　　And bids thee christen it with thy dagger's point.   70
Aar. 'Zounds, ye whore! is black so base a hue?

51. *God . . . lords*] so F; with 52 Qq.   *God*] *Good* Q 3, F.   58. *thy*]
thine Q 2-3, F.   65. *Why . . . dam:* (with 64)| *A . . . issue.* Hanmer.
68. *fair-fac'd*] *N.E.D.* ; *fairfast* Q 1-2; *fairest* Q 3, F.   71. *'Zounds, ye*]
Out you F.

50. *Belike*] probably.

51. *God morrow*] the full expression
is " (God) give you good-morrow,"
which is variously contracted. Cf.
Godden (IV. iv. 42).

53. *more*] With a pun on *Moor*, cf.
Mer. V. III. v. 44-5 : " It is much that
the Moor should be more than
reason " (Delius).

68. *fair-fac'd*] For the Q 1 spelling

cf. Q 1 of *LLL.* v. ii. 836 : *smothfast.*

71. *'Zounds*] The substitution of
Out in the Folio is the only trace in
that text of the influence of the 1606
Act against profanity on the stage,
for which see Chambers, I. 238.
The omission of l. 76 might also look
like bowdlerization, but must be ac-
cidental: two successive lines end
with *mother*, and l. 77 is pointless
without l. 76; cf. l. 8.

Sweet blowse, you are a beauteous blossom, sure.
Dem. Villain, what hast thou done?
Aar. That which thou canst not undo.
Chi. Thou hast undone our mother.   75
Aar. Villain, I have done thy mother.
Dem. And therein, hellish dog, thou hast undone her.
    Woe to her chance, and damn'd her loathed
      choice!
    Accurs'd the offspring of so foul a fiend!
Chi. It shall not live.   80
Aar. It shall not die.
Nurse. Aaron, it must; the mother wills it so.
Aar. What, must it, nurse? then let no man but I
    Do execution on my flesh and blood.
Dem. I'll broach the tadpole on my rapier's point: 85
    Nurse, give it me; my sword shall soon dispatch it.
Aar. Sooner this sword shall plough thy bowels up.
    Stay, murtherous villains! will you kill your
      brother?
    Now, by the burning tapers of the sky
    That shone so brightly when this boy was got,   90
    He dies upon my scimitar's sharp point
    That touches this my first-born son and heir.
    I tell you, younglings, not Enceladus,
    With all his threat'ning band of Typhon's brood,
    Nor great Alcides, nor the god of war,   95
    Shall seize this prey out of his father's hands.
    What, what, ye sanguine, shallow-hearted boys!

76. om. F.   77. *her*] om. Q 3, F.   95. *Alcides*] Alciades Q 1.

72. *blowse*] Normally " a ruddy fat-faced wench " (Johnson, *Dict.*). The application to a black male baby is no doubt a mere joke.

76. *done*] had sexual intercourse with. Puns on this are common. Cf. *Meas.* I. ii. 93-4 : " What has he done?—A woman " (Delius) and Mistress Overdone in the same play. Tilley T200 quotes " the thynge that is done can not be undone " from Taverner's *Proverbs* (1539), and *O.D.E.P.* p. 154 analogous sayings as early as Chaucer.

85. *broach*] " stick on a sword's point as on a spit " (On.).

93. *Enceladus*] One of the Titans (sons of Typhon, l. 94) who fought against the gods.

95. *Alcides*] Heracles, grandson of Alcaeus.

97. *sanguine*] red-faced (in contrast to black).

Ye white-lim'd walls! ye alehouse painted signs!
Coal-black is better than another hue
In that it scorns to bear another hue,   100
For all the water in the ocean
Can never turn the swan's black legs to white,
Although she lave them hourly in the flood.
Tell the empress from me, I am of age
To keep mine own, excuse it how she can.   105
Dem. Wilt thou betray thy noble mistress thus?
Aar. My mistress is my mistress; this my self;
The vigour and the picture of my youth:
This before all the world do I prefer;
This maugre all the world will I keep safe,   110
Or some of you shall smoke for it in Rome.
Dem. By this our mother is for ever sham'd.
Chi. Rome will despise her for this foul escape.
Nurse. The emperor in his rage will doom her death.
Chi. I blush to think upon this ignomy.   115
Aar. Why, there's the privilege your beauty bears.
Fie, treacherous hue, that will betray with blushing
The close enacts and counsels of thy heart!
Here's a young lad fram'd of another leer:
Look how the black slave smiles upon the father,   120
As who should say, " Old lad, I am thine own."

98. *white-lim'd*] F3; *whitelimde* Q 1; *white limbde* Q 2-3; *white-limb'd* F.
115. *ignomy*] *ignominie* F.   118. *thy*] *the* Q 3, F.

98. *white-lim'd walls*] Perhaps a reference to *Matthew* xxiii. 27': " whited sepulchres." Wilson quotes *Piers Plowman* (C) xvii. 264-7 : " Ypocrisie . . . is ylikned in Latyn . . . to a wal white-lymed and were blak with-innes."
alehouse . . . signs] " crudely painted " (Wilson, quoting (after Delius) *2H6* iii. ii. 81: " make my image but an alehouse sign ").
99-100. *Coal-black . . . hue*] See *O.D.E.P.* p. 49 : " Black will take no other hue," first quoted from Heywood (1546). The notion that black is the best colour is found in Sandford's *Garden of Pleasure* (1573) : Tilley G172.

101-2. *For . . . white*] See *O.D.E.P.* p. 693 : " To wash a blackamoor (Ethiopian) white," first quoted from Becon (1543).
110. *maugre*] in spite of.
111. *smoke for it*] suffer for it : see Additional Notes.
113. *escape*] " outrageous transgression " (On., who describes the sense as "peculiarly Shakespearian "). Wilson adds that it is used especially of sexual offences. Delius happily glosses " faux pas."
115. *ignomy*] This shortened form of *ignominy* is common.
118. *close enacts*] secret purposes.
119. *leer*] complexion.

He is your brother, lords, sensibly fed
Of that self blood that first gave life to you;
And from that womb where you imprisoned were
He is enfranchised and come to light: 125
Nay, he is your brother by the surer side,
Although my seal be stamped in his face.
Nurse. Aaron, what shall I say unto the empress?
Dem. Advise thee, Aaron, what is to be done,
And we will all subscribe to thy advice: 130
Save thou the child, so we may all be safe.
Aar. Then sit we down, and let us all consult.
My son and I will have the wind of you:
Keep there; now talk at pleasure of your safety.
Dem. How many women saw this child of his?   135
Aar. Why, so, brave lords! when we join in league,
I am a lamb; but if you brave the Moor,
The chafed boar, the mountain lioness,
The ocean swells not so as Aaron storms.
But say again, how many saw the child?   140
Nurse. Cornelia the midwife, and myself,
And no one else but the delivered empress.

124. *that*] *your* Q 1-2.   136. *we*] *we all* F 2.   *join*] *are join'd* Maxwell
conj.   142. *no one*] *none* F.

122. *sensibly*] " as a creature en-
dowed with feeling " (On.). This
is not entirely satisfactory. Wilson
suggests " plainly " as an alternative,
and Ridley " till capable of sensa-
tion," which is tolerably good sense,
but hard to get out of the word.
    123. *self*] same.
    124. *that womb*] I agree with Dr.
Alice Walker (see p. xii) that *your*,
which I accepted in 1953, is intolerably awkward.
    125. *enfranchised*] Baildon com-
pares *Wint.* II. ii. 59-61 : " This
child was prisoner to the womb
and is | By law and process of
great nature thence | Freed and
enfranchis'd."
    126. *surer side*] *O.D.E.P.* p. 435 and
Tilley M1205 quote from Hall's
Chronicle (1548), in a speech attributed

to Henry V : " if the old and trite
proverb be true that the woman's
side is the surer side."
    130. *subscribe to*] acquiesce in.
    131. *so*] See on II. i. 102.
    133. *have the wind of*] " keep watch
upon (as upon game when following
it down the wind)" (On.).
    136. *join*] The metrical irregularity
may be justified by a pause after *lords*
but I suspect the true reading is *are
join'd* : *ioind* might have been misread as *ioine*, and *are* omitted in
consequence.
    138. *chafed*] enraged, an epithet
frequently used of an animal brought
to bay, as Wilson points out on
John III. i. 259. But that is not to say
that it *means* " brought to bay " as
he glosses it here.

Aar. The empress, the midwife, and yourself:
    Two may keep counsel when the third's away:
    Go to the empress; tell her this I said.   145

                                        [*He kills her.*

    " Wheak, wheak! "
    So cries a pig prepared to the spit.
Dem. What mean'st thou, Aaron? wherefore didst thou
        this?
Aar. O Lord, sir, 'tis a deed of policy:
    Shall she live to betray this guilt of ours,   150
    A long-tongu'd babbling gossip? no, lords, no.
    And now be it known to you my full intent.
    Not far, one Muly lives, my countryman;
    His wife but yesternight was brought to bed.
    His child is like to her, fair as you are: 155
    Go pack with him, and give the mother gold,
    And tell them both the circumstance of all,
    And how by this their child shall be advanc'd,

---

146. *Wheak, wheak*] *N.E.D.*; *Weeke, weeke* Qq, F.   146-7. so Camb.; one
line Qq, F.   153. *Muly lives,*] Steevens conj.; Muliteus Qq, F;
Muliteus lives, Rowe.

143. *empress*] See on I. i. 89.
144. *Two . . . away*] See *O.D.E.P.*
p. 330 : " Three (two) may keep
counsel if two (one) be away," first
quoted from *Romance of the Rose, c.*
1400. Though this is treated as a
single proverb, it is really two proverbs, the point of which is not the
same. We can have, as here, a
proverb asserting that two can keep a
secret whereas three cannot, or else
(as in *Rom.* II. iv. 211 : " Two may
keep counsel, putting one away ")
one asserting, more ironically, that the
only safe secret is one that *no* one
shares.
146. *Wheak*] squeak.
149. *policy*] See on II. i. 104.
151. *babbling gossip*] See on II. iii. 17.
153. *Muly lives*] Steevens's excellent correction. The MS. probably read *Muli leues* (cf. Wilson,
The Manuscript of Shakespeare's Hamlet,

p. 105 for *live* spelt *leue* and set up as
leaue in Q 2 of *Ham.* III. iv. 158), or
conceivably, though this would be
odd, *leus. Muly* as a Moorish name
occurs in Peele's *Battle of Alcazar.*
At the same time, very odd pseudo-
classical names are not surprising in
this play, and " Muliteus my countryman his wife " for " the wife of
Muliteus my countryman " would
not be an abnormal construction, so
that the original text may be sound.
But " not far " goes much more
happily with " lives " than with
" was brought to bed." Qq, F do
not punctuate at the end of the line,
which slightly favours the original
text. Alexander retains " Muliteus "
but puts a dash at the end of the line
to indicate an anacoluthon, thus
making the worst of both worlds.
156. *pack*] conspire, come to an
arrangement.

And be received for the emperor's heir,
And substituted in the place of mine,   160
To calm this tempest whirling in the court;
And let the emperor dandle him for his own.
Hark ye, lords; you see I have given her physic,
And you must needs bestow her funeral;
The fields are near, and you are gallant grooms. 165
This done, see that you take no longer days,
But send the midwife presently to me.
The midwife and the nurse well made away,
Then let the ladies tattle what they please.

Chi. Aaron, I see thou wilt not trust the air   170
With secrets.

Dem.   For this care of Tamora,
Herself and hers are highly bound to thee.

                                        [*Exeunt.*

Aar. Now to the Goths, as swift as swallow flies,
There to dispose this treasure in mine arms,
And secretly to greet the empress' friends.   175
Come on, you thick-lipp'd slave, I'll bear you hence;
For it is you that puts us to our shifts;
I'll make you feed on berries and on roots,
And feed on curds and whey, and suck the goat,
And cabin in a cave, and bring you up   180
To be a warrior, and command a camp.   [*Exit.*

163. *you*] *ye* Q 3, F.   170-1. *Aaron . . . secrets*] so Theobald; one line
in Qq, F.   179. *feed*] *feast* Hanmer.

164. *bestow*] Rare with an in-
direct object instead of with " on,"
but also found in Swift.
165. *grooms*] fellows.
166. *days*] time. Wilson compares *Troil.* IV. v. 12 : " 'Tis but
early days," and *nowadays* implies a
similar use.
167. *presently*] immediately.
173. *as . . . flies*] The same metaphor in II. ii. 24. The comparison
is already proverbial for T. Wilson,
Rule of Reason (1551), cited by Tilley
S1023.
176. *thick-lipp'd*] A typical feature
of a blackamoor also in *Oth.* I. i. 66.

177. *puts . . . shifts*] " bring to
extremity " (*N.E.D.*) : here not
quite so strong, perhaps " cause
trouble." The still more literal
meaning " cause to have recourse to
stratagems " (here and in the
similar phrase at IV. i. 72) makes
good sense, but the idiom seems to
have developed along less specific
lines. Cf. *Revenger's Tragedy* IV. ii.
2 : " How that great villain puts
me to my shifts." The earliest
N.E.D. quotation (1553) is antedated
by one from Borde (1542), cited by F.
P. Wilson, *R.E.S.* N.S. 3 (1952), 198.
180. *cabin*] lodge.

SCENE III.

Enter TITUS, *old* MARCUS, *young* LUCIUS, *and other Gentlemen,*
with bows, and Titus *bears the arrows with letters on the*
ends of them.

Tit. Come, Marcus, come; kinsmen, this is the way.
Sir boy, let me see your archery:
Look ye draw home enough, and 'tis there straight.
Terras Astraea reliquit: Be you rememb'red, Marcus,
She's gone, she's fled. Sirs, take you to your tools.   5
You, cousins, shall go sound the ocean,
And cast your nets;
Happily you may catch her in the sea;
Yet there's as little justice as at land.
No; Publius and Sempronius, you must do it;   10
'Tis you must dig with mattock and with spade,
And pierce the inmost centre of the earth:
Then, when you come to Pluto's region,
I pray you, deliver him this petition;

Scene III

Scene III.] Capell; om. Qq, F.   ends] end F.   2. *let*] *now let* F 2.
4-8. Capell divides after reliquit, *fled, shall, nets, sea.*   7-8. divided
by Maxwell; one line in Qq, F.   8. *Happily*] *haply* F.   catch] *finde* Q 3, F.

Scene III

3. *home*] to the full extent. More
common with verb of striking, and in
metaphors therefrom, but here it refers
to the stretching of the bow necessary
to ensure that the arrow gets "home."
4. Terras . . . reliquit] the goddess
of justice has left the earth (Ovid,
Met. I. 150). See F. A. Yates,
"Queen Elizabeth as Astraea" in
*Journal of the Warburg and Courtauld
Institutes* 10 (1947), 27-82. (I owe
this reference to Mr. Peter Ure.)
Miss Yates deals with the identification of Astraea with the constellation
Virgo (l. 64 below), e.g. in Spenser,
F.Q. v. i. 11, VII. vii. 37, and (p. 71)
suggests that in *Titus* "the good
empire [i.e. the golden age] returns
with Lucius " who bears the name of
the traditional first king of England,

and that " it is perhaps a very
significant detail that it was Lucius
who hit Virgo in the shooting scene
and therefore, presumably, brought
her down to earth." I am sceptical
about this last point.
Be you rememb'red] remember.
7-8. *And . . . sea*] By dividing this
line only, and leaving the earlier
part of the passage lineated as in
Qq, F, I have dealt less violently with
these lines than has been customary
since Capell.
8. *Happily*] perhaps; this form and
" haply " are interchangeable in
Shakespeare's English.
11-12. *'Tis . . . earth*] Titus's behaviour in this scene recalls that of
Hieronymo in Kyd's *Spanish Tragedy*
III. xii-xiii. Robertson quotes xii.
71-5, xiii. 108-10.

Tell him, it is for justice and for aid,   15
And that it comes from old Andronicus,
Shaken with sorrows in ungrateful Rome.
Ah, Rome!   Well, well, I made thee miserable
What time I threw the people's suffrages
On him that thus doth tyrannize o'er me.   20
Go, get you gone; and pray be careful all,
And leave you not a man-of-war unsearch'd:
This wicked emperor may have shipp'd her hence;
And kinsmen, then we may go pipe for justice.

Marc. O Publius, is not this a heavy case,   25
To see thy noble uncle thus distract?

Pub. Therefore, my lords, it highly us concerns
By day and night t' attend him carefully,
And feed his humour kindly as we may,
Till time beget some careful remedy.   30

Marc. Kinsmen, his sorrows are past remedy,
But   *   *   *   31*b*
Join with the Goths, and with revengeful war
Take wreak on Rome for this ingratitude,
And vengeance on the traitor Saturnine.

Tit. Publius, how now! how now, my masters!   35
What, have you met with her?

Pub. No, my good lord; but Pluto sends you word,
If you will have Revenge from hell, you shall:
Marry, for Justice, she is so employ'd,
He thinks, with Jove in heaven, or somewhere else, 40
So that perforce you must needs stay a time.

Tit. He doth me wrong to feed me with delays.
I'll dive into the burning lake below,

---

26. *thus*] *this* Q 2.   27. *lords*] *lord* F 2.   30. *careful*] *cureful* Schmidt
conj. ; *easeful* W. S. Walker.   32. *Join*] *But* Q 1 catchword.

24. *pipe for*] "look for in vain,
'whistle for'" (On.).

26. *distract*] See on I. i. 462.

30. *careful*] " costing   trouble "
(Wilson).

31*b*. *But*] The catchword shows
that at least a line has dropped out
before *Join.* I suspect that it contains the words *let us* and that *Join*

is infinitive.   Q 1 has no punctuation
at the end of l. 31.

33. *wreak*] vengeance. Wilson is
mistaken in saying that the noun does
not occur in Shakespeare outside this
play : cf. *Cor.* IV. v. 91.

43. *burning lake*] Probably Phlegethon, though this is properly a
river. Cf. Marlowe, *Faustus* (ed.
Boas), III. i. 48-9 : " the fiery lake |

And pull her out of Acheron by the heels.
Marcus, we are but shrubs, no cedars we;   45
No big-bon'd men fram'd of the Cyclops' size;
But metal, Marcus, steel to the very back,
Yet wrung with wrongs more than our backs can bear:
And sith there's no justice in earth nor hell,
We will solicit heaven and move the gods   50
To send down Justice for to wreak our wrongs.
Come, to this gear.   You are a good archer, Marcus.

                           [He gives them the arrows.

Ad Jovem, that's for you: here, *Ad Apollinem*:
Ad Martem, that's for myself:
Here, boy, to Pallas: here, to Mercury: 55
To Saturn, Caius, not to Saturnine;
You were as good to shoot against the wind.
To it, boy! Marcus, loose when I bid.
Of my word, I have written to effect;
There's not a god left unsolicited.   60
Marc. Kinsmen, shoot all your shafts into the court:
We will afflict the emperor in his pride.

---

48. *backs*] *backe* F.   56. *Saturn, Caius*] Capell; *Saturnine, to Caius* Qq, F.

Of ever-burning Phlegethon," and
Kyd, *Spanish Tragedy*, III. xii. 11 :
" the lake where hell doth stand,"
as well as " the burning lake "
(*2H6* I. iv. 42).

44. *Acheron*] Apparently used
generally for " hell." Wilson considers that it is a lake here (so in
Sackville, *Induction* 480).

45. *shrubs . . . cedars*] Contrasted
also in *Lucr.* 664 : " The cedar stoops
not to the base shrub's foot "
(Wilson). Tilley C208 quotes various
phrases to the effect that the shrub
can survive where the cedar suc-
cumbs, the earliest *c.* 1592. The
cedar and the hyssop are the extremes
of the vegetable kingdom in *1 Kings*,
IV. 33.

46. *Cyclops'*] Giants in Homer's
Odyssey IX.

47. *steel . . . back*] *O.D.E.P.* p.
620 and Tilley S842 cite " steele

to the backe " from Lyly's *Euphues*
(1578).

49-50. *And . . . gods*] A reversal
of Virgil, *Aen.* VII. 312 : " flectere
si nequeo superos, Acheronta move-
bo " (" If Jove and heaven my just
desires deny, | Hell shall the power of
heaven and Jove supply!" (Dryden)),
as Douce noted, *Illustrations of Shakespeare* (1807), II. 116.

52. *gear*] business, rather than
(Ridley) " arms."

56. *Caius*] The corrections seem
certain, cf. v. ii. 151. For the
" Saturn . . . Saturnine " antithesis,
see Introduction p. xxxiii n. 4.

57. *were . . . shoot*] would do as
much good by shooting. The original
sense of this idiom is literally : " it
would be as good to you," but long
before Shakespeare's time the phrase
had come to be used with a personal
subject.

Tit. Now, masters, draw. O, well said, Lucius!
    Good boy, in Virgo's lap: give it Pallas.
Marc. My lord, I aim'd a mile beyond the moon;   65
    Your letter is with Jupiter by this.
Tit. Ha, ha! Publius, Publius, what hast thou done?
    See, see, thou hast shot off one of Taurus' horns.
Marc. This was the sport, my lord: when Publius shot,
    The Bull, being gall'd, gave Aries such a knock   70
    That down fell both the Ram's horns in the court;
    And who should find them but the empress' villain?
    She laugh'd, and told the Moor he should not choose
    But give them to his master for a present.
Tit. Why, there it goes: God give his lordship joy!   75

Enter the Clown, with a basket, and two pigeons in it.

News, news from heaven! Marcus, the post is come.
    Sirrah, what tidings? have you any letters?
    Shall I have justice? what says Jupiter?

65. *aim'd*] Hudson; *aime* Qq, F.   66. *Jupiter*] Iubiter Q 1.   75. *his*]
your Q 3, F.   76. so Rowe (3rd ed.) ; two lines, divided after *heaven*, in
Qq. F.   *News*] Clowne. *Newes* Q 1.   78. *Jupiter*] Iubiter Q 1.

63. *well said*] well done.
64. *Virgo*] the constellation : see
on l. 4. This passage may be indebted, as R. A. Law suggests (*S.P.*
40 (1943), 150–1) to the Chorus's description of the " disarrangement of
the zodiacal signs in view of Atreus's
crime " in Seneca, *Thyestes* 844 ff.
65. *aim'd*] I think Hudson's correction (implying the corruption *d* : *e*)
is unavoidable. Cf. *O.D.E.P.* p. 81 :
" cast beyond the moon " (i.e.
" indulge in wild conjectures "),
first quoted from Heywood (1546).
Marcus expresses his sense of the
futility of Titus's actions, while at the
same time the literal meaning of his
words is calculated to satisfy Titus.
66. *Jupiter*] Spelt *Iubiter* here and
at ll. 78, 82, 83. Only in the last
of these is it required, as a misunderstanding by the Clown. Wilson
suggests that the other occurrences
are the result of changes " on the

press or in proof." This is not
entirely satisfactory, and implies
more careful proof-correction than
we should expect. Moreover, the
form is not a sheer illiterate blunder,
but a current spelling in Middle
English and later (Wyld, pp. 312–13),
and it is conceivable that Shakespeare
used it throughout to lead up to the
joke in l. 84. But that joke seems to
depend on the Clown's pronunciation
seeming odd to the audience, so
that I have, with some hesitation,
followed Wilson in retaining *Jubiter*
only in l. 83. *by this*] Cf. III. i. 109.
68. *Taurus*] the Bull (sign of the
zodiac). Aries (l. 70) is the Ram.
71. *horns*] The usual joke on
cuckoldry.
72. *villain*] servant, with a play in
the modern sense, as in *AYL.* I. i. 60.
75. *there it goes*] " the hunter's
cry of encouragement " (Wilson,
comparing *Tp.* IV. i. 259).

Clo. Ho, the gibbet-maker? He says that he hath
   taken them down again, for the man must not   80
   be hang'd till the next week.

Tit. But what says Jupiter, I ask thee?

Clo. Alas, sir, I know not Jubiter; I never drank
   with him in all my life.

Tit. Why, villain, art not thou the carrier?   85

Clo. Ay, of my pigeons, sir; nothing else.

Tit. Why, didst thou not come from heaven?

Clo. From heaven? alas, sir, I never came there.
   God forbid I should be so bold to press to heaven
   in my young days. Why, I am going with my   90
   pigeons to the tribunal plebs, to take up a matter of
   brawl betwixt my uncle and one of the emperal's
   men.

Marc. Why, sir, that is as fit as can be to serve for
   your oration; and let him deliver the pigeons to   95
   the emperor from you.

Tit. Tell me, can you deliver an oration to the emperor
   with a grace?

---

79. *Ho,*] *Who?* Rowe; *O*, Camb.   82. *Jupiter*] Iubiter Q 1.   83-4.
prose Capell; verse, divided after *Jupiter*, Qq, F.   83. *Jubiter*] Iupiter Q
2-3, F.   87. *Why,*] *Why* Q 1.   88. *From . . . there*] prose Pope;
separate line of verse Qq, F.   90. *Why*] begins new line in Qq.
92. *emperal's*] *Emperialls* Q 2-3, F.

---

79. *Ho*] An exclamation of mild surprise at the question seems in place, hence (with Delius and Alexander) I return to the Qq F text.

gibbet-maker] The same misunderstanding, also by a Clown, occurs in Heywood's *Golden Age* (*a.* 1611), Act III. (*Sh. Soc.* ed., 1851, p. 46).

83. *Jubiter*] See on l. 66.

91. *take up*] settle (amicably).

91-2. *tribunal plebs . . . emperal's*] Malapropisms for *tribunus plebis* and *emperor's*. Wilson (who compares Launce's " Imperial's court," *Gent.* II. iii. 5) notes that " the Clown is also seeking for justice," but, more realistically than Titus, " with a bribe."

97-8. *Tell . . . grace?*] Wilson notes

that this question is virtually repeated at l. 106, and suggests " duplication owing to revision," with ll. 94-100 and ll. 101-7 as alternatives, the latter being the later " because it is not, like the other, detachable from the text." It looks to me more like " foul papers " not finally tidied up— the dividing line between this and revision is never easy to draw. The lines that could be most easily dispensed with are ll. 97-100 : the pun on *grace* may be an afterthought, to which the rest of the passage was not adjusted. I cannot see that Marcus's speech, ll. 94-6, goes any more closely with ll. 97-100 than with what follows.

Clo. Nay, truly, sir, I could never say grace in all my
    life.   100
Tit. Sirrah, come hither: make no more ado,
    But give your pigeons to the emperor:
    By me thou shalt have justice at his hands.
    Hold, hold; meanwhile here's money for thy charges.
    Give me pen and ink.   105
    Sirrah, can you with a grace deliver up a supplication?
Clo. Ay, sir.
Tit. Then here is a supplication for you.   And when
    you come to him, at the first approach you must
    kneel; then kiss his foot; then deliver up your   110
    pigeons; and then look for your reward.   I'll be
    at hand, sir; see you do it bravely.
Col. I warrant you, sir; let me alone.
Tit. Sirrah, hast thou a knife?   Come, let me see it.
    Here Marcus, fold it in the oration;   115
    For thou hast made it like an humble suppliant:
    And when thou hast given it to the emperor,
    Knock at my door, and tell me what he says.
Clo. God be with you, sir; I will.   [*Exit.*
Tit. Come, Marcus, let us go.   Publius, follow me.   120
                                          [*Exeunt.*

106. *up*] om. Q 2-3, F.   116. *For*] *So*, Maxwell conj.   117. *to*] om. 3, QF.

104. *Hold*] here you are.
meanwhile] Rather obscure whether
it is taken (Qq, F and most editors)
with what follows or (Delius) with
Hold. Perhaps it means " to keep
you going until you get justice."
    112. *bravely*] in good style (Rolfe,
who compares *Tp.* III. iii. 83-4 :
" Bravely the figure of this harpy hast
thou | Perform'd ").
    113. *let me alone*] See on I. i. 449.
    116. *For . . . suppliant*] I do not
understand this. Is " it " the knife
or the oration? If the latter, we
have the difficulty noted by Wilson
that this " seems to imply that Marcus
wrote the letter," which disagrees
with l. 105. (I cannot see why Wilson
thinks it is even in agreement with
ll. 94-6.) In either case, what is the

point of " for "?   I am tempted to
suggest that between ll. 115 and 116
Marcus does as Titus has asked him,
and that Titus then says : " So [i.e.
' that's good,' as in *H8* IV. ii. 3-4 :
' Reach a chair : | So '], thou hast
etc." (" For " and " So " are confused in Donne's *Extasie*, l. 59.)
With this interpretation, " it " would
be " the knife wrapped in the
oration." Or, with the same interpretation, we could read " Now."
The only permissible alternative,
which seems very weak but does give
a meaning to " for," is to take " it "
as the oration (with the difficulties
mentioned), and to suppose Titus to
be asking Marcus to fold the knife in
it in order that it may *no longer* be a
humble suppliant.

K

SCENE IV.

Enter Emperor and Empress and her two sons; the Emperor brings
the arrows in his hand that Titus shot at him.

Sat. Why, lords, what wrongs are these! Was ever seen
  An emperor in Rome thus overborne,
  Troubled, confronted thus; and, for the extent
  Of egal justice, us'd in such contempt?
  My lords, you know, as know the mightful gods,   5
  However these disturbers of our peace
  Buzz in the people's ears, there nought hath pass'd
  But even with law against the wilful sons
  Of old Andronicus. And what and if
  His sorrows have so overwhelm'd his wits?   10
  Shall we be thus afflicted in his wreaks,
  His fits, his frenzy, and his bitterness?
  And now he writes to heaven for his redress:
  See, here's to Jove, and this to Mercury;
  This to Apollo; this to the god of war;   15
  Sweet scrolls to fly about the streets of Rome!
  What's this but libelling against the senate,
  And blazoning our unjustice every where?
  A goodly humour, is it not, my lords?
  As who would say, in Rome no justice were.   20

Scene IV

Scene IV.] Capell; om. Qq, F.   5. *know, as know*] Camb.; *know* Qq, F.
18. *unjustice*] *Iniustice* F.

Scene IV

3. *extent*] exercise.
4. *egal*] equal : this form, through
French instead of direct from Latin,
was still common.
8. *even*] " in exact agreement "
(On.).
11. *wreaks*] " vindictive acts "
(On.); cf. on IV. iii. 33.
17. *libelling*] making libellous state-
ments. This line may be echoed in
Marlowe's *Edward II* (ed. Charlton
and Waller) II. ii. 34-5 : " What

call you this but private libelling |
Against the earl of Cornwall and my
brother? " (cited by Verity).

18. *blazoning*] proclaiming; a
metaphor from heraldry.

20. *were*] For subjunctive *be* and
were after *say*, *think* etc., see Franz
§ 640, Abbott §§ 299, 301: cf. *1H4*
II. i. 15-16 : " I think this be the
most villainous house in all London
road for fleas "; *1H6* II. i. 46 : " I
think this Talbot be a fiend of hell."

But if I live, his feigned ecstasies
Shall be no shelter to these outrages;
But he and his shall know that justice lives
In Saturninus' health; whom, if she sleep,
He'll so awake, as she in fury shall   25
Cut off the proud'st conspirator that lives.

Tam. My gracious lord, my lovely Saturnine,
Lord of my life, commander of my thoughts,
Calm thee, and bear the faults of Titus' age,
Th' effects of sorrow for his valiant sons,   30
Whose loss hath pierc'd him deep and scarr'd his
    heart;
And rather comfort his distressed plight
Than prosecute the meanest or the best
For these contempts. [*Aside.*] Why, thus it shall
    become
High-witted Tamora to gloze with all: 35
But, Titus, I have touch'd thee to the quick;
Thy life-blood out, if Aaron now be wise,
Then is all safe, the anchor in the port.

Enter Clown.

How now, good fellow! would'st thou speak
    with us?

24. *whom*] *who* (retaining *he . . . he*) Capell.   *she*] Rowe; *he* Qq, F.
25. *she*] Rowe; *he* Qq, F.   34. [Aside.]] F (end of 35); om. Qq.
36-7. *quick; . . . out,*] Maxwell; *quicke, . . . out:* Qq, F.   *life-blood*] *life-blood's*
Koeppel conj.   38. *anchor*] *Anchor's* Q 3, F.

21. *feigned ecstasies*] Baildon notes
that Saturninus alone, being "of
a suspicious and cowardly temperament," seems to suspect that Titus's
madness is not genuine. On *ecstasies,*
cf. IV. i. 125.

25. *she*] Almost certainly correct
here, I think, as well as in l. 24.
The one corruption would naturally
lead to the other, and the sense is
much better. With Capell's *who*
the antecedent is *Saturninus,* but there
seems no reason why Saturninus
should grant, even for the sake of
argument, that he himself is asleep.

Cf. *R3* I. iii. 287-8 : " I will not
think but they [i.e. my curses] ascend
the sky, | And there awake God's
gentle-sleeping peace."

35. *gloze*] use fair words.

36. *touch'd*] wounded. The phrase
" touch on the quick " is quoted by
Tilley Q 13 from Skelton's *Magni-
ficence* (c. 1516).

37. *Thy . . . out*] I think this
means " once thy life-blood is out,"
and is subordinate to " Then all is
safe." Koeppel's conjecture is in
Englische Studien 35 (1906), 126.

Clo. Yea, forsooth, and your mistress-ship be emperial.   40
Tam. Empress I am, but yonder sits the emperor.
Clo. 'Tis he.   God and Saint Stephen give you godden.
    I have brought you a letter and a couple of
    pigeons here.   [*He reads the letter.*
Sat. Go, take him away, and hang him presently.   45
Clo. How much money must I have?
Tam. Come, sirrah, you must be hanged.
Clo. Hang'd, by' lady! then I have brought up a
    neck to a fair end.   [*Exit.*
Sat. Despiteful and intolerable wrongs!   50
    Shall I endure this monstrous villainy?
    I know from whence this same device proceeds.
    May this be borne as if his traitorous sons
    That died by law for murther of our brother
    Have by my means been butchered wrongfully?   55
    Go, drag the villain hither by the hair;
    Nor age nor honour shall shape privilege.
    For this proud mock I'll be thy slaughterman,
    Sly frantic wretch, that holp'st to make me great,
    In hope thyself should govern Rome and me.   60

Enter ÆMILIUS.

What news with thee, Æmilius?

40. *mistress-ship*] Johnson ; *Mistriship* Q 1 ; *Mistership* Q 2-3, F.   42.
godden] *good den* Q 3, F.   45-6. *presently. . . . have?*] *presently? . . . haue.*
Q 1-2.   48. *by' lady*] *be Lady* Qq ; *ber Lady* F.   53. *borne*] *borne,*
Q 2-3 ; *borne?* F.   55. *butchered*] *butcher'd* F.   *wrongfully?*] *wrongfully.* Q 1-2.
60. *ÆMILIUS*] Theobald ; Nutius (Nuntius Q 2-3, F) Emillius Qq, F.

42. *godden*] See on IV. ii. 51.
48. *by' lady*] The Q spelling is
paralleled in another text probably
printed from Shakespeare's MS.,
Q 2 of *Ham.* II. ii. 454 : " by lady "
(Q 1 : *burlady* ; F : *Byrlady*). It
also occurs in the early editions of
The Batchelars Banquet (1603), p. 10,
l. 13, of F. P. Wilson's edition (1929),
and in *Eastward Ho* (ed. Herford and
Simpson), II. ii. 374.
53. *this . . . as if*] Virtually
" this accusation that " ; cf. on III.
ii. 72.

57. *shape privilege*]   create im-
munity.
58. *slaughterman*]   executioner :
deathsman also occurs in this sense,
2H6 III. ii. 217.
59. *holp'st*] Still commoner in Shakespeare than the modern (weak) past.
60. S.D. app. crit. Nutius] In error
for " Nuntius " (= messenger), contracted " Nūtius." The use of this
word is no indication of classical
imitation : it is found already in
Miracle Plays, cf. *York Mystery Plays*,
ed. L. Toulmin Smith, p. 148.

Æmil. Arm, my lords! Rome never had more cause.
The Goths have gathered head, and with a power
Of high-resolved men, bent to the spoil,
They hither march amain, under conduct   65
Of Lucius, son to old Andronicus;
Who threats, in course of his revenge, to do
As much as ever Coriolanus did.
Sat. Is warlike Lucius general of the Goths?
These tidings nip me, and I hang the head   70
As flowers with frost, or grass beat down with
storms.
Ay, now begins our sorrows to approach:
'Tis he the common people love so much;
Myself hath often heard them say,
When I have walked like a private man,   75
That Lucius' banishment was wrongfully,
And they have wish'd that Lucius were their
emperor.
Tam. Why should you fear? is not your city strong?
Sat. Ay, but the citizens favour Lucius,
And will revolt from me to succour him.   80
Tam. King, be thy thoughts imperious, like thy name!
Is the sun dimm'd, that gnats do fly in it?
The eagle suffers little birds to sing,

62. *Arm*] *Arm, arm* Warburton (Ravenscroft).   *lords*] *lord* Capell
(Ravenscroft).   63. *gathered*] *gather'd* F.   67. *his*] Rowe; *this* Qq, F.
78. *your*] *our* F.

62. *Arm . . . lords*] The corrections by Warburton and Capell are
both plausible.
67. *his*] The confusion of *this* and *his*
is so common that I accept Rowe's
correction, which gives a more normal
expression.
72. *begins*] See on II. i. 26.
74-5. *Myself . . . man*] A curious
isolated reference to the theme of the
disguised ruler (in the manner of
Harun al Rashid), common on the
English stage in Shakespeare's time;
e.g. *Measure for Measure*, Chapman's
Blind Beggar of Alexandria, Middleton's
Phoenix. See W. Creizenach, *The*

English Drama in the Age of Shakespeare
(1916), pp. 221-3. The practice is
recommended by Sir Thomas Elyot
in his *Governour* (1531), III. xxvi.
76. *wrongfully*] See on I. i. 475-6.
82-3. *Is . . . sing*] Wilson compares *Lucr.* 1014-15 : " Gnats are
unnoted whereso'er they fly, |
But eagles gaz'd upon with every
eye." The link between eagles and
gnats is probably (Tilley E1) by way
of the Erasmian proverb : " Aquila
non captat muscas " (*O.D.E.P.* p.
163 : " Eagles catch no flies," first
quotation from Pettie, 1581 :
O.D.E.P., wrongly, 1586).

And is not careful what they mean thereby,
Knowing that with the shadow of his wings   85
He can at pleasure stint their melody;
Even so mayest thou the giddy men of Rome.
Then cheer thy spirit; for know thou, emperor,
I will enchant the old Andronicus
With words more sweet, and yet more dangerous,   90
Than baits to fish, or honey-stalks to sheep,
When as the one is wounded with the bait,
The other rotted with delicious feed.

Sat. But he will not entreat his son for us.

Tam. If Tamora entreat him, then he will: 95
For I can smooth and fill his aged ears
With golden promises, that, were his heart
Almost impregnable, his old ears deaf,
Yet should both ear and heart obey my tongue.
Go thou before, be our ambassador: 100
Say that the emperor requests a parley
Of warlike Lucius, and appoint the meeting
Even at his father's house, the old Andronicus.

Sat. Æmilius, do this message honourably,
And if he stand on hostage for his safety,   105
Bid him demand what pledge will please him
          best.

Æmil. Your bidding shall I do effectually.   [*Exit.*

88. *know thou,*] Kittredge; *know thou* Qq, F; *know, thou* F 4.   93. *feed*]
Q 3; *seede* Q 1-2; *foode* F.   96. *ears*] *eare* Q 3, F.   98. *ears*] *yeares* Qq.
100. *before, be*] Capell; *before to be* Qq; *before to* F.   103. om. Q 3, F.
105. *on*] F 4; *in* Qq, F.   *safety*] *saftie* Q 1.

86. *stint*] stop.
91. *honey-stalks*] stalks of clover.
Not found elsewhere, though " honey-
suckle " is found for " red clover " in
Warwickshire (On.). A surfeit of it
is sometimes fatal to sheep : Wilson
compares Thomas Hardy's *Far from
the Madding Crowd.*
92. *When as*] when. The phrase is
fairly common in Shakespeare, and as
it is now obsolete there seems no point
in spelling it *whenas.*
96. *smooth*] flatter.

98. *ears*] See on II. iii. 160 for the
Q spelling.
100. *be our ambassador*] F's *to* is
perhaps just possible, in the sense
" in the capacity of," but would be
intolerably ambiguous after *Go.* On
the other hand *to* would be readily
inserted by a compositor if his copy
had no comma after *before.*
105. *stand on*] insist on. *safety*]
For the Q 1 spelling cf. *Ham.* (Q 2),
I. iii. 21 : " safty " (where, however,
the text is suspect).

Tam. Now will I to that old Andronicus,
 And temper him with all the art I have,
 To pluck proud Lucius from the warlike Goths. 110
 And now sweet emperor, be blithe again,
 And bury all thy fear in my devices.
Sat. Then go incessantly, and plead to him. [*Exeunt.*

113. *incessantly*] Capell; *sucessantly* Q 1 ; *successantly* Q 2-3, F. *to*] *for* F.

109. *temper*] work on, cf. *Gent.* III.
ii. 64-5 : " temper her, by your per-
suasion, | To hate young Valentine."
 113. *incessantly*] immediately (a
rare but authenticated sense). There
is better evidence for Capell's
conjecture than he himself knew.
The substantive Q 1 text is *sucessantly*,
which could arise from a misreading

of *Jn* as *Su* (the capital *J* is admittedly
unexpected). Q 2 then emends to
successantly, which has been variously
interpreted as " following after another " and " successfully." Wilson,
p. lvi, in accordance with his theory
of Shakespeare's burlesque intention,
treats it as a deliberate *vox nihili*.

ACT V

SCENE I.

Enter LUCIUS *with an army of Goths, with drums and soldiers.*

Luc. Approved warriors and my faithful friends,
I have received letters from great Rome
Which signifies what hate they bear their emperor
And how desirous of our sight they are.
Therefore, great lords, be, as your titles witness,   5
Imperious, and impatient of your wrongs;
And wherein Rome hath done you any scath,
Let him make treble satisfaction.
First Goth. Brave slip, sprung from the great Andronicus,
Whose name was once our terror, now our comfort,   10
Whose high exploits and honourable deeds
Ingrateful Rome requites with foul contempt,

ACT V

Scene 1

ACT V. *Scene* 1.] Rowe; Actus Quintus. F ; om. Qq.   Enter]
Flourish. Enter. F. drums] Drum Q 3, F.   9. First Goth] Capell (so
121, 162); Goth Qq, F. *sprung*] *sprong* Q 1.

Scene 1

soldiers] An " army with soldiers "
is an odd expression, and Capell
substituted *colours* for *soldiers*. Wilson
suggests that " Drums and Soldiers "
was " a prompter's marginal note "
—for such notes made on author's
" foul papers " while, or before,
preparing the prompt-copy, see Greg,
Editorial Problem, pp. 123-4 (*Merchant
of Venice*), 140 (*Comedy of Errors*).
Wilson's reference to p. 96 of his
edition is misleading, since what is
there discussed is the copy for F 1,
not Q 1.

1. *Approved . . . friends*] Wilson finds
this construction and rhythm characteristic of Peele, but cf. also *2H6* 1. i.

24 : " Great king of England, and
my gracious lord "; *R3* v. ii. 1 :
" Fellows in arms, and my most
loving friends "; Marlowe, *I Tam-
burlaine* (ed. Ellis-Fermor), III. i. 1 :
" Great kings of Barbary, and my
portly bassoes." *Approved*] tried.

2. *letters*] As often, for a single
communication.

3. *signifies*] See on II. i. 26. The
singular meaning of *letters* may make
this a little more natural.

7. *Rome*] Not, I think (Wilson), equivalent to *Saturnine*. Rather, the
Goths are to revenge on Saturnine all
the wrongs Rome has *ever* done them.
scath] harm.

9. *slip*] scion.

Be bold in us: we'll follow where thou lead'st,
Like stinging bees in hottest summer's day
Led by their master to the flow'red fields,	15
And be adveng'd on cursed Tamora.
Goths. And as he saith, so say we all with him.
Luc. I humbly thank him, and I thank you all.
But who comes here, led by a lusty Goth?

Enter a Goth, leading of AARON *with his Child
in his arms.*

Second Goth. Renowned Lucius, from our troops I stray'd	20
To gaze upon a ruinous monastery;
And as I earnestly did fix mine eye
Upon the wasted building, suddenly
I heard a child cry underneath a wall.
I made unto the noise, when soon I heard	25
The crying babe controll'd with this discourse:
"Peace, tawny slave, half me and half thy dame!
Did not thy hue bewray whose brat thou art,
Had nature lent thee but thy mother's look,
Villain, thou might'st have been an emperor:	30
But where the bull and cow are both milk-white,
They never do beget a coal-black calf.

13. *Be bold*] Behold F.	*us:*] us; Theobald; *vs* Q 1-2; *vs,* Q 3, F.
16. *adveng'd*] auengd Q 3, F.	17. Goths] F 2 (Omn.); om. Qq, F.
20. Second Goth] Capell; Goth Qq, F.	*Renowmed*] Renowned Q 3, F.
23. *building, suddenly*] building suddenly, Q 1-2.	27. *dame*] dam Q 2-3, F.

13. *bold*] confident.

15. *master*] i.e. the queen, or, as it was believed in Shakespeare's time, the king. In *H5* I. ii. 190 and 196, he is their "king" and "emperor", and in *2H6* III. ii. 126 "their leader."

16. *adveng'd*] A Latinate form of *aveng'd.*

cursed Tamora] She is evidently thought of as a renegade to her nation. If the chap-book (see Introduction, p. xxx) represents Shakespeare's immediate source, we cannot explain the epithet from the German version, in which she has poisoned the Gothic king.

22. *earnestly*] attentively.

26. *controll'd*] See on III. i. 259.

27. *tawny*] black; not (Herford) "a hue between black and white," cf. H. T. Price, *Papers of the Michigan Academy* 21 (1935), 505-6, who cites examples to show that *tawny* could often mean *black* in Elizabethan English, and quotes R. Scot, *Discovery of Witchcraft*, p. 312 for the belief that the children of a black father and a white mother were always black, which, however, Shakespeare does not share—cf. IV. ii. 155.

dame] mother, cf. *2H4* III. ii. 125, *Lucr.* 1477. There is no need to read *dam* here or at V. ii. 144.

28. *bewray*] make known.

brat] Not necessarily a term of abuse.

Peace, villain, peace! " even thus he rates the babe,
" For I must bear thee to a trusty Goth,
Who, when he knows thou art the empress' babe,   35
Will hold thee dearly for thy mother's sake."
With this, my weapon drawn, I rush'd upon him,
Surpris'd him suddenly, and brought him hither
To use as you think needful of the man.

Luc. O worthy Goth, this is the incarnate devil   40
That robb'd Andronicus of his good hand:
This is the pearl that pleas'd your empress' eye,
And here's the base fruit of her burning lust.
Say, wall-ey'd slave, whither would'st thou convey
This growing image of thy fiend-like face?   45
Why dost not speak? What, deaf? not a word?
A halter, soldiers, hang him on this tree,
And by his side his fruit of bastardy.

Aar. Touch not the boy, he is of royal blood.

Luc. Too like the sire for ever being good.   50
First hang the child, that he may see it sprawl—
A sight to vex the father's soul withal.
Get me a ladder.

> [*A ladder brought, which Aaron is made to ascend.*

Aar.   Lucius, save the child;
And bear it from me to the empress.
If thou do this, I'll show thee wondrous things   55
That highly may advantage thee to hear:
If thou wilt not, befall what may befall,
I'll speak no more but " Vengeance rot you all! "

37. *drawn*] *drawen* Q 1.   43. *her*] Q 1-2 (Capell); *his* Q 3, F.   53.
[A ladder . . . ascend.]] Capell substantially; om. Qq, F.   Aar.
Lucius] Theobald; Qq, F give whole line to Aaron.   58. *more but*
" *Vengeance . . . all!*"] Globe; *more, but vengeance . . . all.* Q 1-2; *more but
vengeance . . . all.* Q 3; *more: but vengeance . . . all.* F; *more: but Vengeance
. . . all.* F 4.

39. *use . . . of*] deal with.
42. *pearl . . . eye*] See *O.D.E.P.*
p. 48 : " A black man is a pearl in a
fair woman's eye." This is the
earliest quotation, and the next is
also Shakespearian, *Gent.* v. ii. 12.
44. *wall-ey'd*] fierce-looking (lit.
with the iris of the eye discoloured).

51. *sprawl*] " struggle in the death
agony " (On.). Cf. *3H6* v. v. 39.
58. " *Vengeance . . . all!*"] I think
F 4 intended to represent this as a
quotation, by printing *Vengeance* with
a capital. This persists in some
eighteenth-century editions, but eventually disappears.

Luc. Say on, and if it please me which thou speak'st,
  Thy child shall live, and I will see it nourish'd.   60
Aar. And if it please thee! why, assure thee, Lucius,
  'Twill vex thy soul to hear what I shall speak;
  For I must talk of murthers, rapes, and massacres,
  Acts of black night, abominable deeds,
  Complots of mischief, treason, villainies,   65
  Ruthful to hear, yet piteously perform'd ;
  And this shall all be buried in my death,
  Unless thou swear to me my child shall live.
Luc. Tell on thy mind; I say thy child shall live.
Aar. Swear that he shall, and then I will begin.   70
Luc. Who should I swear by? thou believest no god:
  That granted, how canst thou believe an oath?
Aar. What if I do not? as, indeed, I do not;
  Yet, for I know thou art religious,
  And hast a thing within thee called conscience,   75
  With twenty popish tricks and ceremonies,
  Which I have seen thee careful to observe,

65. *treason*] *treasons* Maxwell conj.   67. *in*] *by* Q 3, F.

59. *and*] A genuine connective, I think, though some editors, influenced by Aaron's repetition in l. 61, write " an." What the repetition actually shows is the absence of any sense in sixteenth-century English that two different " words " are in question.

60. *nourish'd*] Perhaps monosyllabic, cf. l. 84, and *2H6* III. i. 348 : " Whiles I in Ireland nourish a mighty band." This pronunciation is represented by the earlier spelling *nursh*.

65. *treason*] The isolated singular is suspicious, and the plural, for *acts of treason*, is common, cf. *Mer. V.* v. i. 85 : " fit for treasons, stratagems, and spoils."

66. *Ruthful*] lamentable.
piteously] so as to excite pity.

71-2. *Who . . . oath?*] There is an interesting parallel in Machiavelli's *Arte of Warre*, translated by Peter Whithorn (2nd ed., London, 1588),

p. 106 (end of Bk. VII), on the subject of mercenaries : " By what God or by what sainctes may I make them to sweare? By those y[t] they worship, or by those that they blaspheme ? Who they worship I know not any : but I know well they blaspheme all. How should I beleeue that they will keepe their promise to them, whom euery hower they dispise. How can they that dispise God, reuerence men? Then what good fashion should that bee, which might be expressed in this matter?" Wilson compares *R3* IV. iv. 369 ff. but the point is not quite the same.

74. *for*] because.

76. *popish*] Wilson sees in this the hand of the anti-papal Peele. But considering who the speaker is, it would be at least as appropriate from a writer sympathetic to Catholicism.

Therefore I urge thy oath; for that I know
An idiot holds his bauble for a god,
And keeps the oath which by that god he swears,   80
To that I'll urge him: therefore thou shalt vow
By that same god, what god soe'er it be,
That thou adorest and hast in reverence,
To save my boy, to nourish and bring him up;
Or else I will discover nought to thee.   85

Luc. Even by my god I swear to thee I will.

Aar. First know thou, I begot him on the empress.

Luc. O most insatiate and luxurious woman!

Aar. Tut, Lucius, this was but a deed of charity
To that which thou shalt hear of me anon.   90
'Twas her two sons that murdered Bassianus;
They cut thy sister's tongue and ravish'd her,
And cut her hands and trimm'd her as thou sawest.

Luc. O detestable villain! call'st thou that trimming?

Aar. Why, she was wash'd, and cut, and trimm'd, and
        'twas   95
Trim sport for them which had the doing of it.

Luc. O barbarous beastly villains like thyself!

Aar. Indeed, I was their tutor to instruct them.

88. *and*] om. Q 3, F.   93. *hands*] *hands off* F.   95-6. divided by
Capell; Qq, F divide after *trimm'd*.   96. *which*] *that* Q 2-3, F.
97. *barbarous*] *barberous*, Qq.

78-81. *for . . him*] I now (1961)
follow H. F. Brooks in the interpretation of this passage. It is
addressed to Lucius, and contains a
parallel to the oath Aaron is urging
upon him: " because I know an
idiot . . . swears, to that oath I will
(when occasion arises) urge him.
Therefore (on the same principle)
thou shalt etc."

79. *bauble*] the court fool's stick.

82-3. *what . . . reverence*]   Alexander punctuates with a dash before
and after these words, since Qq, F
put no comma after " be." But I
think " what . . . be " must (as
earlier editors have taken them) be
parenthetic.

84. *nourish*] See on l. 60.

88. *luxurious*] lustful; the normal
Shakespearian sense, as with
" luxury," e.g. *Ham.* I. v. 83.

90. *To*] compared with.

93. *wash'd . . . trimm'd*] " As by a
barber " (Wilson). But *trim* also
has a bawdy sense, as in Fletcher,
Loyal Subject, II. i. 92 (cited by
Delius), *False One*, II. iii. 88; Dekker,
Match Me in London, I. i. 53-5. E.
Partridge, *Dictionary of Slang and
Unconventional English*, cites " trim
the buff " in this sense.

94. *detestable*] Stress on first syllable.

97. *barbarous*] A pun on " barber "
in the Q spelling is unlikely. The
spelling occurs also at v. iii. 4, and in
Jack Straw (also a Danter play, 1593),
sig. D2ᵛ.

That codding spirit had they from their mother,
As sure a card as ever won the set;   100
That bloody mind I think they learn'd of me,
As true a dog as ever fought at head.
Well, let my deeds be witness of my worth.
I train'd thy brethren to that guileful hole
Where the dead corpse of Bassianus lay;   105
I wrote the letter that thy father found,
And hid the gold within that letter mentioned,
Confederate with the queen and her two sons:
And what not done, that thou hast cause to rue,
Wherein I had no stroke of mischief in it?   110
I play'd the cheater for thy father's hand,
And, when I had it, drew myself apart,
And almost broke my heart with extreme laughter.
I pry'd me through the crevice of a wall
When, for his hand, he had his two sons' heads;   115
Beheld his tears, and laugh'd so heartily

---

107. *that*] *the* Q 2-3, F.   *mentioned*] *mention'd* F.   110. *it?*] Rowe; *it,*
Q 1-2; *it.* Q 3, F.

---

99. *codding*] Usually glossed " lustful " (from *cod* = testicle), but not
recorded elsewhere. Ridley suggests
" eager to ' cod ' " in the dialect
sense of " score off." This is attractive (though not recorded before the
nineteenth century) and I think a
pun on both senses is possible.

100. *sure . . . card*] " expedient
certain to obtain its object " (*N.E.D.*).
Both *O.D.E.P.* p. 632 and Tilley C74
cite *Thersytes* (*c.* 1560) which ante-
dates the earliest *N.E.D.* quotation. A " Master Surecard " is
mentioned in *2H4* III. ii. 96.

set] game.

102. *at head*] A reference to bull-
dogs " whose generosity and courage
are always shown by meeting the
bull in front and seizing him by the
nose " (Johnson). Cf. Jonson (ed.
Herford and Simpson), *Epicoene*,
IV. ii. 31-3 : " TRV. You fought
high and faire, sir IOHN. CLE. At

the head. DAV. Like an excellent
beare-dog."

104. *train'd*] enticed.

109-10. *what . . . it?*] A mixture
of constructions, (*a*) " what was not
done . . . rue?" (*b*) " what was
done wherein, etc. ?"

111. *cheater*] " officer appointed to
look after property forfeited to the
Crown (escheats) ; hence, because of
his opportunities, fig. in the modern
sense " (Wilson based on On.).

113. *broke my heart*] died. H. T.
Price (*Papers of the Michigan Academy*,
21 (1935), 504) compares Marlowe,
Massacre at Paris (ed. Bennett), x. 15 :
" my heart doth break : I faint and
die."

114. *I . . . wall*] Was this shown
on the stage, from behind the
traverse, in III. i. ? It would be an
effective piece of stage-business.

me] For this idiom see Abbott
§ 220, Franz § 294.

That both mine eyes were rainy like to his:
And when I told the empress of this sport,
She sounded almost at my pleasing tale,
And for my tidings gave me twenty kisses.   120
First Goth. What, canst thou say all this, and never
        blush?
Aar. Ay, like a black dog, as the saying is.
Luc. Art thou not sorry for these heinous deeds?
Aar. Ay, that I had not done a thousand more.
        Even now I curse the day, and yet, I think,   125
        Few come within the compass of my curse,
        Wherein I did not some notorious ill:
        As kill a man, or else devise his death;
        Ravish a maid, or plot the way to do it;
        Accuse some innocent, and forswear myself;   130
        Set deadly enmity between two friends;
        Make poor men's cattle break their necks;
        Set fire on barns and haystalks in the night,
        And bid the owners quench them with their tears.
        Oft have I digg'd up dead men from their graves,   135
        And set them upright at their dear friends' door,
        Even when their sorrows almost was forgot,
        And on their skins, as on the bark of trees,
        Have with my knife carved in Roman letters,
        " Let not your sorrow die, though I am dead."   140

121-4. Qq centre prefixes.   126. *the*] *few* F.   132. *break*] *stray
and break* Z. Jackson conj.; *fall and break* Hudson.   133. *haystalks*]
haystakes Q 2; *haystackes* Q 3, F.   134. *their*] *the* F.

119. *sounded*] swooned. It is
pointless to half-modernize to
swounded, itself obsolete.
        122. *like . . . dog*] See *O.D.E.P.*
p. 53, where the first quotation is
from Gosson (1579).
        125-7. *Even . . . ill*] See Introduc-
tion, p. xxii. " Within the compass of
my curse " recurs in *R3* I. iii. 284.
        132. *break their necks*] Hudson in
explaining his conjecture (which is as
good as any) suggests that Aaron set
pitfalls for the cattle.

133. *haystalks*] The *English Dialect
Dictionary* records this form of " stack "
for Hertfordshire (1750).
        135-7. *Oft . . . forgot*] The fact
that a comparable incident actually
occurs on the stage in Marlowe's *Jew
of Malta* IV. ii suggests the priority of
Marlowe : cf. L. Kirschbaum, *Modern
Language Quarterly* 7 (1946), 56.
        136. *friends'*] probably " rela-
tions' " : a sense still current in
Scotland.
        137. *sorrows*] See on II. i. 26.

But I have done a thousand dreadful things
As willingly as one would kill a fly,
And nothing grieves me heartily indeed
But that I cannot do ten thousand more.
Luc. Bring down the devil, for he must not die   145
So sweet a death as hanging presently.
Aar. If there be devils, would I were a devil,
To live and burn in everlasting fire,
So I might have your company in hell,
But to torment you with my bitter tongue!   150
Luc. Sirs, stop his mouth, and let him speak no more.

Enter ÆMILIUS.

Goth. My lord, there is a messenger from Rome
Desires to be admitted to your presence.
Luc. Let him come near.
Welcome, Æmilius: what's the news from Rome?   155
Æmil. Lord Lucius, and you princes of the Goths,
The Roman emperor greets you all by me;
And, for he understands you are in arms,
He craves a parley at your father's house,
Willing you to demand your hostages,   160
And they shall be immediately delivered.
First Goth. What says our general?
Luc. Æmilius, let the emperor give his pledges
Unto my father and my uncle Marcus,
And we will come.   March away.   [*Exeunt.* 165

141. *But*] *Tut,* Q 2-3, F.   165. *March away*] *Away.* [March. Exeunt.]
Capell. Exeunt.] om. Q 1-2; Flourish. Exeunt F.

141. *But*] The sense seems to be
" but why should I go on itemizing? "
(H. F. Brooks). Q 2's *Tut* has some
attractiveness, but the compositor
may have recalled l. 89.

146. *presently*] immediately.

148-50. *To live . . . tongue*] The
resemblance (Noble) to *Rev.* xx. 10
is not very close.

149. *So*] See on II. i. 102.

151. Enter ÆMILIUS] It has been
customary here to give an entry for

" a Goth " and to transfer Æmilius's
entry to after l. 154. This is unnecessary. One of the Goths already
on the stage announces Æmilius's
arrival to Lucius. Wilson satisfac-
torily expands the Qq, F direction by
reading here : *A Goth comes up* and
after l. 154 *ÆMILIUS is brought
forward*; but it is a little anomalous
not to give Æmilius a formal entry.

165. *March away*] The absence of
an *Exeunt* in Q 1-2 (not known to
Capell) tells in favour of his correction.

SCENE II.

Enter TAMORA, *and her two sons, disguised.*

Tam. Thus, in this strange and sad habiliment,
　　I will encounter with Andronicus,
　　And say I am Revenge, sent from below
　　To join with him and right his heinous wrongs;
　　Knock at his study, where they say he keeps,   5
　　To ruminate strange plots of dire revenge;
　　Tell him Revenge is come to join with him
　　And work confusion on his enemies.

　　　　　　　[*They knock, and Titus opens his study door.*

Tit. Who doth molest my contemplation?
　　Is it your trick to make me ope the door,   10
　　That so my sad decrees may fly away
　　And all my study be to no effect?
　　You are deceiv'd; for what I mean to do
　　See here in bloody lines I have set down;
　　And what is written shall be executed.   15

Tam. Titus, I am come to talk with thee.

Tit. No, not a word; how can I grace my talk,
　　Wanting a hand to give it action?

Scene II

Scene II.] Rowe; om. Qq, F.   1. *habiliment*] *habilliament* Qq 1, 3, F.;
habillament Q 2.   18. *it action*] F; *that accord* Qq; *it that accord* Pope.

Scene II

1. *sad*] dismal; Wilson compares
R2 v. v. 70-1 : "that sad dog That
brings me food."

2. *encounter with*] meet.

5. *keeps*] dwells ; cf. *Ham.* II.
i. 7-8 : "what Danskers are in Paris
. . . where they keep."

9. *Who . . . contemplation*] This
line is quoted from memory (" Whoe
does molest o^r Contemplations "),
and in jest, by a clown in *The Welsh
Embassador* (Malone Society Reprint),
l. 1963. See on IV. i. 102.

11. *That . . . away*] Possibly an
allusion to the Sibyl's leaves : see
on IV. i. 105.

sad decrees] " solemn resolutions "
(Ridley).

18. *Wanting . . . action*] I accept
the F reading with some confidence.
Q cannot be accepted as it stands,
but would need to be emended as
by Pope. The MS. may have read
giue yt acc(i)on(e). The *cc* spelling is
common and so is *-con* for *-cion*, and a
final *e*, which could be corrupted to
d, is not inconceivable (for " super-
fluous *e* mute " see J. D. Wilson,
The Manuscript of Shakespeare's Hamlet,
p. 116). For the meaning, see B. L.
Joseph, *Elizabethan Acting* (London,
1951), especially p. 39, quoting John
Bulwer, *Chironomia* (London, 1644),
p. 16 : " The moving and significant

Thou hast the odds of me; therefore no more.

Tam. If thou didst know me, thou would'st talk with me. 20

Tit. I am not mad; I know thee well enough:
Witness this wretched stump, witness these crimson
   lines;
Witness these trenches made by grief and care;
Witness the tiring day and heavy night;
Witness all sorrow that I know thee well 25
For our proud empress, mighty Tamora.
Is not thy coming for my other hand?

Tam. Know thou, sad man, I am not Tamora;
She is thy enemy, and I thy friend:
I am Revenge, sent from th' infernal kingdom 30
To ease the gnawing vulture of thy mind
By working wreakful vengeance on thy foes.
Come down and welcome me to this world's light;
Confer with me of murder and of death.
There's not a hollow cave or lurking-place, 35
No vast obscurity or misty vale,
Where bloody murther or detested rape
Can couch for fear, but I will find them out,
And in their ears tell them my dreadful name,
Revenge, which makes the foul offender quake. 40

Tit. Art thou Revenge? and art thou sent to me
To be a torment to mine enemies?

28. *Know thou,*] F 4; *Know thou* Qq, F ; *Know, thou* Capell.   31. *thy*] *the* F.
32. *thy*] *my* F.   40. *offender*] *offenders* Q 3, F.   42. *mine*] *thine* Q 2 (Edin.
copy).

extension of the *Hand* is knowne to be
so absolutely pertinent to speech, that
we together with a speech expect the
due motion of the *Hand* to explaine,
direct, enforce, apply, apparrell, & to
beautifie the words men utter, which
would prove naked, unless the
cloathing *Hands* doe neatly move to
adorne and hide their nakednesse,
with their comely and ministeriall
parts of speech." Dr. Joseph discusses
both the Quarto and Folio readings
(pp. 53, 59) : cf. also *2H6* v. i. 8-9 :
" I cannot give due action to my
words | Except a sword or sceptre
balance it." W. F. Schirmer (*Sh. Jb.*

81 (1935), 21 n. 4) cites Quintilian
XI. 3 [65 ff. and 85], and Wilson,
Arte of Rhetorique (ed. G. H. Mair,
Oxford, 1909), pp. 220-1. There is
an allusion to this scene in Middleton's
Father Hubburd's Tales (Works, ed.
Bullen, VIII. 94) : " my lamentable
action of one arm, like old Titus
Andronicus."

19. *odds of*] advantage over.

31. *gnawing vulture*] An allusion to
the Prometheus story (see on II. i. 17).

32. *wreakful vengeance*] This sort of
pleonasm is normal in the minor
drama of the time.

L

Tam. I am; therefore come down and welcome me.
Tit. Do me some service ere I come to thee.

Lo, by thy side where Rape and Murder stands;   45
Now give some surance that thou art Revenge:
Stab them, or tear them on thy chariot-wheels,
And then I'll come and be thy waggoner,
And whirl along with thee about the globe.
Provide two proper palfreys, black as jet,   50
To hale thy vengeful waggon swift away,
And find out murderers in their guilty caves:
And when thy car is loaden with their heads,
I will dismount, and by thy waggon-wheel
Trot like a servile footman all day long,   55
Even from Hyperion's rising in the east
Until his very downfall in the sea:
And day by day I'll do this heavy task,
So thou destroy Rapine and Murder there.

---

49. *globe.*] Capell conj.; *globes.* Qq, F; *globe,* W. S. Walker conj.   50.
two] Rowe; *thee two* Qq, F.   *black*] *as blacke* Q 3, F.   52. *murderers*]
Capell; *murder* Qq, F.   *caves*] F 2; *cares* Qq, F.   54. *thy*] Q 1 (Rowe);
the Q 2-3, F.   56. *Hyperion's*] F 2 (Hiperions); *Epeons* Qq; *Eptons* F.
57. *very*] *weary* Wilson conj.

46. *surance*] assurance.

49. *globe*] I think this correction is certain : only the terrestrial globe can be in question. Capell wrote : "'*globes*,' (if not a mistake), implies a plurality of worlds constituted as earth is " : for this reason I credit him with the conjecture. Walker may well have been right in further proposing to replace the full-stop at the end of this line by a less heavy stop, and to treat *Provide* as infinitive, parallel to *come* and *whirl*.

50. *proper*] handsome; frequent in Shakespeare.

56. *Hyperion's*] The MS. probably read " Epions," using the customary abbreviation for " per " (J. G. McManaway in *Shakespeare Survey* 3 (1950), p. 144). Hyperion is the sun-god.

57. *very*] Wilson's conjecture is attractive but not essential; cf. *Err.* i. ii. 7 : " Dies ere the weary sun set in the west."

59. *So*] See on ii. i. 102.

Rapine] rape : so only in this scene, ll. 83, 103. If Shakespeare consulted Gower's version of the Tereus story (*Confessio Amantis* v), he may have recalled the use of *Ravine* there, in the sense " robbery by violence "; cf. especially ll. 5523-8 : " So ben ther in the same wise | Lovers, as I thee schal devise, | That whan noght elles mai availe, | Anon with strengthe thei assaile | And gete of love the sesine [possession], | Whan thei se time, be Ravine," also ll. 5530, 5627, 5919 (*raviner*), and 5650, 6050 (noted by Steevens), 6064 (*ravine*).

Tam. These are my ministers, and come with me.   60
Tit. Are they thy ministers? what are they call'd?
Tam. Rape and Murder; therefore called so
       'Cause they take vengeance of such kind of men.
Tit. Good Lord, how like the empress' sons they are,
       And you the empress, but we worldly men   65
       Have miserable, mad, mistaking eyes.
       O sweet Revenge, now do I come to thee;
       And, if one arm's embracement will content thee,
       I will embrace thee in it by and by.   [*Exit.*
Tam. This closing with him fits his lunacy.   70
       Whate'er I forge to feed his brain-sick humours,
       Do you uphold and maintain in your speeches,
       For now he firmly takes me for Revenge;
       And, being credulous in this mad thought,
       I'll make him send for Lucius his son,   75
       And whilst I at a banket hold him sure,
       I'll find some cunning practice out of hand

---

61. *they*] F 2; *them* Qq, F; *these* Dyce.   62. *Rape*] *Rapine* F 2.
65. *worldly*] *wordlie* Q 1.   66. *mad, mistaking*] *mad mistaking* Qq, F; *mad-
mistaking* W. S. Walker.   69. Exit] Exit above Rowe (but see Add. Notes).
71. *humours*] *fits* Q 2-3, F.   76. *banket*] *banquet* Q 2-3, F.

61. *Are they*] I cannot quite believe
in Qq, F's *them*, though F has *them*
as nominative in *John* IV. ii. 50-1: "for
the which myself and them | Bend
their best studies," where some
editors think it to have been errone-
ously repeated from the previous line.
   what . . . call'd ?] Wilson calls
this question "an inconsistency surely
too glaring to be explained as Titus's
lunacy." In my 1953 edition, I
wrote, "It is not at all clear, though
the editors do not comment on it,
how Titus knows at l. 45 who
Tamora's attendants are." In this
edition, I am privileged to publish in
an Appendix an admirable solution
by Dr. H. F. Brooks.
   62. *Rape . . . so*] An effectively
solemn headless line.
   65. *worldly*] of this world; without
the modern connotations. In 1953 I
retained the Q1 form as an archaism

(see *N.E.D.*), but at this date it is
almost certainly a misprint.
   70. *closing*] agreeing, cf. *Meas.* v. i.
341 : "Hark how the villain would
close ('climb down,' On.) now."
   71. *forge*] invent; cf. Falstaff's
"apprehensive, quick, forgetive"
(*2H4* IV. iii. 107).
   humours] Q 2's *fits* is not just
(Wilson) "repeated by the compositor from l. 70," though that line
no doubt influenced his choice of a
word. But the corruption of the
corresponding word on the verso
(l. 106 : *shalt* Q 1 ; *maist* Q 2) shows
that the word was illegible (it is
very badly printed in the surviving
copy). The line begins a new page.
   76. *banket*] See on III. ii. S.D.
before 1, and cf. ll. 194, 203.
   77. *practice*] scheme.
   out of hand] on the spur of the
moment.

To scatter and disperse the giddy Goths,
Or, at the least, make them his enemies.
See, here he comes, and I must ply my theme.   80

Enter TITUS.

Tit. Long have I been forlorn, and all for thee:
Welcome, dread Fury, to my woeful house:
Rapine and Murther, you are welcome too.
How like the empress and her sons you are.
Well are you fitted, had you but a Moor: 85
Could not all hell afford you such a devil?
For well I wot the empress never wags
But in her company there is a Moor;
And would you represent our queen aright,
It were convenient you had such a devil: 90
But welcome as you are: what shall we do?
Tam. What would'st thou have us do, Andronicus?
Dem. Show me a murtherer, I'll deal with him.
Chi. Show me a villain that hath done a rape,
And I am sent to be reveng'd on him.   95
Tam. Show me a thousand that hath done thee wrong,
And I will be revenged on them all.
Tit. Look round about the wicked streets of Rome,
And when thou find'st a man that's like thyself,
Good Murther, stab him; he's a murtherer.   100
Go thou with him; and when it is thy hap
To find another that is like to thee,
Good Rapine, stab him; he is a ravisher.
Go thou with them; and in the emperor's court
There is a queen attended by a Moor;   105
Well shalt thou know her by thine own proportion,
For up and down she doth resemble thee:
I pray thee, do on them some violent death;
They have been violent to me and mine.

80. *ply*] *play* F.   Enter *TITUS*] Rowe; om. Qq, F.   91. *are: what*]
Pope; *are, what* Qq, F.   96. *hath*] *haue* Q 2-3, F.   97. *I will*] *Ile* F.
106. *shalt*] *maist* Q 2-3, F.   *thine*] *thy* Q 3, F.

87. *wags*] goes about.   106. *shalt*] See on l. 71.
96. *hath*] See on II. iv. 17.   107. *up and down*] exactly.

Tam. Well hast thou lesson'd us; this shall we do.   110
     But would it please thee, good Andronicus,
     To send for Lucius, thy thrice-valiant son,
     Who leads towards Rome a band of warlike Goths,
     And bid him come and banquet at thy house,
     When he is here, even at thy solemn feast,   115
     I will bring in the empress and her sons,
     The emperor himself, and all thy foes,
     And at thy mercy shall they stoop and kneel,
     And on them shalt thou ease thy angry heart.
     What says Andronicus to this device?   120
Tit. Marcus, my brother, 'tis sad Titus calls.

Enter MARCUS.

     Go, gentle Marcus, to thy nephew Lucius;
     Thou shalt inquire him out among the Goths:
     Bid him repair to me and bring with him
     Some of the chiefest princes of the Goths;   125
     Bid him encamp his soldiers where they are.
     Tell him, the emperor and the empress too
     Feast at my house, and he shall feast with them:
     This do thou for my love; and so let him,
     As he regards his aged father's life.   130
Marc. This will I do, and soon return again.   [*Exit.*
Tam. Now will I hence about thy business,
     And take my ministers along with me.
Tit. Nay, nay, let Rape and Murder stay with me,
     Or else I'll call my brother back again   135
     And cleave to no revenge but Lucius.
Tam. [*Aside to her sons.*] What say you, boys? will you
          abide with him,
     Whiles I go tell my lord the emperor
     How I have govern'd our determin'd jest?

121. Enter *MARCUS*] so Theobald; after 120 Qq, F.   128. *Feast*]
Feasts F.   131. Exit] om. Qq, F.   136. *Lucius*] *Lucius'* W. S. Walker.
137. [Aside . . . sons.]] Hanmer; om. Qq, F.   *abide*] Q1 (Rowe);
bide Q 2-3, F.

139. *govern'd our determin'd jest*] put
into practice the jest we determined
on.

Yield to his humour, smooth and speak him fair,   140
And tarry with him till I turn again.
Tit. [*Aside.*] I knew them all, though they suppos'd me
     mad,
And will o'erreach them in their own devices,
A pair of cursed hell-hounds and their dame.
Dem. Madam, depart at pleasure; leave us here.   145
Tam. Farewell, Andronicus: Revenge now goes
To lay a complot to betray thy foes.
Tit. I know thou dost; and, sweet Revenge, farewell.

                                        [*Exit Tamora.*

Chi. Tell us, old man, how shall we be employ'd?
Tit. Tut, I have work enough for you to do.   150
Publius, come hither, Caius, and Valentine.

               Enter PUBLIUS *and others.*

Pub. What is your will?
Tit. Know you these two?
Pub. The empress' sons, I take them, Chiron and
     Demetrius.
Tit. Fie, Publius, fie, thou art too much deceiv'd;   155
The one is Murder, and Rape is the other's name;
And therefore bind them, gentle Publius;
Caius and Valentine, lay hands on them.
Oft have you heard me wish for such an hour,
And now I find it: therefore bind them sure,   160
And stop their mouths if they begin to cry.   [*Exit.*
Chi. Villains, forbear, we are the empress' sons.
Pub. And therefore do we what we are commanded;
Stop close their mouths, let them not speak a word;
Is he sure bound? look that you bind them fast.   165

---

140. *Yield*] *Yeede* Q 2 (*Yeeld* with imperfect *l* resembling an apostrophe Q 1).
142. [*Aside.*]] Rowe, om. Qq, F.   *knew . . . suppos'd*] *know . . . suppose*
Q 2-3, F.   144. *dame*] *Dam* Q 3, F.   148. Exit Tamora.] Capell
(after 147 Rowe); om. Qq, F.   150 *Tut*] *But* Q 3.   152. Enter
. . . others] Rowe substantially; om. Qq, F.   154. *and*] Theobald; om.
Qq, F.   156. *and*] om. Q2-3, F.   161. om. F (but with comma at end of
160).   Exit] Rowe; om. Qq, F.   165. *fast.*] *fast.* Exeunt. F.

140. *smooth*] See on IV. iv. 96.   144. *dame*] See on V. i. 27.
speak him fair] humour him.   163. *therefore*] for that very reason.

Enter TITUS ANDRONICUS *with a knife, and* LAVINIA *with a basin.*

Tit. Come, come, Lavinia; look, thy foes are bound.
Sirs, stop their mouths, let them not speak to me,
But let them hear what fearful words I utter.
O villains, Chiron and Demetrius,
Here stands the spring whom you have stain'd with
    mud,   170
This goodly summer with your winter mix'd:
You kill'd her husband, and for that vild fault
Two of her brothers were condemn'd to death,
My hand cut off and made a merry jest:
Both her sweet hands, her tongue, and that more dear   175
Than hands or tongue, her spotless chastity,
Inhuman traitors, you constrain'd and forc'd.
What would you say if I should let you speak?
Villains, for shame you could not beg for grace.
Hark, wretches, how I mean to martyr you.   180
This one hand yet is left to cut your throats,
Whiles that Lavinia 'tween her stumps doth hold
The basin that receives your guilty blood.
You know your mother means to feast with me,
And calls herself Revenge, and thinks me mad.   185
Hark, villains, I will grind your bones to dust,
And with your blood and it I'll make a paste,
And of the paste a coffin I will rear,
And make two pasties of your shameful heads,
And bid that strumpet, your unhallowed dam,   190

182. *Whiles*] *Whilst* Q 2-3, F.

170. *spring . . . mud*] Parrott, p. 35, cites *Lucr.* 577 : "Mud not the fountain that gave drink to thee," noting that in both passages the words are addressed to a ravisher (or would-be ravisher) and refer to his victim. The *Lucr.* lines refer more specifically to ingratitude, and I believe they combine a recollection of the *Titus* line with a recollection of Southwell's *St. Peter's Complaint*, st. 18, which ends : "But I, that drunk the drops of heavenly flud, | Bemyr'd the Giver with returning mud." On the relationship between Southwell and *Lucr.*, see Fr. Christopher Devlin in *The Month*, Sept. 1950. Tilley, D 345, quotes "Cast no dirt into the well that has given you water" as a proverb first recorded by Ray in 1678.

188. *coffin*] The normal word for a pie-crust, not a sinister metaphor, though perhaps with double sense.

Like to the earth swallow her own increase.
This is the feast that I have bid her to,
And this the banket she shall surfeit on;
For worse than Philomel you us'd my daughter,
And worse than Progne I will be reveng'd.   195
And now prepare your throats—Lavinia, come,
Receive the blood: and when that they are dead,
Let me go grind their bones to powder small,
And with this hateful liquor temper it,
And in that paste let their vile heads be bak'd.   200
Come, come, be every one officious
To make this banket, which I wish may prove
More stern and bloody than the Centaurs' feast.

> [*He cuts their throats.*

So, now bring them in, for I'll play the cook,
And see them ready against their mother comes.   205

> [*Exeunt.*

SCENE III.

Enter Lucius, Marcus, *and the Goths, with* Aaron,
prisoner.

Luc. Uncle Marcus, since 'tis my father's mind
     That I repair to Rome, I am content.
Goth. And ours with thine, befall what fortune will.

---

191. *own*] om. F.   193. *banket*] *banquet* Q 2-3, F.   200. *vile*] *vilde*
Q 3; *vil'd* F.   202. *may*] *might* F.   204. *I'll*] *I will* W. S. Walker.
206. *against*] *gainst* F.

Scene III

Scene III.] Capell; om. Qq, F.   with *Aaron*, prisoner] Rowe; om. Qq, F.

191. *Like . . . increase*] See on II.
iii. 239.

194-5. *Philomel . . . Progne*] See
on II. iv. 26.

199. *temper*] moisten.

201. *officious*] busy, without the
hostile modern implication.

203. *Centaurs' feast*] A battle between the Centaurs and the Lapithae
followed the marriage of Pirithous and
Hippodamia : see, amongst other
sources, Ovid, *Met.* XII. 210 ff.

204. *So . . . cook*] With normal

scansion, we get an inappropriate
stress on *them*. Walker, followed by
H. T. Price (*English Institute Essays,
1947*, p. 152), and by Alexander,
may be right in treating *So* as
extrametrical and reading *I will*.

205. *against*] by the time that.

Scene III

3. *ours*] Prob. " our mind " from
l. 1 (Delius) rather than (Malone)
" our content," supplied out of adj.
" content " in l. 2.

Luc. Good uncle, take you in this barbarous Moor,
This ravenous tiger, this accursed devil;   5
Let him receive no sust'nance, fetter him,
Till he be brought unto the empress' face,
For testimony of her foul proceedings:
And see the ambush of our friends be strong;
I fear the emperor means no good to us.   10
Aar. Some devil whisper curses in my ear,
And prompt me that my tongue may utter forth
The venomous malice of my swelling heart!
Luc. Away, inhuman dog, unhallowed slave!
Sirs, help our uncle to convey him in.   15
                              [*Exeunt Goths with Aaron.*
The trumpets show the emperor is at hand.

Sound trumpets.   Enter Emperor and Empress, with ÆMILIUS,
Tribunes and others.

Sat. What, hath the firmament mo suns than one?
Luc. What boots it thee to call thyself a sun?
Marc. Rome's emperor, and nephew, break the parle;
These quarrels must be quietly debated: 20
The feast is ready which the careful Titus
Hath ordain'd to an honourable end,

7. *empress*'] Q 1-2 (*Empresse*), Malone; *Emperours* Q 3; *Emperous* F.
11. Aar.] Moore. Qq.   *my*] Q 1, F; *mine* Q 2-3.   15. Exeunt . . . Aaron.]
Rowe (after 14); om. Qq, F; F adds Flourish at end of this line.   16.
ÆMILIUS,] Dyce; om. Qq, F.   17. Sat.] King. Qq.   *mo*] *more* F.
22. *ordain'd*] ordained Q 3, F.

13. *The . . . heart*] Verity quotes
1H6 III. i. 26 : " From envious malice
of thy swelling heart," and Wilson
[Peele], *Alcazar* II. iii. 3. Add
(Robertson) *Arden of Feversham* I.
327 : " the rancorous venome of thy
mis-swolne hart."

17. *mo*] more, usually of number.
From O.E. *ma*, originally an adverb
constructed with genitive, like Latin
plus. Tilley S992 compares *1H4*
v. iv. 65 : " Two stars keep not their
motion in one sphere," and quotes
Erasmus, *Similia* 608B : " Ut plures
apparere Soles prodigium est : Ita

plures esse Monarchas aut Impera-
tores," and Young, *Civile Conversation*
(1586) : " Two kinges in one
kingdome doe not agree well
together." Sidney plays on the
notion in some verses in the *Arcadia*
(*Works*, ed. Feuillerat, II. 38).

19. *break*] interrupt; see Add. Notes.
21. *careful*] Probably " afflicted
with cares " rather than " taking
trouble." There might be an ironic
pun, though it could only be Shakespeare's irony, not Marcus's, as he
does not know the special kind of care
that Titus has taken.

For peace, for love, for league, and good to Rome:
Please you, therefore, draw nigh, and take your places.
Sat. Marcus, we will.   25

Trumpets sounding, enter TITUS, *like a cook, placing the dishes, and*
LAVINIA, *with a veil over her face.*

Tit. Welcome, my lord; welcome, dread queen;
Welcome, ye warlike Goths; welcome Lucius;
And welcome, all: although the cheer be poor,
'Twill fill your stomachs; please you eat of it.
Sat. Why art thou thus attir'd, Andronicus?   30
Tit. Because I would be sure to have all well
To entertain your highness and your empress.
Tam. We are beholding to you, good Andronicus.
Tit. And if your highness knew my heart, you were.
My lord the emperor, resolve me this: 35
Was it well done of rash Virginius
To slay his daughter with his own right hand,
Because she was enforc'd, stain'd, and deflow'r'd?

25. Sat.] King. Q 1; Empe. Q 2.   *will.*] *will.* Hoboyes. A Table
brought in. F.   Trumpets sounding, enter] Sound trumpets, enter
(euter Q 2) Q 2-3; Enter F.   dishes] meate on the table Q 2-3, F.
26. *lord*] *gracious Lord* Q 2-3, F.   28. *all:*] *all* Q 1-2; *all,* Q 3.
30. Sat.] King. Q 1-2 (so 39, 41, 48, 53 (Q 3), 59).   *attir'd*] *attired* Qq.

33. *beholding*] See on 1. i. 396.

36-8. *Was* . . . *deflow'r'd?*] A difficult passage. Virginius killed his
daughter to protect her from being
ravished, and this seems to be implied
in ll. 50-2 : Titus has *more* reason
than Virginius to kill his daughter
because she (Lavinia) has actually
been ravished. Wilson thinks that
Shakespeare here revised, and got
wrong, a Peele original. I think
Delius's *Before* in l. 38 may be right.
The corruption could have occurred
either accidentally, by anticipation of
l. 41, *or* deliberately by someone who
took for granted that ll. 41-2 meant
that the girl had actually undergone
her shame and tampered with l. 38
to make it fit. This latter explanation would imply more editorial
attention in Q 1 than seems likely.

Baildon's view that l. 38 may be an
interpolation is improbable in view
of the probable "foul papers"
origin of the text. A final com-
plication is introduced by Robertson's
reference (*Introduction to the Study of the
Shakespeare Canon*, pp. 154-5) to the
play attributed to Chapman, *Alphonsus
Emperor of Germany* (in *Tragedies of
George Chapman*, ed. Parrott) IV. iii. 64.
There the Duke, who believes his
daughter has been dishonoured, says:
" Then, like Virginius, will I kill
my child." Robertson assumes (*a*)
that the parallel is intended to be
perfect, (*b*) that Peele wrote *Alphonsus*
—therefore also wrote this passage
of *Titus*. But (*b*) is improbable,
while (*a*) is uncertain, and even if it
is right, the author of *Alphonsus*
might be recalling *Titus*.

Sat. It was, Andronicus.

Tit. Your reason, mighty lord?   40

Sat. Because the girl should not survive her shame,
And by her presence still renew his sorrows.

Tit. A reason mighty, strong, and effectual;
A pattern, president, and lively warrant
For me, most wretched, to perform the like.   45
Die, die, Lavinia, and thy shame with thee;
And with thy shame thy father's sorrow die!

[*He kills her.*

Sat. What hast thou done, unnatural and unkind?

Tit. Kill'd her for whom my tears have made me blind.
I am as woeful as Virginius was,   50
And have a thousand times more cause than he
To do this outrage: and it now is done.

Sat. What, was she ravish'd? tell who did the deed.

Tit. Will't please you eat? will't please your highness
feed?

43. *and*] om. Hanmer.   47. He kills her.] om. Q 1-2.   48. *thou*]
om. F.   52. om. F.   *now is*] *is now* Q 3.

41. *Because . . . shame*] Perhaps, simply, "because it was not right that she should survive," but I suspect, rather, an elliptical construction. Titus has asked "why do you say he was right" and Saturninus answers : [He was right because he acted] in order that, etc. Such a telescoping is facilitated by the double sense of "because" in Elizabethan English. A writer can pass from one to the other in the same sentence : cf. Sidney's Dedication of *Arcadia* (ed. Feuillerat, p. 4) : "this say I, because it may be ever so; or to say better, because it will be ever so." A passage in Shakespeare very similar to the present is *1H6* III. i. 36-7 : "It is not that that hath incens'd the duke : | It is because no man should sway but he," where we move from cause in the first line to purpose in the second. *N.E.D.*, Schmidt, Onions and Franz fail to quote Shakespearian instances of "because" = in order that. Abbott (§ 117) quotes *2H6* III. ii.

99-100, to which add *Troil.* III. ii. 216-18. The easy transition from one sense of *because* to the other is also illustrated in Jonson, *Neptune's Triumph* 228-9, and in Dekker, *Foure Birds of Noah's Arke* (1609), sig. A5 (ed. F.P. Wilson, pp. 9-10) : "Nothing that is set downe is tedious, because I had a care of thy memorie. Nothing is done twice, because thou mayst take delight in them."

43. *and*] Hanmer's deletion of this may well be right.

44. *president*] precedent; the most usual Shakespearian spelling with this meaning.

lively] striking (Wilson); Greg, *R.E.S.* 1 (1925), 477 notes that this is *N.E.D.*'s sense 4c, the first quotation for which postdates *Titus* but illustrates it well : "they shew the Indians their blind errors, by lively and plain reasons" (E. Grimstone, *D'Acosta's Hist. Indies*, 1604). There is perhaps play on the literal sense "living" (cf. III. i. 105), to which On. refers this passage.

Tam. Why hast thou slain thine only daughter thus?   55
Tit. Not I; 'twas Chiron and Demetrius:
    They ravish'd her, and cut away her tongue;
    And they, 'twas they, that did her all this wrong.
Sat. Go fetch them hither to us presently.
Tit. Why, there they are, both baked in this pie;   60
    Whereof their mother daintily hath fed,
    Eating the flesh that she herself hath bred.
    'Tis true, 'tis true; witness my knife's sharp point.
                     [*He stabs the Empress.*
Sat. Die, frantic wretch, for this accursed deed.
                     [*Kills Titus.*
Luc. Can the son's eye behold his father bleed?   65
    There's meed for meed, death for a deadly deed.
                     [*Kills Saturninus.*
Marc. You sad-fac'd men, people and sons of Rome,
    By uproars sever'd, as a flight of fowl
    Scatter'd by winds and high tempestuous gusts,
    O, let me teach you how to knit again   70

---

55. *thus*] om. Q 3 (with no stop after *daughter*), F.   60. *are, both*]
Grey; *are both* Q 1; *are both*, Q 2-3, F.   *this*] *that* Q 2-3, F.   64. Sat.]
Emperour. Q 1; Empe. Q 2-3.   Kills Titus] Rowe substantially; om.
Qq, F.   66. Kills Saturninus] Rowe substantially; om. Qq, F.   68.
as] *like* Q 3, F.   69. *Scatter'd*] *Scattered* Q 3, F.   *tempestuous*] *tempestious* Q 2-3.

---

59. *presently*] immediately.
60. *are, both*] I credit this punctuation to Zachary Grey since it appears
(but without comment) in his
Notes on Shakespeare (1754), II. 136.
Professor Alexander adopts it and it
seems to me rhythmically superior to
the Q 2 punctuation.
    this] See Introduction, p. xiii.
66. *Kills Saturninus*] It has been
customary since Capell to send
" Lucius, Marcus and others " to the
upper stage at this point, and bring
them down again at l. 145. This
is no doubt based on ll. 130 ff.
I am not convinced that those lines
require the speaker and his friends
to be visibly higher than their
audience : on the dangers of in-
ference to staging from dialogue

interpreted too naturalistically, see
G. F. Reynolds, *J.E.G.P.* 42 (1943),
124. Neither ascent nor descent is
here covered by dialogue, as is usual:
cf. G. F. Reynolds, *The Staging of
Elizabethan Plays* (New York, 1940),
pp. 99-100; at v. ii. 70 (*possibly* a
descent) Titus has eleven lines for
coming down. If it is felt that
ll. 130 ff. demand some sort of
raised position, one might suggest a
movable scaffolding. There is
evidence for the existence of this,
though its nature is obscure : cf.
W. Smith, *R.E.S.* n.s. 2 (1951),
22-6, especially the reference to
Troil. I. ii. 191-5 : " Shall we stand
up here? . . . there's an excellent
place; here we may see most
bravely."

This scattered corn into one mutual sheaf,
These broken limbs again into one body;
Lest Rome herself be bane unto herself,
And she whom mighty kingdoms cur'sy to,
Like a forlorn and desperate castaway,   75
Do shameful execution on herself.
But if my frosty signs and chaps of age,
Grave witnesses of true experience,
Cannot induce you to attend my words,
Speak, Rome's dear friend, as erst our ancestor,   80
When with his solemn tongue he did discourse
To love-sick Dido's sad-attending ear
The story of that baleful burning night
When subtle Greeks surpris'd King Priam's Troy.
Tell us what Sinon hath bewitch'd our ears,   85
Or who hath brought the fatal engine in
That gives our Troy, our Rome, the civil wound.
My heart is not compact of flint nor steel,
Nor can I utter all our bitter grief,

71. *scattered*] *scattred* Q 2-3, F.   72-3. *body; Lest*] Capell; *bodie.*
Romane Lord. *Let* Qq; *body.* Goth. *Let* F.   74. *cur'sy*] Qq, F (*cursie*);
curtsie F 3.   75. *castaway*] *cast away* Qq.   82. *sad-attending*] W. S.
Walker; *sad attending* Qq, F.   83. *baleful burning*] *baleful-burning* W. S.
Walker.

71. *mutual sheaf*] a sheaf whose
parts belong together (Delius, quoting
Ant. I. i. 37 : " such a mutual pair ").
Not quite the same sense as in l. 134.

72. *broken limbs*] Cf. Seneca, *Thyestes*
432-3 : " lacerae domus | componit
artus."

73. *Lest*] Capell's emendation
is in itself satisfactory, but does
not explain everything. Wilson
suggests that " 'Romane Lord' was
Shakespeare's heading to a marginal
addition, or slip, which he intended
to be tacked on to Marcus's lines
67-72." But he would surely never
have referred to Marcus in such an
impersonal fashion. If the lines were
on a loose sheet, they most likely had
no heading at all. *bane*] destroyer.

74. *cur'sy*] this phonetic spelling
(cf. Wyld, p. 302) seems worth
preserving.

77. *frosty . . . chaps*] white hair
and cracks in the skin.

80. *ancestor*] Aeneas.

82. *sad-attending*] seriously attending.

85. *Sinon*] whose false story in-
duced the Trojans to admit the
wooden horse.

86. *fatal engine*] Virgil's *fatalis
machina* (*Aen.* II. 237), as J. A. K.
Thomson points out, *Shakespeare and
the Classics* (1952), p. 56. J. M.
Robertson, *Introduction to the Study of
the Shakespeare Canon* (1924), p. 183,
cites some rather striking parallels
to this passage in Peele's *Tale of Troy*
(1589), 400 ff.

87. *civil*] inflicted in civil war; cf.
Rom. Prol. 4. : " Where civil blood
makes civil hands unclean."

88. *compact*] composed. See on I.
i. 462, and cf. *MND.* v. i. 8 : " of
imagination all compact."

But floods of tears will drown my oratory,   90
And break my utt'rance, even in the time
When it should move ye to attend me most,
And force you to commiseration.
Here's Rome's young captain, let him tell the tale,
While I stand by and weep to hear him speak.   95
Luc. Then, gracious auditory, be it known to you,
That Chiron and the damn'd Demetrius
Were they that murdered our emperor's brother;
And they it were that ravished our sister.
For their fell faults our brothers were beheaded,   100
Our father's tears despis'd, and basely cozen'd
Of that true hand that fought Rome's quarrel out
And sent her enemies unto the grave.
Lastly, myself unkindly banished,
The gates shut on me, and turn'd weeping out,   105
To beg relief among Rome's enemies;
Who drown'd their enmity in my true tears,
And op'd their arms to embrace me as a friend:
I am the turn'd forth, be it known to you,
That have preserv'd her welfare in my blood   110
And from her bosom took the enemy's point,
Sheathing the steel in my advent'rous body.
Alas, you know I am no vaunter, I;

91. *my*] *my very* Q 3, F.   92. *ye*] *you* Q 2-3, F.   93. *And force you to*]
Lending your kind (F adds *hand*) Q 2-3, F.   94. *Here's Rome's young*] *Here is
a* (*our* W. S. Walker) Q 2-3, F.   95. *While I stand by*] *Your harts will throb*
Q 2-3, F.   96. *Then*] *This* F.   *gracious*] *noble* Q 2-3, F.   97. *Chiron
and the damn'd*] *cursed Chiron and* Q 2-3, F.   98. *murdered*] Rowe ; *murdred*
Qq, F.   100. *faults*] *fault* Hudson.   109. *I*] *And* (*and* Q 3) *I* Q 3, F.
the] om. F.   *turn'd*] F 4 ; *turned* Qq, F.

93-7. *And . . . Demetrius*] See
Introduction, p. xiii. In l. 94
Walker (and Dyce who followed him)
deserves credit for not acquiescing in
the traditional text.

98. *murdered*] Qq, F's *murdred* cannot represent an alternative pronunciation, so I have normalized.

99. *they it were*] For this agreement
of the verb with the complement instead of the subject, already archaic
at this time, see *N.E.D.* *it*, 2.

100. *faults*] *Fault* would be more
natural in modern English, but ap-

parently the share of the guilt
belonging to each is thought of
separately (cf. on III. i. 238). But the
emendation may be correct : cf.
II. iii. 291.

101. *cozen'd*] cheated. According
to sense this goes with *father*. In l.
105, *turn'd* is in a similar loose
construction.

104. *unkindly*] unnaturally (this is
at least part of the sense : cf. II. i. 116
for the noun *kind*).

112. *advent'rous*] See on II. iii. 285.

My scars can witness, dumb although they are,
That my report is just and full of truth.   115
But soft, methinks I do digress too much,
Citing my worthless praise: O, pardon me;
For when no friends are by, men praise themselves.
Marc. Now is my turn to speak.   Behold the child;
Of this was Tamora delivered,   120
The issue of an irreligious Moor,
Chief architect and plotter of these woes.
The villain is alive in Titus' house,
And as he is to witness, this is true.
Now judge what cause had Titus to revenge   125
These wrongs unspeakable, past patience,
Or more than any living man could bear.
Now have you heard the truth: what say you, Romans?
Have we done aught amiss, show us wherein,
And, from the place where you behold us pleading, 130
The poor remainder of Andronici
Will hand in hand all headlong hurl ourselves,
And on the ragged stones beat forth our souls,

119. *the*] *this* Q 3, F.   124. *And . . . is to witness,*] Maxwell; *And . . .*
is to witnes Qq; *And . . . is, to witnesse* F ; *Damn'd . . . is, to witness* Theobald.
true.] *true,* Qq.   125. *cause*] F 4; *course* Qq, F.   *revenge*] *reuenge.*
Q 1-2.   127. *bear.*] *beare,* Q 1.   128. *have you*] *you haue* Q 2-3, F.
truth:] *truth.* Wilson; *truth,* Qq, F.   129. *amiss,*] *amisse?* Q 3, F.
130. *pleading*] *now* Q 2-3, F.   131. *Andronici*] *Andronicie* Qq.   132.
hurl ourselves] *cast vs downe* Q 2-3, F.   133. *souls*] *braines* Q 2-3, F.

118. *when . . . themselves*] O.D.E.P.
p. 447 and Tilley N117 cite from
Barclay's *Ship of Fools* (1509) : " Men
. . . | In theyr olde prouerbes often
comprehende | That he that is among
shrewyd neyghbours | May his
owne dedes laufully commende."

124. *And . . . true*] I think these
are the only changes required in the
Q text. It could, as Delius saw, be
construed without any changes,
making " As he is to witness [that]
this is true " subordinate to " Now
judge, etc." But " Now judge "
seems to begin a new sentence—
he has given all the facts and now he
asks for a verdict—and the Q
punctuation is certainly faulty at the
end of ll. 125 and 127. With the

text printed, the meaning is *either* " as
he is to witness " exactly as in modern
English, *or*, if this seems a little tame,
the *as* may be the *as* of asseveration,
= " as surely as." A comparable
(though not closely similar) line is
R2 III. iii. 119 : " This swears he, as
he is a prince, is just." Theobald's
forcible-feeble *Damn'd* has been sur-
prisingly popular, but is not ade-
quately supported by comparing
Oth. I. ii. 63 : " Damn'd as thou
art," though both are applied to
Moors. For misplaced ingenuity,
Kellner's *Audashious* (for *And as he is*)
is worth mentioning.

130-33. *And . . . souls*] See Introduction, p. xiii.

133. *ragged*] See on II. iii. 230.

And make a mutual closure of our house.
Speak, Romans, speak, and if you say we shall,   135
Lo, hand in hand, Lucius and I will fall.

Æmil. Come, come, thou reverent man of Rome,
And bring our emperor gently in thy hand,
Lucius our emperor; for well I know
The common voice do cry it shall be so.   140

All. Lucius, all hail, Rome's royal emperor!

Marc. [*To Attendants.*] Go, go into old Titus' sorrowful
house,
And hither hale that misbelieving Moor,
To be adjudg'd some direful slaught'ring death,
As punishment for his most wicked life.   145

[*Exeunt Attendants.*

All. Lucius, all hail, Rome's gracious governor!

Luc. Thanks, gentle Romans: may I govern so,
To heal Rome's harms, and wipe away her woe.
But, gentle people, give me aim awhile,

---

137. *Come, come,*] *Come, Marcus, come,* Maxwell conj.   141. All.] Rom.
Capell (Omnes Ravenscroft); Marcus. Qq; Mar. F.   142. Marc. [To
Attendants]] Capell; om. Qq, F.   144. *adjudg'd*] *adiudge* Q 1-2.   *direful
slaught'ring*] *direful-slaught'ring* W. S. Walker.   *slaught'ring*] *slaughtering* F.
145. Exeunt Attendants.] Camb.; om. Qq, F.   146. All.] Rom. Capell;
om. Qq, F.   *Rome's*] Q 1 (Rowe); *to Romes* Q 2-3, F.

---

134. *mutual closure*] common end. This meaning of *mutual*, " now regarded as incorrect," is " the commonest Shakespearian sense " (On.).

137. *Come, come*] An odd repetition, though cf. l. 160. For my conjecture, cf. IV. iii. 1, and III. i. 143 : " Mark, Marcus, mark." It is conceivable that *Marcus* was abbreviated to M. in the MS. and that the compositor did not know what to make of it. *reverent*] See on II. iii. 296.

141. All] Knight's argument that here and at l. 146 " Marcus is the tribune of the people, and speaks authoritatively what ' the common voice ' has required " is unconvincing, with its sharp transition from l. 141 to l. 142. Capell had already written : " the pretence that Marcus speaks for them is indeed foolish, and will never be set up by persons of understanding." More likely the change of speaker at both points was inadequately indicated in the MS., perhaps only by a dash, and the compositor had to do his best.

149. *give me aim*] The literal meaning of this idiom is (On.) " to guide someone in his aim by informing him of the result of a preceding shot," but something less specific is required here, and a number of passages in Dekker give a clue. " The English, the Dutch, and the Spanish, stoode aloofe

For nature puts me to a heavy task.   150
Stand all aloof; but, uncle, draw you near
To shed obsequious tears upon this trunk.
O, take this warm kiss on thy pale cold lips,
These sorrowful drops upon thy blood-stain'd face,
The last true duties of thy noble son.   155

Marc. Tear for tear and loving kiss for kiss
Thy brother Marcus tenders on thy lips:
O, were the sum of these that I should pay
Countless and infinite, yet would I pay them.

Luc. Come hither, boy; come, come and learn of us   160
To melt in showers: thy grandsire lov'd thee well:
Many a time he danc'd thee on his knee,
Sung thee asleep, his loving breast thy pillow;
Many a story hath he told to thee,
And bid thee bear his pretty tales in mind,   165
And talk of them when he was dead and gone.

Marc. How many thousand times hath these poor lips,
When they were living, warm'd themselves on
thine!
O now, sweet boy, give them their latest kiss.

---

153. *pale cold*] *pale-cold* W. S. Walker.   154. *blood-stain'd*] F 3 ; *blood slaine* Q 1-2 ; *bloud-slaine* Q 3, F.   163. *Sung*] *Song* Q 1.   164. *story*] *matter* Q 2-3, F.   165-9. *Meete and agreeing with thine infancie,* | *In that respect then, like a louing child,* (*child.* Q 2) | *Shed yet some small drops from thy tender spring,* | *Because kind nature doth require it so,* | *Friends should associate friends in grief and woe.* Q 2-3, F.

and gaue ayme, whilst thou shotst arrowes vpright, that fell vpon thine owne head " (*The Seven Deadly Sins of London*, ed. H. Brett-Smith, p. 9) ; " France, Spaine, and Belgia, lift vp their heads, preparing to do asmuch for *England* by giuing ayme, whilst she shot arrowes at her owne brest " (*Plague Pamphlets*, ed. F. P. Wilson, p. 20) ; " *England* hath stood and giuen aime, when Arrowes were shot into all our [? their *or* other] bosomes " (*ibid*, p. 142) ; " they that are ful of coyne, *draw* : they that haue little, stand by & giue *ayme* " (*Lanthorn and Candlelight*, 1608, sig. D2). In all these passages (I owe

the second and fourth to Professor F. P. Wilson) the sense seems weakened to little more than " encourage," which would suit the *Titus* passage well. If this is so, emendations, none of them satisfactory, may be ignored, as may Schmidt's vague paraphrase : " give room and scope to his thoughts."

150. *puts me to*] imposes on me.

152. *obsequious*] dutiful towards the dead, with no unfavourable implication.

164-9. *Many . . . kiss*] See Introduction, p. xiii.

167. *hath*] See on II. iv. 17.

M

Bid him farewell; commit him to the grave;   170
Do them that kindness, and take leave of them.

Boy. O grandsire, grandsire, ev'n with all my heart
Would I were dead, so you did live again !
O lord, I cannot speak to him for weeping;
My tears will choke me if I ope my mouth.   175

Re-enter Attendants, with AARON.

Æmil. You sad Andronici, have done with woes:
Give sentence on this execrable wretch
That hath been breeder of these dire events.

Luc. Set him breast-deep in earth, and famish him;
There let him stand and rave and cry for food.   180
If any one relieves or pities him,
For the offence he dies.   This is our doom.
Some stay to see him fast'ned in the earth.

Aar. Ah, why should wrath be mute, and fury dumb?
I am no baby, I, that with base prayers   185
I should repent the evils I have done;
Ten thousand worse than ever yet I did
Would I perform, if I might have my will.
If one good deed in all my life I did,
I do repent it from my very soul.   190

Luc. Some loving friends convey the emperor hence,
And give him burial in his fathers' grave.
My father and Lavinia shall forthwith
Be closed in our household's monument.
As for that ravenous tiger, Tamora,   195

171. *them . . . them*] Qq; *him . . . him* F.   172. Boy.] Puer. Qq.   175.
Re-enter . . . *AARON*] Rowe (substantially); om. Qq. F.   176. Æmil.]
Dyce (Ravenscroft); Romane. Q 1; Romaine. Q 2-3; Romans. F.   184.
Ah] O F.   192. *fathers'*] Anon. (in Camb.); *fathers* Qq, F; *father's* Rowe.
195. *ravenous*] Q 1 (Collier MS.); *hainous* Q 2-3, F.

171. *them . . . them*] With Alexander
and Sisson, I now revert to Q,
treating as parenthetic l. 170 (which
I still think may have been an afterthought, to take the place of l. 171,
or to follow it).

173. *so*] See on II. i. 102.

176. Æmil.] It seems most unlikely that an otherwise mute character should make this speech.   On the
other hand, if it is meant for Æmilius,
the vague reference is exactly what

we expect in this sort of text (see on
I. i. 299).   Hence I follow Dyce
with some confidence.

184-90. *Ah . . . soul*] Recalls v.
i. 124-44 (Wilson).

192. *fathers'*] More probable than
father's.   What is important is that
it is the ancestral tomb.

195. *ravenous*] One of the few correct guesses attributed by Collier to
his mythical MS.; no doubt from l. 5

No funeral rite, nor man in mourning weed,
No mournful bell shall ring her burial;
But throw her forth to beasts and birds to prey.
Her life was beastly and devoid of pity;
And being dead, let birds on her take pity. 200

[*Exeunt.*

Finis the Tragedy of Titus Andronicus.

196. *rite*] *right* Q 1-2. *mourning*] *mournefull* Q 3, F. *weed*] *weeds* Q 2-3, F.
198. *to prey*] *of prey* F. 199. *beastly*] *Beast-like* F. 200. *dead . . . pity*]
so, shall haue like want of pitty Q 2-3, F. After this line Q 2-3, F add: *See
iustice done on Aron that damn'd Moore,* | *By (From F) whom our heauie haps had
their beginning:* | *Then (Than Q 2) afterwards to order well the state,* | *That like
euents may nere it ruinate.* Exeunt.] om. Q 2-3. the Tragedy of Titus
Andronicus] om. Q 2-3, F.

196. *No . . . rite*] Not, strictly, an
appropriate subject to *shall ring*, but
the transition through *man . . . weed*
makes the expression natural. For
the Q 1-2 spelling *right* see on I.
i. 78.

198. *to prey*] With Neilson and Hill,
I see no objection to this in the sense
" for them to prey on." For what
may be an echo in *Troublesome Reign
of King John,* see Introduction,
p. xxiii.

APPENDIX

(Contributed by Harold F. Brooks)

(*a*) Ravenscroft on *Titus*,[1] and Cowley on the posthumous Folio editions of Beaumont and Fletcher, Jonson, and Shakespeare.

When Ravenscroft calls *Titus* " rather a heap of Rubbish than a Structure," it is pretty clear that he is remembering the passage where Cowley, in 1656, censured what he regarded as the uncritical inclusiveness of posthumous collected editions like the First Folio Shakespeare.[2] Posthumous editions of poets, above all, Cowley complains are

> stuffed out, either with counterfeit pieces, . . . or with such, which though of their own *Coyn*, they would have called in themselves for the baseness of the Alloy; whether this proceed from the indiscretion of their *Friends*, who think a vast heap of Stones or Rubbish a better Monument than a little *Tomb* of *Marble*, or by the unworthy avarice of some *Stationers*, who are content to diminish the value of the Author, so they may encrease the price of the Book. . . . This has been the case with *Shakespeare*, *Fletcher*, *Jonson*, and many others, part of whose Poems I should take the boldness to prune and lop away, if the care of replanting them in print did belong to me; neither would I make any scruple to cut off from some the unnecessary yong *Suckers*, and from others the old withered Branches.[3]

The passage was most likely brought to Ravenscroft's mind by a citation of part of it in Joseph Hindmarsh's " Advertisement " to the *Remains* of John Oldham, 1684; Hindmarsh published Ravenscroft's *Titus*;[4] and a second edition of the *Remains*, both in 1687. Ravenscroft's actual echo is not from the *Remains*, but apparently from Cowley at first hand.[5]

[1] See above, p. xxi, and R. F. Hill in *Shakespeare Survey*, 10 (1957), 70, n. 7.

[2] See p. 132, n. 1 below.

[3] Abraham Cowley, *Poems*, 1656, preface; repr. *Critical Essays of the 17th Century*, ed. J. E. Spingarn, II. 78 f.

[4] Also his *London Cuckolds*, 1682, 1688; *Dame Dobson*, 1684; and the Prologue and Epilogue to *Dame Dobson*, s. sh. fol., 1683.

[5] In the *Remains* " heap of Rubbish " is not quoted: Hindmarsh dissociates himself from those publishers who " (as the incomparable Mr. *Cowley* has exprest it) think a rude heap of ill-placed Stones a better Monument than a neat Tomb of Marble." Dryden had previously adopted the phrase in justifying (like Ravenscroft) an adaptation from Shakespeare: cf. *Troilus and Cressida*, preface (*Essays*, ed. W. P. Ker, I. 204): " I undertook to remove that

No doubt he saw, or chose to see, in *Titus*, an instance not only of the inferior but also of the unauthentic work which Cowley had stigmatised in his preface; and he may have been reading Cowley correctly. Yet it is not certain that Cowley meant to say that anything spurious had been included in the Shakespeare First or Second Folio.[1] A collected edition, he contends, should admit neither the unauthentic, nor the inferior (for example, the juvenile or the senile). The reference to senile work must be specifically to Jonson; to what Dryden called " his dotages ":[2] and there is nothing unauthentic in the 1640 Folio, nor yet juvenile; it follows Jonson's own well-considered edition of 1616 in excluding his immature comedy, *The Case is Altered*.[3] If only one of Cowley's objections is aimed at the posthumous Jonson Folio, the same may hold good for Shakespeare. The Beaumont and Fletcher Folio of 1647 notoriously contained, without identifying them, Fletcher's collaborations with others besides Beaumont—Sir Aston Cockayne protested at the wrong done to both authors, and to Massinger also, by the want of proper attributions.[4] This uncertainty in which the Fletcher canon was left may perhaps be the sole point concerning the dramatists named by Cowley to which his general stricture about " counterfeit pieces " has relevance. When he comes to these dramatists in particular, he thinks chiefly of lopping away their senilia and juvenilia. Subsequently, some of Fletcher's plays were classed by Dryden as immature;[5] and Dryden may have been personally acquainted

heap of rubbish under which many excellent thoughts lay wholly buried." Ravenscroft probably knew this passage too: but his " structure " corresponds to Cowley's " Monument," and, as antithesis to " heap," with Cowley's " Tomb of Marble."

[1] It was not till the second issue of the Third, 1664, that *Pericles* and six apocryphal plays were added.

[2] *Essays, ed. cit.* I. 81.

[3] *Ben Jonson*, ed. Herford and Simpson, IX. 14, 89-91, 104-6. Two spurious pieces appeared in the 1640 collections of his poems (*ibid.* 126, 128), but I doubt whether Cowley was thinking of those.

[4] His authorities were Massinger himself, and Cotton: cf. " To my Cousin Mr. Charles Cotton, " and " To Mr. Humphry Mosley and Mr. Humphrey Robinson " (the publishers of the Folio): *Poems*, 1662, pp. 91, 217; cf. p. 186. Cockayne's occasional poems witness to epistolary and conversational discussion.

[5]   Your *Ben* and *Fletcher*, in their first young flight
        Did no *Volpone*, no *Arbaces* write.

Prologue to *Circe*, 1677 ll. 11 f.), cf. *Essays, ed. cit.* I. 81 : " The first play that brought Fletcher and [Beaumont] in esteem was their *Philaster*, for before that, they had written two or three very unsuccessfully."

with Cowley's views.[1] It is to immaturity, again, that Dryden attributes what he considers inferior plays by Shakespeare: *Pericles*, History plays, *Troilus and Cressida*.[2] In censuring the Shakespeare Folio, it may have been the inclusion of immature, not of spurious pieces, that Cowley had in mind. But one cannot be sure.

One cannot be sure, either, of the bearing of Ravenscroft's Cowleian reminiscence upon his denial of *Titus* to Shakespeare. It allows us to argue that part of the shaky support he relied on was the statement he read into Cowley that the Folio included " counterfeit pieces." Alternatively, however, it allows us to argue that far from misreading Cowley he had indeed the support of a complaint against the canon of the Folio, made thirty years before the date of his own Address: thirty years nearer to Shakespeare's lifetime.[3] Yet although, so far as I can see, no conclusion favourable or unfavourable to Ravenscroft's assertions can safely be drawn from it, his debt to Cowley, if we are to discuss what the assertions rest upon, cannot be left out of account.

(*b*) Act V, Scene II. Chiron and Demetrius as Rape and Murder.[4]

The editor and I no longer believe that Titus's identification of Tamora's sons with Rape and Murder constitutes a puzzle, nor his subsequent question, " What are they calld? " an inconsistency pointing perhaps to corruption in the text. Commentators set themselves an insoluble problem if they take Tamora's plan of presenting herself to Titus as Revenge,[4] to include presenting her sons as Rape and Murder. If it is assumed that the disguises into which she has put them are emblematic of those crimes, Titus's identification of them is

---

[1] They both took part in the meetings to consider the founding of an English Academy (Spingarn, *op. cit.*, II. 328 f., 337).

[2]   Shakespeare's own Muse her *Pericles* first bore:
       The Prince of *Tyre* was elder than the Moore.
       'Tis miracle to see a first good Play.

(Prologue to *Circe*, ll. 16-18). He criticizes the plots of Elizabethan dramatists, " especially those which they writ first. . . . I suppose I need not name *Pericles Prince of Tyre* nor the historical plays of Shakespeare." And again: " in his latter plays he had worn off somewhat of the rust; but the tragedy which I have undertaken to correct was in all probability one of his first endeavours on the stage . . . Shakespeare . . . in the apprenticeship of his writing, modelled " the story " into that play, . . . now called *Troilus and Cressida* " (*Essays*, ed. cit. I. 165, 203). Dryden's ignorance of Shakespearian chronology only emphasises his correlation of the inferior with the immature as he conceives them. He is generalizing from his own long apprenticeship, but may be following Cowley too.

[3] The ground of the complaint, if Cowley intended it, is another question.

[4] See above v. ii. 61, n., " *what . . . call'd?*"

explained, it is true, but at the cost of making it impossible to understand the discussion of their names later on; whereas once it is realized that the disguises and her intentions cast them only for the rôle of Revenge's ministers, the development of the scene becomes perfectly intelligible.

In announcing herself as Revenge, Tamora speaks of rape and murder, not of course as her companions, but as villainies (half-personified) which she will persecute.[1]   Titus responds:

> Lo, by thy side where Rape and Murder stands.

He has recognized, not impersonations designed by Tamora, but the men themselves, and, under cover of his supposed madness,[2] christens them after his knowledge of what they have done.   For her, this is at most a madman's intuition: she cannot know he knows.   She is faced, however, with his awkward demand that she should prove herself Revenge, and fulfil her promise, by falling upon Rape and Murder in the persons of her companions. She begins to deny the identifications:

> These are my ministers, and come with me;

that is, she assigns them the rôle she has envisaged them in all along.   And Titus replies as though shaken in his madman's rash assurance:

> Are they thy ministers?   what are they call'd?

" They are your ministers, then, are they?   Well, if I was wrong about them, what do you say their names really are? "   But now Tamora decides she can accept the names he has bestowed, while maintaining her explanation: " Rape and Murder," she answers,

> therefore called so
> 'Cause they take vengeance of such kind of men.

Thus she accommodates her original conception to what she regards as Titus's " brainsick humours."

That this is the right interpretation is clear from Tamora's own comment, aside to her sons:

> This closing with him fits his lunacy.

" This closing with him " is her pretence that he was right after all about the names.   They do not originate with her: to humour Titus she accepts them, as the phrase implies, from him.

----

[1] Ll. 35, 40.

[2] If something of real madness clings about Titus in the scene, one need not, for the present purpose, try to say how much.   He is sane enough to see through Tamora, to play up to her belief that he is lunatic, and to organize his (surely not altogether sane) revenge.

ADDITIONAL NOTES

I. i. 35. *at this day.* W. W. Greg, *M.L.R.* 48 (1953), 439-40 (so also Baldwin (1959), p. 431) conj. " as this day," noting that if this means " as he has already done," it supports the view of Dover Wilson and others that the sacrifice of Alarbus (ll. 96-119) is a later insertion in the scene as originally conceived; but that if it means " as he proposes to do " (so Baldwin), it supports the integrity of the scene. H. F. Brooks suggests that " at this day " could mean " on the day corresponding to this "—i.e. always on the very day of return; then " at last " (l. 36) could mean " for the final time."

I. i. 40. *Whom . . . succeed.* Stoll, with no support from *N.E.D.*, gives the original text the sense of Capell's emendation by treating " succeed " as a past participle. H. F. Brooks suggests that the meaning is: they want whoever is chosen to succeed " worthily," and this requires that the election should be carried on peacefully and without intimidation.

I. i. 71. Other examples of similar mixtures are: Bacon, *Advancement of Learning*, II. xxii. 1 (ed. Aldis Wright, p. 203): " so as it may yield of herself "; Nashe, *Lenten Stuffe* (ed. McKerrow, III. 157, ll. 25-7): " vesselles . . . it hath given shelter to at once in her harbour."

I. i. 83. *latest home.* The *Ecclesiastes* quotation is from Coverdale's version (retained in A.V.): see *N.E.D. home* sb. 6. Tilley, H533, has quotations with " longest " (a. 1594) and " last " (1611). *Locrine* (*Sh. Apocrypha*, ed. Tucker Brooke), v. iv. 237 has " latest home."

I. i. 94. *in store.* " laid up as in a storehouse " (On.). Schmidt compares *Mac.* II. iv. 34, " The sacred storehouse of his predecessors."

I. i. 110. Most editions (including my 1953 one) accept Theobald's repunctuation. But " triumphs and return " is an awkward hendiadys for " triumphal return," and there is really nothing wrong with saying that she and her sons " return captive with thee " when the meaning is that he returns with them as his captives. There may also be a suggestion of the sense given by Schmidt 1 d as " fall to, become the share of ": *Ham.* I. i. 91-2, " which had return'd / To the inheritance of Fortinbras." Kittredge and Alexander retain the original punctuation.

I. i. 230. *of every sort.* from all classes of the community, patrician and plebeian alike (Delius).

I. i. 236. *in part of.* For this curious expression, cf. a 1601 quotation in J. E. Neale, *Elizabeth I and her Parliaments, 1584-1601* (1957), p. 427, " in part of the charges bestowed for their defence "; Dryden, *All for Love*, Act III (ed. Scott-Saintsbury, v. 392), " Take this in part of recompense."

I. i. 310. *flourish'd.* The sense " swaggered " is probably also present: cf. *Caes.* III. ii. 193, with *New Shakespeare* Glossary.

I. i. 358. *shall.* For the peremptory implications, cf. *Cor.* III. i. 87 ff. (G. K. Hunter).

I. i. 409-10. *short . . . sharp.* Cf. Tilley, A168, " All that is sharp is short " (F. P. Wilson).

I. i. 449. *let me alone.* In this sense already in Chaucer, *Troilus*, II. 1401, III. 413 (where see Robinson's note).

I. i. 491. *love-day.* The word is exhaustively discussed by Josephine W. Bennett, *Speculum* 32 (1958), 351-70.

II. i. 71. Qq, F have commas after " I " and " world ", leaving the attachment of " knew . . . world " uncertain. Editors have generally, and I believe rightly, joined it to what precedes. Certainly Sisson, who removes the comma after " world," has no grounds for his implied claim (*New Readings*, II. 137) that he is more faithful to the original than " recent editors."

II. i. 103. *join . . . jar.* For the jingle, A. Koszul, *Etudes Anglaises* 7 (1954), 325, refers to *N.E.D. jar* 13, Sylvester, " We build and balter, ioyne and iarre."

II. i. 106-7. Tilley cites this passage under M 554, but the Heywood one under M 769. For the earlier history of the saying in Greek, see Plato, *Hippias Major* 301c, with note in D. Tarrant's edition (1928).

II. i. 112. *solemn hunting.* The phrase occurs also in R. Wilson, *The Cobbler's Prophecy* (1594), Malone Soc. Reprint, l. 716.

II. iii. 1 ff. For the burying of gold to incriminate an innocent person, cf. the story of Ulysses and Palamedes, referred to in Ovid, *Met.* XIII. 60 (G. K. Hunter).

II. iii. 8. *repose . . . unrest.* Delius on IV. ii. 31 quoted both these passages. Steevens had already quoted *Spanish Tragedy* III. xiii. 29, " Thus therefore will I rest me in unrest."

II. iii. 12-15. Herford, Introduction, p. 292, compares this with Seneca, *Phaedra*, 508-9, " hinc aves querulae fremunt / ornique ventis lene percussae tremunt."

II. iii. 31. *Saturn.* See also McKerrow's Nashe, IV. 117-18 (G. K. Hunter).

II. iii. 93 ff. Richard Hurd in his " Discourse on Poetical Imitation " (*Q. Horatii Flacci Epistolae*, etc., ed. 3 (1757), II. 115) cites this passage as " an *Anti-tempe.*"

II. iii. 152. *paws par'd.* Cf. T. Fuller, *Comment . . . St. Matthew's Gospel* (1652), p. 28, " Christ's innocence . . . pared the Lions paws." Versions of the proverb " Leonem ex unguibus aestimare " vary between *claws* and *paws* (Tilley, L 313).

II. iii. 231. I would agree with Greg (see p. viii above) that the supposition of a lost corrected state of Q 1 is probably otiose.

II. iii. 260. I retain my conjecture, but feel bound to record the spelling *griue* in *Per.* (Q 1), I. ii. 100, and the rhyme *grife/life* in Daye's translation of *Daphnis and Chloe* (ed. 1890), p. 37.

II. iii. 287. Cf. Tilley, M 1315, " Murder will out," citing this and other Shakespeare passages.

II. iii. 291-2. H. F. Brooks points out that the *Richard III* exchange cited goes back to More (in a passage which is the first quotation in Tilley, I 16, " If's and and's "). He also quotes the interruption in Kyd, *Spanish Tragedy*, II. i. 76-7, " If Madame *Bel-imperia* be in love—/What, Villaine, ifs and ands ? "

II. iii. 294. As Delius noted, this is in conflict with the plan outlined at . 46, unless Tamora deliberately dropped the letter again. This is the sort of anomaly that could survive in foul papers but would be cleared up in production.

III. i. 36. On this problem see W. W. Greg, *The Shakespeare First Folio* (1955), pp. 206-7. Greg suggests that F got the words not in Q 3 from an annotated copy of Q 2 used as prompt-book, by which a scribe corrected the copy of Q 3 from which F was set up. He assumes, what is less than certain, that F's " oh " in l. 34 is a misprint for " or " and not of independent origin. He is unwilling to admit a manuscript prompt-book, which would have made possible the correction of Q 2 corruptions (p. 205), but admits that a corrector would not necessarily have accepted the prompt-book readings (p. 209, Note E); the same, surely, applies to the variant stage directions at V. iii. 26, where there would be no strong inducement to reinstate " the dishes " for Q 2's " The meate on the table," which Greg (p. 209, Note C) calls spurious, but which might have commended itself as more explicit. Even if, as Greg thinks, the company was using an annotated Q 2 as a prompt-book, and this was all that was available for correction of the copy of Q 3 used by the printer of F, it would be rash to assume that *no* authoritative corrections were made to that copy of Q 2, which must on any showing have been accompanied by the manuscript from which F printed III. ii. See especially I. i. 398, and v. ii. 18 (where, *pace* Greg, I still believe that F has the true text).

III. i. 96. *Expecting when.* Later examples: Scott, *Redgauntlet*, ch. 1, " expecting any moment when he would start off "; Carlyle, *French Revolution*, III. iv. 6 (Temple Classics ed., III. 235), " expecting when the end will be "; Tennyson, *The Vision of Sin*, l. 8, " Expecting when a fountain should arise."

III. ii. In my 1953 edition, I dismissed too hastily the possibility that this scene is a later addition. E. K. Chambers, *William Shakespeare*, I. 316, had noted the " distinct scribal origin " reflected in the S.D. forms " Andronicus " and " Tamira." Moreover, as N. S. Brooke has pointed out to me—and as I now find C. M. Haines had noted in " The ' Law of Re-entry ' in Shakespeare " (*R.E.S.* 1 (1925), 449-50)—the end of III. ii is the only place in the play where characters exit to re-enter immediately; whereas the end of III. i makes a natural break, and points forward to the revenge theme. Is it a serious objection that without sc. ii the Folio Act III would be only 300 lines long? As Greg points out, the Folio act-division is certainly wrong at the end of Act I (*The Shakespeare First Folio* (1955), p. 205). Altogether, the date of the scene remains very much an open question—it would be convenient, but hazardous, to make its addition the justification for Henslow's " ne " of 24 Jan. 1594—and if so, its authorship must also be uncertain. There is no positive reason to deny it to Shakespeare, or to attach much weight to the " fancy " Chambers records having had that it is by Webster (*William Shakespeare*, I. 321).

III. ii. 15. *Wound . . . sighing.* Sighs were thought to drain the heart of blood; cf. *2 H 6* III. i. 61, 63, *3 H 6* IV. iv. 22 (Verity; Stoll).

III. ii. 80. *shadows . . . substances.* The *substance/shadow* antithesis is very common in Shakespeare; this instance is particularly close to Ovid, *Met.* III. 417 (Narcissus), " corpus putat esse quod umbra est."

IV. ii. 10. *well-advis'd.* Not pre-Shakespearian in *N.E.D.*, but Palsgrave, *Acolastus* (E.E.T.S.), 26. 34, translates " male sanus " by " not wel advysed "; Cooper, *Thesaurus*, s.v. *sanus, pro sano aliquid facere*, " To doe a thing as it becometh one well advised or in his right minde."

IV. ii. 65. *devil's dam.* See Tilley, D225.

IV. ii. 67. *loathsome as a toad.* See Tilley, T361.

IV. ii. 101-3. Either this, or a common proverbial source, must lie behind Heywood, *The Captives* (Malone Soc. Reprint), 14-16, " The stayneles swanne,/ wth all the Oceans water canott wash/the blacknes ffrom her ffeete, tis borne with her."

IV. iii. 89-90. *God . . . days.* Greg, *The Shakespeare First Folio* (1955), pp. 203-4, taking up a suggestion he first made in *The Library*, 4 Ser. 13 (1922-3), 141, notes that " the typographical arrangement [as a separate paragraph] suggests that this unquestionably Shakespearian sally was a marginal addition."

IV. iii. 91-2. *Gent.* II. iii. 5 was already cited by Delius.

IV. iii. 92. *emperal's.* This malapropism recurs in Beaumont and Fletcher, *Knight of the Burning Pestle*, II. i (ed. Waller, VI. 183).

IV. iv. 48. I now find that " by (be) lady " is quite common: *The Trial of Treasure*, sig. C3ᵛ; *Jack Straw* (Malone Soc. Reprints), l. 505; *Locrine*, II. iv. 90; *Mucedorus*, II. ii. 42; R. Johnson, *Tom a Lincoln*, in *Early English Prose Romances*, ed. W. J. Thoms, p. 640; Beaumont and Fletcher, *Knight of the Burning Pestle*, I. i (ed. Waller, VI. 176); *Wild Goose Chase*, III. i (ed. Waller, IV. 357). I multiply examples in the hope of ensuring that the expression never again gets emended.

IV. iv. 105. *stand on. N.E.D., stand* 72e, retains " stand in " as the only example of " insist upon having." No editors have followed, and the F4 correction seems more probable, though perhaps some weight should be given to the fact that F2-3 did not make it.

IV. iv. 111. *smoke for it. N.E.D.* 4 notes " in early use with allusion to actual burning," but links one later quotation with sense 2, under which Heywood, 1533, is specially relevant, " When I have beten her tyll she smoke." This may be the force of the figure here. On. glosses " have a ' warm ' time of it."

IV. iv. 113 *incessantly*. As H. F. Brooks points out to me, a word of Lady Wishfort's: *The Way of the World*, IV. xiii, end; V. viii (the latter cited in *N.E.D.*).

V. ii. 50. *black as jet*. See Tilley, J49.

V. ii. 69. The whole question of the gallery has been re-opened by R. Hosley in *Shakespeare Quarterly*, 8 (1957) and *Shakespeare Survey*, 10 (1957). In the latter article (p. 86, n. 4) Hosley rejects the use of the gallery in this scene. Certainly it is unproved, and Titus can perfectly well withdraw into a "study" behind the main stage. I am glad that Hosley also agrees that the gallery is not called for in v. iii (see my note on l. 66).

V. ii. 188. In Dekker (ed. Bowers), *Patient Grissil*, IV. iii. 124-5, there is a pun on this sense of coffin: " the coffins of pyes, wherein the dead bodies of birdes should have been buried." See also Oppel, p. 50.

V. iii. 19. *break the parle*. I think " interrupt " is probably right, the " parle " being the slanging-match that ll. 17-18 have initiated; but I ought to have noted that Johnson interpreted " begin the parley," and On. 4 gives " open (negotiations) " as his first gloss, though adding " (or? = ' break off ')."

V. iii. 41. *Because*. For the double function, see also Donne, *Sermons* (ed. Simpson and Potter), VIII. 8. 696-8, " Neither does it become us in any case, to say God layes this upon him, because he is so ill, but because he may be better." So in Latin, *causa* can be followed by *quod* and *ne* in the same sentence: Caesar, *B.G.* VI. ix. 1-2.

V. iii. 66. *meed for meed*. Cited by Tilley, M 800, " Measure for measure."

V. iii. 73. Sisson (*New Readings*, II. 144-5) has a defence of Q which I find quite unconvincing. H. F. Brooks suggests that some tangle of corrections at the beginning of the line might have seemed to give " L. Rom." or the like, expanded to " Romane Lord " as a speech-prefix.

V. iii. 179. H. F. Brooks notes that in Lodge's *Wounds of Civil War* the traitor page is to be famished to death.

I. i. 214 The corrected state of F has " Friend? " for the uncorrected " Friend, ": a misunderstood attempt at proof-correction.

I. i. 259 Only the (mis)corrected state of F has " you "; the uncorrected has, rightly " your ".

III. ii. 39 " complainet " arises from a misunderstood attempt at proof-correction of the uncorrected " complaine ".   [1963]